I'm all yours

KOKO HEART

❀ Created with Vellum

For Jo, Valerie, Melanie and Angela. Four people who have encouraged and supported me throughout this journey. I love that I get to call you family!

Prologue

I close the door quietly and tiptoe down the stairs, breathing a huge sigh of relief that I've made it out of there on my own. I love my son, but mumma needs a break. Teething is a bitch. My one year old son, Ben, has been cutting his back teeth and is in so much pain. I haven't slept in what feels like years. I know it's only been a few days, but he's gone from sleeping through the night to waking up every half hour. It's brutal, and I feel like I've been shoved back into that newborn zombie stage.

I stretch my legs out on the sofa and then curl them underneath me. The silence is a welcome retreat from the non-stop screaming of the past hour. I look over at my now cold tea and really wish it was a big glass of red wine. Biting my bottom lip, I weigh up the pros and cons of going into the kitchen to pour myself one. Yes, it'll help me to unwind, but I can't have a glass knowing I'm here on my own with Ben. I'm already feeling tired, the wine will just make it worse when he inevitably wakes up screaming again in a few minutes.

Shaking my head to clear the thought, I pick up the cold tea and scoot into the kitchen to flick the kettle on. When I make my way back to the sofa with a new hot cup, I quickly check the baby monitor and, seeing my beautiful boy sleeping peacefully, I throw a silent thank you and plea to God that he's settled for a while now. I grab my phone and see a text from my gorgeous husband:

Steve: Hey baby, just wanted to tell you I love you and I'll be heading home soon. I miss you. Snuggling on the sofa with you is a much better idea than being here. Keep it warm for me. Xxx

I'm beaming from ear to ear, happiness oozing from me. Even after fourteen years together he still makes me swoon. My man. Steve and I met as thirteen-year-old kids in high school, fell instantly in love with each other, and have been together ever since.

Smugly, I place my phone back on the table without responding, as I know he won't hear it over the noise in the pub. Steve is out with some work colleagues and even though he didn't want to go, I made him. He never goes out. Neither of us do, really, unless we've been dragged out by one of my sisters, which used to happen more frequently before I had Ben. I knew I'd get a text saying he was going to be home early though. I chuckle at his predictability, but I'm comforted by it too.

Ben starts to stir just as I finish my last sip of tea, but by some miracle he soothes himself before I can even get up to go to him. I sigh again, pulling the blanket from the back of the sofa over myself to get cosy, and grab my tatty old copy of a *Midsummer Night's Dream*, knowing I'll be asleep within minutes. I don't want to go to bed on my own. I can't sleep without Steve, so I'll just rest my eyes on the sofa until he gets home.

BANG! BANG! BANG!

I jump up, disoriented, startled awake by a sound I can't place, and it takes a second to realise I'm downstairs on the sofa and not in my bed. A quick glance over to the monitor confirms Ben is thankfully still asleep, not crying for my attention. I yawn as I reach for my phone to see the time, wondering if there even was a noise or if maybe I dropped my book on my face, when I hear *BANG! BANG! BANG!*

That must have been the noise that woke me up. I'm feeling sick to my stomach as I walk to the street door. Knocks in the middle of the night are never a good thing. I hope it's not my mum or dad or one of my sisters. "God please let them be okay," I whisper out loud as I get to the door. With the security chain on, I peek out to see two police officers standing there.

"Hello? Can I help you?" My voice sounds small, worried. *Please be at the wrong door, please be at the wrong door*, I think in my head over and over.

A kind and soothing voice breaks through my thoughts. "Good evening, are you Mrs. Vickers?"

Shit, not at the wrong door.

"Yes, I am. Can I help you?" Frozen to the spot now, I know they aren't going to tell me anything I want to hear.

"Can we come inside please?"

I want to stamp my foot and tell them no. No, you're not coming into my home to tell me something awful has happened. Who do they think they are? This is my home and Steve will be here soon. Surely they can wait until he's here to share their bad news with me. God, I hope it's not my Mum or Dad.

While my brain is screaming all these thoughts at me, my hands are slowly undoing the security chain and my feet are retreating into the front room, the officers following close behind. Once inside I sit on the sofa and look up at them, leaving them standing awkwardly in front of the tv.

"Mrs. Vickers, I'm afraid we have some bad news for you. Your husband..."

I don't hear the rest. I hear a wail, the sound of someone's heart breaking, and as I look around the room, I realise the awful sound is coming from me.

I'm in a daze. I can't take anything in. I just hear the words husband, dead, stabbed and sorry.

I must give them my mum's details because the next thing I know I'm engulfed in her strong arms, her comforting voice in my ear, "Shh, my girl, shh. Mum's here baby. I've got you, my girl."

She sounds so far away but I know from the warmth surrounding me that she's holding me close. My soul feels like it's been ripped out of me and I don't know what to do, so I let her cradle me, and cry like I used to as a kid.

I'm vaguely aware of my dad coming into the front room carrying Ben, and I jump up and grab him. I cuddle him tightly and sob into his beautiful blond hair. His blond hair, just like his daddy's. The daddy he'll never remember. The one who isn't here anymore.

My sobs get louder and my breath racks through my body. I drop to my knees, still clinging to our boy, the one who's now crying with me. I look down at his beautiful face and see the confusion and sadness etched there. He feels my pain. He knows I'm breaking. He's losing the one parent he has left.

That thought spears my already broken heart and shatters it all over again. I'm all he has. I can't break.

Pulling myself to my feet, I square my shoulders, swipe at the tears on my face, and take a deep breath. "I'm so sorry my boy, mummy's here. I promise," I whisper as I give him a kiss on his head.

Mustering every ounce of strength I have left, I confront my new reality. "Mum, I'm going to take him back upstairs. Please, can you deal with the police and phone Steve's mum and dad?"

My mum grabs my hand and pulls me into a cuddle with Ben between us. "You are so strong my girl, remember that. Cuddle that boy of yours tightly and know that we are here for you always," she whispers into my ear before pulling away and kissing Ben on the head.

I walk up the stairs and turn into Ben's bedroom, automatically switching his night-time music on to soothe him. I hum along with the familiar tune as I sway with him in my arms, clutching him tightly to me. My legs feel like jelly, so I settle into the rocking chair with him, watching his face turn peaceful as his eyes start to close. Once I know he's asleep, I let my silent tears fall.

"Why did you leave us, Steve? You promised me forever," I whisper as Ben stirs in my arms. "Shh, baby boy. I've got you. I promise I won't leave you. Even though mummy's heart is breaking right now, I'll always be here for you. I'm sorry you saw me fall apart. I swear to you that's the last time you'll see that. I'll be strong. I'll be your constant in this world. I promise you." I rock with him in my arms all night, sleep not even factoring in my brain.

Ben wakes up when the morning light shines through the blinds, giving me a big smile, completely oblivious of the chaos and heartbreak that surrounds him. And I'm jealous of the fact that I'm not.

～

The weeks fly by in a blur of phone calls, sympathy cards, flowers and people turning up with food that I have no interest in eating. I have no interest in practically anything. All I want to do is focus my attention on my boy.

When Steve's parents arrived, they dealt with the funeral arrangements and liaising with the police. I couldn't handle it, it was all too much. They told me that Steve had simply been in the wrong place at the wrong time. He tried to stop a fight, which was typical Steve, and was stabbed in the process. The only consolation is that the police arrested the young guy that did it and he's been charged with murder. It brings little joy to me, but at least I know he won't be able to inflict this pain on another family.

I've also been informed that as Steve's wife I'm entitled to his life insurance pay out. His parents aren't happy about that fact, but I don't have the energy to care. The insurance will enable me to pay off the mortgage on the house so that Ben will always have a home. And I'll be able to stay at home and look after him instead of having to rush back to work. He needs me now more than ever. But I'd give it all up in a heartbeat if it meant I could have my Steve back.

Sometimes the pain catches me unaware, and I have to stop what I'm doing. The physical ache that I have in my chest burns through my very fibre. I can't stop the hurt, but I can hold it in. I can keep it locked away, only allowing myself to give in and feel it when Ben's asleep. I keep the tears away from him. I don't want him to see his mummy sad all the time. He deserves the best version of me, even though I feel like she died the day Steve did. I'll work at getting her back though, for Ben's sake.

Today I'm supposed to say goodbye. I won't shed a tear, not when I know everyone is watching me. Not when Ben is here. I'll say my goodbyes when he's asleep.

The funeral is a blur of sympathetic faces and disapproval from Steve's parents. They don't like that I'm going home with our son instead of attending the wake at a local pub. I don't give a fuck. I want to tell everyone to leave me the fuck alone, but I don't. Because that would be making a scene, and I don't want Steve's funeral to become all about the weeping widow. His parents made it abundantly clear that there was to be no dramatics today.

After the funeral, I leave all my family downstairs, and with Ben asleep in his room I retreat to my bedroom. I lay down on Steve's side of the bed, curl into a ball, and sob. All the emotions of the day are finally set free, knowing that Ben isn't here to see me.

I hear my bedroom door open and feel the bed dip behind me as Emilia spoons into me. A second later, Cleo enters and lays on the bed in between mine and Emilia's legs and holds on to me. Right on cue the door opens one more time and Juliet, our baby sister, walks around the bed to the front of me and climbs on, so she's the little spoon.

No talking is necessary. We just lay there cuddling and crying together as we have done through all our sad times. Through break-ups and fall outs, if one of us is upset, this is where you'll find all of us. The Cooper circle of comfort, as we've called it. My sisters are my world. I don't think I'd be able to face this without them. And they are once again proving, I don't have to.

CHAPTER 1

Nell

3 YEARS LATER...

"We're nearly there, bud. Nanny's picking you up today, so try not to eat too many sweets with her."

"Okay, Mumma, I won't."

I look at my sweet boy in the rear-view mirror and see him grinning back at me. His smile lights me up and makes me happy. It also knocks me for six sometimes. He has the exact same smile as his daddy. I miss him so much, but I'll be forever thankful that I have a piece of him in Ben.

Pulling up to his nursery I turn the ignition off and head out of the car to unstrap Ben from his car seat. He jumps down and bounces onto his toes, excitement radiating from him. I've never known a kid that likes nursery as much as mine. It kind of bums me out if I'm honest though. Of course, I'm happy that he's happy and likes it there, but it also makes me sad that he doesn't need me as much.

For the past three years I've focused all my energy and attention on Ben. I was on maternity leave from my teaching job when Steve died, and I never went back afterwards. I wanted to spend every second I could with him. He was already missing one parent, and I didn't want him to miss me as well.

Apart from when my mother forced me to leave him with her once a week to give me a break, we were never separated. Even then, I just stayed in the house, keeping myself busy sorting his clothes or tidying his room and counting down the time until he'd be back with me. I know it wasn't the healthiest thing to do, but I clung to him. Whilst he needed me, I couldn't fall apart. And if I'm honest, he saved me.

When I reach down to take his hand and walk towards the building where his nursery is, he looks up at me and smiles. I smile back asking, "Why are you so happy this morning, buddy?"

He starts jumping beside me talking hurriedly. "Because I love my nursery, I'mma big boy, Miss Ali teached me numbers."

"Taught you numbers honey, she taught you, not teached." He frowns at me, then says the sentence again with the correction and resumes beaming up at me.

Some people think it's cute when their kids use incorrect grammar, but it's my worst nightmare. My love for words, grammar, punctuation, all of it, led me to become an English teacher for high school children. But trying to get them to use the right pronouns and grammar was harder work than I had anticipated. It's probably why I'm harder on Ben than most parents are when it comes to his speech, but in all fairness, I do it to everyone. I'm a bit like Ross from Friends, I correct everyone, and I'm really not sorry about it either.

"So, is Miss Ali why you like nursery so much? She seems to be your favourite." I nudge him with my hip a little bit.

He giggles at me and says, "She's my favourite, mummy. She's so kind and helps me wiv everyfing." I try to ignore the little stab of jealousy I feel when he talks about his teacher. I know it's ridiculous, it just feels like I'm being replaced in some small way. And that stings a bit.

Standing outside his classroom I say hello to a couple of other parents but never take my eyes off Ben who's chatting and playing with his friends. Seeing him happy, confident and laughing makes me happier than anything else could in the world.

As the doors open, I grab the back of Ben's shirt to stop him from running into class without giving me a kiss, and bend down so that I'm eye level with him. I squeeze his little body tightly, savouring just one more moment with him. But as soon as I let him go he bounds inside, carefree and eager to start his day. I'm in awe of this little boy who doesn't know how much he's loved and needed.

After reminding Miss Ali that my mum is picking him up today, I head outside to my car, Ben's happy voice fading into the chaos of the classroom behind me.

Halfway back to my house my phone starts ringing and connects through the car's speakers. Before I can even speak, my sister Juliet's voice comes through.

"Please tell me you are on your way back home from dropping my little guy to school already. I'm outside your house. And I'm freezing."

I shake my head and laugh at her. "Are you mad? It's not even cold, it's the middle of spring for god's sake."

"Yeah, but I've just spent the past three years in paradise and now I'm cold. Where are you?" She's whining, and I can't help laughing at her. She's definitely the baby of the family.

"Juliet, I've just dropped him off. I just started the car when you called. Why did you leave Mum's so early?" I know why, my mum is driving her mad.

Three years ago, before Juliet decided to go gallivanting around the world, and before my world came crashing down on me, Princess, as she's known, was the last one of us girls still living at home. To say she enjoyed the luxury of being spoiled rotten is an understatement. My mum and dad doted on her.

In the few months since she's been back not much has changed with them, but Juliet has. She's used to living on her own, doing everything for herself, and my mum and dad are finding that a bit difficult. She phoned me the other day complaining that Mum wouldn't let her cook her own dinner. Mum justified her actions with "you're my baby and it's my job as your mummy to feed you, my little girl." Juliet didn't find my laughter helpful and hung up on me when I snorted. She later told me she had images of Mum chewing her food up and spitting it into her mouth like mother birds do. Which only made me laugh harder.

"You know why I'm here waiting for you Nell, please tell me you're nearly here."

"Stop whining at me, Princess. I'm round the corner. I don't know why you don't just stay here with me," I say as I turn the corner into my street. She's standing on my doorstep, in a thick winter coat, hopping from one foot to the other to keep warm. I hang up when she waves at me, and as I step out of my car, in my long sleeved t-shirt, she shoots me a dirty look.

"Rude! You hung up on me and called me Princess." She raises her hand to silence my protests and continues, "To answer your question, I want to stay here, believe me, I really do. However, when I mentioned it to Mum, she got all upset and said she doesn't understand why I don't want to live with her again and then went on about only just getting me back and how if I wanted to live with Cleo or Emilia, ha imagine me and Emilia living together, then she'd be okay as they're in London, but because you only live round the corner it makes no sense. So big sis, it's your fault for living so damn close to them. Now please open the door so I can put your heater on."

I stand and stare at her in a daze at how much information she's just thrown at me. I'm not even sure she took a breath the entire time. I open the front door and follow her into my home. True to her word, she makes a bee-line to my marble fireplace and flicks the electric fire on.

"So why don't you?"

She stops midway from taking her coat off and grunts "huh?" as I sit on the arm of the sofa, already feeling warmer than I should be.

"Why don't you move in with Cleo? Move to London. You won't need to pay her rent as it's covered by her and Verity, so you'd only have to figure out food. But once you're there you can look for work. I know you don't know what you want to do, but you can temp for a while. Plus, I'm sure between Emilia and Cleo they'd be able to help you find a job."

She looks at me like I've grown two heads, then plonks onto the floor so the heat is blasting at her head and blowing her hair into her face. She huffs as she reaches to turn it off.

"Do you think Cleo would let me?"

"You won't know unless you ask her. Think about it." I look down at her and smile to myself, thinking how remarkable she is. At the age of twenty two she's already travelled and experienced so many amazing things, and all I've done is move round the corner from where I grew up.

"I'm so proud of you, Juliet. You've had so many life experiences already. You're so brave for doing what you did."

She stares at me in bewilderment. "Are you for real? All I did was jump on a plane and enjoy myself for a few years. You are amazing. You have a brilliant career, that you need to revive by the way, an amazing home, the most beautiful little man that has ever lived, EVER. You've faced the worst thing imaginable and did it with so much decorum and strength. You're my superhero, Nell."

Tears pool in my eyes. I give her a big hug and tell her to text Cleo while I go in the kitchen to make tea. Really, I need a few minutes to compose myself as her words hit home, especially about reviving my career.

Before I had Ben, I was a teacher at the same secondary school we all attended as teenagers. I absolutely loved teaching English Lit, and I had every intention of going back after my maternity leave ended. My mum was all set to look after Ben for me. But after Steve died, I couldn't.

There were a lot of things I couldn't do after Steve died. And a lot of things I had to learn how to do, as well. I wasn't always the 'prepared for anything person' I now am.

Lately, since Ben has started nursery full-time and is enjoying it so much, I've been thinking about getting back into the swing of things. I've got an email drafted, all ready to send to the head teacher, my old boss, who's familiar with my circumstances. I just haven't had the balls to press send. Something's holding me back, though I'm not ready to delve into what that is just yet.

Taking two cups of tea into the front room, I find Juliet still on the floor, chatting on FaceTime with Cleo. She turns the screen to me so I can see her.

I blow my sister a kiss hello. "Are you still coming over tonight? You staying?"

She vigorously nods her head yes at me and smirks. "Definitely! We have lots to discuss and lots of wine to consume so yep, definitely staying. I mean it's only once that your biggest sister turns thirty for god's sake."

I roll my eyes at her as my baby sisters giggle and talk about what ridiculous things they want to plan for me. I plop down on the floor next to Juliet and she moves the phone back so Cleo can see us both.

"Why can't you get it into your heads that I don't want a fuss made. It's just another day." I know I'm fighting a losing battle, but I try anyway.

"Pfft. Another day my arse, girl. You never make a fuss unless it's about Ben. You deserve what we have planned so just shush will you." Cleo very firmly puts me in my place.

Just as Juliet is about to join in with scolding me, a man's voice bellows off screen. "Is that Nell and Princess? Let me talk to them." Juliet jumps up and mumbles "toilet" at me as she scurries out, saying something about 'fucking Princess,' just as Connor's face squashes in next to Cleo's. Connor has been Cleo's best friend, and our honorary brother, since Cleo first met him in school. Princess owes her royal moniker to him.

"Hey Nell, how you doing? Why are you sitting on the floor? Where's Princess?"

I blow out a breath and shrug my shoulders at him. "If she hears you call her that you'll be in so much trouble. Her royal highness was cold, so she sat in front of the fire. I just joined her. She, er, nipped to the loo." I hesitate in saying that as I notice Juliet walk past and head into the kitchen.

"Oh. I haven't seen her since she got back. Anyway, how's my main man?"

I could have sworn there was a flicker of sadness in his eyes when he spoke of Juliet.

"He's okay. Replaced me with his teacher, but it's all good."

Connor laughs as someone calls his name. He apologises and says his goodbyes before disappearing back into the room behind him. Cleo's back on screen for a moment before telling me she has to go too, and she'll see me tonight.

I hang up and call out to Juliet, "He's gone now Juliet. You can come back in."

She stomps into the front room with a frown on her face.

15

"I wasn't avoiding him. I have a headache from the cold and heat, so I went to get some painkillers. Why would I need to avoid Connor Shay?" Her voice has gone all squeaky, like when someone is trying to convince you they're fine when they're not, so I decide not to push her.

"What do you want to do today then? Do we need to hit the shops for wine and nibbles for tonight?"

CHAPTER 2

Nell

"I'm not having strippers. Nope, no way. You can think again if you think I'll let any of those greased up, naked men gyrate at me, thank you very much. And I don't care what any of you three say." I hold my hand with my wine glass up and point my finger accusingly at each of them in turn. Emilia shakes her head at me in disgust whilst Juliet blushes and Cleo merely shrugs her shoulders.

"Was worth a shot. Em, we'll save them for your thirtieth, then she won't be able to stop us." Cleo shoots a wink over to Emilia.

"Is it really that hard to say Emilia? Em-ee-lee-ah! It's not hard to say, you know," she chides us, complete with an eye roll and melodramatic sigh. Emilia is probably the only one of us who likes her name and doesn't like it shortened. Our mum and dad are huge Shakespeare fans and named us after characters from his works. I don't have the worst name going, my sister Cleopatra can claim that one.

I roll my eyes back at her and throw a pillow at her head. "Lighten up, you fucking tight arse." She frowns at me but then sticks her middle finger up and pokes her tongue out at the same time.

"See if I had said and done that, she would have scratched my eyes out. Why can she get away with it Em-ee-lee-ah?" Cleo says exaggerating her name right back at her to annoy her even more.

"Because, sweet middle sister, I shared a room with her. She knows all my secrets. I spent most of my teenage life annoying and winding her up and took quite a few hits from her. I respect the hierarchy of this family. You should too." She picks the pillow up and throws it at Cleo's head, but she ducks out of the way and it hits Juliet straight in the face. We all erupt into laughter.

Except for Juliet.

She stands up, hands on her hips and snaps, "Really mature guys, grow the fuck up," then storms out of the front room and into the kitchen.

"That girls got a serious attitude problem. What's with her, the brat?" Emilia asks, but Cleo and I can only shrug our shoulders.

I offer to go after her, but Cleo says she will. There's only a couple of years between them and they've always been close.

I settle back into my seat and tell Emilia, "Please don't do anything I'll hate for my birthday."

Another eye roll accompanies a sip of her wine. "Nell, come on. You know I won't let them hire strippers, even though I'd love nothing more than a naked greased up man gyrating on me. But I know you'll hate that. I will say though, I am on board with 'getting you out of your comfort zone.' It's time.

"You've devoted your entire life to Ben since Steve died, and now he's at nursery and on his way to school soon. You need to learn how to be Nell again. You need to get back to work, get back out into the real world. Start thinking about dating again." She says the last part hesitantly, avoiding eye contact with me, but looks up when she hears me sniff and realises I'm crying.

"Oh, shit Nell, I'm sorry. I didn't mean to make you cry. I'm such a bitch, even when I'm not meaning to be." She gets up, sits next to me and I place my head on her shoulder.

As if they can sense my despair, Cleo and Juliet come in and sit around me too. All of them touching me at some point to show that they're there. The Cooper circle of comfort. I notice Juliet nudge Emilia's leg and Emilia nudge her back, their way of saying everything is fine between them now.

"I can't leave you with any of your sisters now, Em-ee-lee-ah can I?" Cleo states and over dramatically flings her arms out causing all of us to laugh.

"She didn't do anything apart from voice what's been inside my head for the last month or so. I know I need to get out more and start thinking about me instead of Ben, especially as he's getting more independent and needs me less now. It's just hard. When I start thinking of going back to work something holds me back, and I don't know what. I can't even bear to think about dating, even though I miss being held by a man and kissed and... you know. I feel guilty for thinking like that though. I honestly believed Steve was it for me."

With more tears streaming down my face my sisters squeeze me tighter than ever and then Emilia, always the straight talker with the stoic expression, speaks.

"Nell, Steve was it for you for that part of your life. You were destined to be together for the time you had. Now you need to trust in fate and find someone to spend the rest of your forever with. Steve would want it and you know that. Just because he's dead doesn't mean you have to give up your life too. You're alive! And you're the kindest, most caring person. The best sister and mummy to us and Ben. You deserve to be happy. If that means on your own then great. But you weren't made to be alone, Sis, none of you are."

She looks pointedly at all three of us as we stare back at her with our mouths wide open. She flips her long, shiny, platinum blonde hair and takes a long swallow of wine.

When none of us speak through the shock of what we've just heard, she speaks again. "Anyway, birthday plans. I think we should have a spa day and then go shopping. All the girls and Mum of course. And then, because little Miss Prissy-pants doesn't want too much of a fuss, we head to the pub and get absolutely shit faced. We'll come back here and pass out. What do we think?"

Cleo's nodding her head, a little stunned still. Juliet is smiling like a madwoman, in complete agreement with the plan, but adds, "And we get to dress the birthday girl. Nothing too outrageous but no granny clothes either."

Taking huge offence to being told my style is granny-like, I stick my tongue out at her. "I'm not dressing like a stripper. If you can remember that, I'll wear what you want. God help me, I'm going to regret this aren't I?!"

CHAPTER 3
William

"Well?"

I chuckle at the question from my lifelong friend Marcus. "Four years cancer free, brother. Fuck you, cancer! Yeah, you may have stolen my ball, but you aren't getting my life."

Marcus jumps on to my back and shouts, "Yes! I'm so fucking happy. I knew you'd be fine, but these check-ups always get me nervous."

I smile at him because I know exactly what he means. Ever since I was told I had cancer, I've dreaded coming to the hospital for my check-ups. I've been prodded about, poked with needles, had drugs pumped into me, been sick and tired, lost my hair, lost my ball and was at death's door... but I beat it. Coming back here always makes me scared they'll tell me it's back. Thankfully I haven't heard those words, and for another year I can rest easy.

"So, big man, are we out celebrating tonight then?" I glance skyward then nod my head at him.

Again, he jumps onto my back. "Tonight, my aim is to get you laid. One ball or not, you're going to get it on with some-one. I'm making sure of it."

"And how exactly are you going to do that?" I ask him. "You going to hire me a stripper who does extras?"

He turns to me, feigning a shocked expression as he clutches his fake pearls in dramatic fashion. "William, how dare you? I would never do such a thing..."

I raise my eyebrow at him, and he smirks at me.

"But only because it'd be wasted on you, Bro."

He isn't wrong. I'm not that type of guy. Yes, I've had my fair share of experiences with the fairer sex, but I've never paid for it and never would. And ever since a one night stand screamed at my 'deformity' as I took my pants off, I haven't done any of those either. I mean I know it's not pretty, but come on. I didn't scream when one of her chicken fillet things flopped out of her bra. Obviously, I have manners and she didn't.

It's hard having such an intimate piece of your anatomy removed to begin with. And when people see it, they instantly know it was cancer, and the pity looks begin. I hate the pity looks. Head tilted to the side, little awkward smile on their face, and the aww that follows always drives me mad. I know people aren't doing it to be mean or malicious, well except the screaming no tits witch, it just gets annoying after the millionth time. I tend to avoid sex now. My dick and ball aren't happy with my decision, but they'll get over it.

"I'm heading to the gym, you coming?" I ask Marcus who's nodding at me.

"Yeah, what else am I going to do on a Saturday afternoon?"

Before I can reply with a sarcastic comeback of my own, my attention is caught by a group of women, laden with shopping bags, heading towards us like they're going to charge right through us without stopping. It's impossible to hear what any of them are saying because there are so many of them talking at once, but the lady towards the back, who has her head down examining her phone, catches my eye immediately.

She's breathtaking.

Her long dark blonde hair is flowing around her face and she has a cute little button nose that turns up at the tip. I can't see the colour of her eyes, as they're glued to her phone, but if I had to hazard a guess it would be green or hazel. I quickly glance at her body and blow out a deep breath. Her long slender legs are clad in dark blue jeans, and a long sleeved black shirt is clinging to her tiny waist and very full looking tits.

I can't wait for her to walk past me so I can see her arse, but first I need to catch her attention. I can't help thinking what a great meet cute story this could be to tell our grandkids one day.

I shake my head a bit to clear my thoughts. I've been reading way too many romance novels for my mum's virtual book club.

The ladies at the front of the gaggle seem to quiet down a bit as they approach us. They stare at us, devouring our bodies with their eyes. An amused look flits across my face.

There are six of them in total, some look very similar and I can't help wondering if they're all related. I hit Marcus in the shoulder, a not-so-subtle indication for him to step to the side so they can carry on their stampede.

As I move to the left, my leg brushes against something and I look down and see flowers propped up in a bucket. I chuckle as I quickly scan my surroundings and realise I'm in front of a florist. You couldn't make this shit up. I reach down and grab a single white rose from the display just as the woman at the back looks up and her eyes meet mine. Her green eyes, I might add.

She's beautiful.

I can finally fully appreciate how Romeo must have felt

seeing Juliet for the first time. Right now, I'd gladly change my name and deny my father too. Wait, that was Juliet's line. Damn, this woman has got me mixing up Shakespeare. My students are going to love that.

The blonde lady with her hair in a bun smirks at us. "Thanks boys." She gives us a wink as she struts past us. The confidence oozing from her.

When my lady walks past me, she shyly smiles and mumbles, "Thank you."

"You're most welcome," I smile at her, "but parting is such sweet sorrow." I wink as I offer her the rose and swallow nervously as she just stares at me with wonder and appreciation in her eyes. She accepts the flower and before her head tips back down to her phone, I notice the pink tint that's now in place on her beautiful face.

As the women disappear around a corner Marcus slaps me on the shoulder trying to gain my attention. "What the hell was that, man?"

"I think I'm in love." I shrug at him.

"Oh, shut up, you saw her for a second."

"Whoever loved that loved not at first sight?" I grin at him knowing he hates it when I speak in 'Shakespeare talk', his words not mine.

"Speak in modern day English man," he shakes his head at me, "instead of that shit Shakespeare shite."

I clutch my chest and stagger slightly. "I'm wounded. You hurt me. Nice alliteration though." I offer a high five but he ignores it. Marcus doesn't enjoy words and grammar quite as much as I do.

"There was something about her." I look in the direction of where the girls went, but before I can think about walking after them, Marcus grabs me in a headlock. I struggle against him for a second before stepping inside the florist to pay for the flower I took. Then I let Marcus drag me down the road toward the gym, my thoughts all on the girl with the green eyes, who stole my heart.

∾

Our two-hour workout didn't do anything to help me get over my temporary madness of thinking I was in love with a woman I'd seen only once. My mind keeps drifting back to her. Why didn't I say more instead of that stupid Shakespeare quote? Why didn't I ask her name or for her number? Or even out for dinner or a drink? Because I'm an idiot, that's why. My only hope is to go out tonight and get drunk enough to obliterate my sheer stupidity and the image of green eyes from my mind.

Standing in my bedroom I look in the mirror. My dark blonde hair is styled into a messy look. I've got a crisp white shirt on with the sleeves rolled up and black jeans. I look good. I spray a bit of my favourite aftershave on and grab my phone and wallet from the side of my bed before heading downstairs. I know that I won't find Marcus ready yet, he always takes longer than me. Apparently, as he's told me on more than one occasion, "Being as gorgeous as this takes time".

I sit on the sofa and check my emails while I wait for Mr. Gorgeous to make his appearance. There's one from the head teacher at the school I work in informing me, as the department head, that a fellow English teacher has resigned. Fuck! This is the last thing I need. I've been trying to build our department up ever since my predecessor left due to a family bereavement. I've slowly managed to get a team of teachers that work nicely together and now one of them has quit. I send a quick reply asking to be kept informed of any decisions regarding filling the role. I know any information he decides to give me is out of courtesy rather than necessity. It's his role to hire, not mine, even though it's my fucking team. I fight the urge to run my hand through my hair so I don't ruin the look I just spent the past twenty minutes achieving, and blow out an exasperated breath just as Marcus walks down the stairs.

"Jeez what crawled up your arse and died?" He asks, shaking his head at me.

"Just got an email about work, it's fine, I'll deal with it Monday." I sigh getting up from the sofa.

"Yes, you will, pretty boy. Tonight is going to be lit. We're getting drunk AF."

I look at Marcus and roll my eyes at him. "Marcus, you're thirty-three, man. Thirty-three! It's time to start talking like a grown up now."

"Would thy preferest it if I spoketh liketh this, -eth?"

I laugh at him and push him in the chest. "Nope, just don't use colloquial slang like lit and AF, just say 'as fuck.' Next you'll be saying OH, EM, GEE, instead of oh my god. I'm telling you now, you speak like that and I'm done. I'll move out and leave your arse on your own. You hear me?" I point at him and frown to show him I mean business.

"Alright babes." He grins at me, winks and picks up his keys and phone heading for the door.

Looking back at me he says, "You're gonna get laid tonight, Bro." I groan and shake my head at him, secretly thinking maybe that's exactly what I need to get those eyes out of my mind once and for all.

CHAPTER 4
Nell

"I. AM. NOT. WEARING. THAT!" Hands on my hips, a fierce frown firmly set on my face, I pin Juliet in place and gesture at the minuscule piece of fabric she's trying to pass off as a dress.

"What? It's really in. You've got a banging body, what's wrong with it?" She looks around at my mum, sisters and Cleo's best friend and business partner Verity and they all nod their heads at her in agreement.

"You did say we could dress you, Nell." Cleo reminds me.

I balk at her, "Within reason. I said within fucking reason." They all erupt into fits of laughter whilst I'm standing in the middle of the shop, hands still on my hips, face flushed and swear words still ringing around me.

"You lot suck. You're all going to burn in hell for being bitches."

"Nell, I'm shocked! How could you say that about your mummy?" My mother scolds me, fake clutching her pearls, but I just grin at her.

"Well mother, as your first born, on my birthday, you

should have my back instead of colluding with those little harlots over there."

She doesn't want to, but she grins back at me. "Such lovely vocabulary Nelly. You are definitely your mother's daughter, aren't you?" She gives me a little cuddle and I stick my tongue out at my sisters over her shoulder.

Juliet smirks at me and, true to form, Cleo rolls her eyes. Emilia, already done with all of us, has picked up three dresses and a pair of boots and is walking over to me.

"Try these. Changing rooms are over there. Go, or we'll be late for the spa. And if I miss my massage because you're cuddling Mum, I won't be held responsible for my actions." I chuckle as Mum tuts at her, and I take the dresses into the changing room.

They're all very pretty, flowy in a boho chic kind of way. Definitely more my style. As I start to change, my mind drifts off to think about Steve. I wonder what his plans for me would have been today. Would he have taken me away somewhere or would we have stayed local? Steve was never a spontaneous guy, and liked everything planned, so he would have had things in place for months in advance. I smile thinking about his meticulous planning and sigh because I miss him, but I notice the ache isn't as prominent anymore and that worries me. Am I forgetting what we had? Am I losing him all over again?

"Are you going to show us how they look or what, Nell?" Emilia's sharp voice drags me out of my silent panic. I have a dress on but I'm just standing in front of the mirror, and I honestly have no idea how long I've been here like this.

"Yeah I'm just putting the boots on." I shove my feet inside them and open the curtain. They all look at me and nod their heads.

"Nice. It looks good on you. Do you like it? Well, it's kind of tough because we don't have time to try anything else on and you did say we could dress you." Juliet's babbling.

I laugh and shake my head at her. "Princess, take a breath, I like it. I'll wear it tonight. Let me change so we can get to the spa before Emilia pops a vein in her head." I get into my own clothes as quickly as I can and head over to the cashier to pay for my new purchases, when Emilia stands in front of me.

"Hand them over, I'm paying for these for your birthday."

"No, you guys paid for the spa treatments. Emilia, let me pay for the clothes." She shakes her head at me, sighs, takes the clothes and turns her back on me. The argument is over, and I apparently lost. My family is nuts, but I love them so bloody much.

When I step outside to join the rest of the gang and wait for Emilia, I take my phone out of my back pocket and see a notification for a missed call from my old boss. I sigh and ignore it, typing a message to my dad asking how Ben is instead.

I wait for a reply, but nothing comes straight through. Dammit I don't want to phone him. He'll moan at me for not trusting him, but I need to know if Ben's okay.

I'm vaguely aware of Emilia joining us, and I start walking when I notice they're moving on without me, but my focus is still on my phone and the lack of reply from my dad. Trailing behind them, I try to tune them out as they very loudly talk and gossip about god knows what. Finally, my dad responds with, "We're fine. Stop stressing. I've raised four girls and a Connor. I know what I'm doing."

I chuckle at the Connor comment, as my mum and dad did practically raise him, and look up just as the girls have gone quiet. My gaze focuses on the most amazing chocolate brown eyes I have ever seen in my life, my mouth goes dry and I can barely remember how to walk. As I near him, he smiles, and I almost lose my footing and face plant in front of him. He's tall and athletic looking, not in a big and bulky muscles way, but lean and tight. His dark blonde hair is just the right amount of messy and his jaw is dotted with a couple day's worth of stubble.

I notice he's moved aside for us, and mumble thank you at him before glancing back down at my phone again, when he responds with a fucking Shakespeare quote and hands me a white rose. Surely, I just imagined that. No man his age would quote Shakespeare. And where did the bloody flower come from? I must be dehydrated or something else that's made me delirious. I look back at him with a confused look on my face, and I'm met with another smile. Before I can do anything else, my phone vibrates with a picture of Ben smiling with my dad. All my unease disappears as I look at two of my favourite men on the screen in front of me, and I forget about the very handsome man standing behind me.

CHAPTER 5

William

Our local pub is busy, as it always is on a Saturday night, and we slowly make our way to the classic old-style wraparound bar, winding through the tables and chairs scattered around for when people order food. The dartboard in the corner is wisely shuttered to the Saturday night crowd. White walls and spotlights in the ceiling, as well as light fixtures that hang down, showcase the dark mahogany tables. Through an arch in the wall, there's a small stage area where the live bands or karaoke set up, and just behind that are two pool tables.

The barman grabs our attention and I order us two beers when Marcus shouts over me, "And shots man, we want shots too."

I shake my head laughing, as does the barman. "Let's start with beer and pace ourselves, we have all night."

Marcus shakes his head at me in disgust and orders two jaeger bombs. I'm still chuckling at him when the barman brings our drinks and puts them, shots and all, in front of us.

"Come on lad, drink up. There are some seriously hot ladies in here for you tonight, some I haven't seen before."

Taking a sip of my beer I look around at the people for the first time tonight. I see Smithy at the bar in his usual spot and nod my head in hello to him. I scan over the bar and my gaze falls onto the pool area. A few girls are lingering there, either waiting for the live music or waiting to play pool, but they barely look older than my students.

"Way too young for me." I say to Marcus pointedly, directing his gaze to the girls.

He chokes on his beer. "Shit Will, do you think I want you to go to prison? No, I mean the ones behind us and to the left. A group of them. Be subtle. But first, shot."

I roll my eyes yet again, sure they're going to get stuck there one day being friends with Marcus. I lift the Jaeger to my mouth and down it, chasing it with a gulp of my beer, before I casually glance around and see the group of ladies he's talking about. A closer look has the hairs on the back of my neck stand up. I feel a shiver through my body and my gaze meets the same green eyes that I've been seeing since this morning.

"No, fucking, way." I mutter to myself.

"What? What's up?" Marcus's gaze follows mine and he smirks when he spots my lady. "No way, Will. Is that the lady from earlier? Go talk to her. I had to listen to you talk about her for two hours in the gym so you better man up and go over there."

I shake my head in amazement and turn back to the bar, motioning for the barman to come over. I order another shot and knock it back.

Marcus turns back to me. "Dude, she's wearing a sash that says birthday bitch. It's perfect. Buy her a drink and get the barman to take it over saying it's from you for her birthday. She'll have to come over and talk to you then. Do it, if you don't I will."

My head snaps up and I glare. "Don't even think about it," I grit my teeth and tell him. God knows what he'd say to her. The challenge in his eyes is telling me he isn't joking, and I've known him long enough to know he won't back down from this, so I do as he says.

"Hey, do you know what the birthday girl over there is drinking?" I ask the barman, trying to sound casual but not sure if it's coming across that way.

"The rest of them have been downing shots and wine like it's going to run out, but she's been drinking vodka and cranberry juice as well as doing a few shots. I also know it's her thirtieth birthday if that helps you." He wiggles his eyebrows at me and smirks, and I laugh and put my hand out to shake his.

"My man, send over a shot and a vodka cranberry and give her this please." He grins back at me and gets to work as I write my note on a napkin.

As he leaves the bar, nerves start to spread through me. What if she sends it back? Or doesn't understand the note. I know it's risky quoting Shakespeare. Most people don't get it, but something's telling me she will.

"What did you write?" Marcus asks me.

"Happy birthday, there was a star danced, and under that was you born." I grimace as I tell him, and the dick starts laughing.

"God, you need fucking help. It's a good job you're pretty, man."

I glance over to the ladies. They've all gone silent and are looking at the note and then at me. The one with the bun high fives another lady, who is the image of her but with dark hair. They must all be sisters.

My lady stands up, turning to face me, and a look of recognition flashes across her face. She remembers me from this morning. I tip my drink at her and smile. She tilts her head to the side with a little frown on her beautiful face before she turns back to the ladies, says something, and then turns and heads my way.

Shit! I start to panic and my tongue sticks to the roof of my mouth. I feel like a nervous teenager again. I sip my beer and give Marcus daggers when he starts to say something. He mumbles that he needs the gents and heads off, leaving me alone, as the most beautiful woman I've ever laid eyes on approaches me. I hear the Bruno Mars song "Marry You" playing in the background and I smile to myself, liking the sound of that.

CHAPTER 6
Nell

"Go, go, go, go!" I'm on my third shot and I know without a doubt this will be my last one. The girls won't notice when I make the switch. I've already told the barman after this one to make sure my 'sambuca' shot is filled with water. I know it's sneaky, but these girls need someone to look after them. And I'm the big sister, it's my job to do so. Plus, I hate getting drunk. I'll get tipsy, but I refuse to get off my face drunk where I can't remember what happened, just in case something happens to Ben and I'm needed.

I sit back in my chair with a happy smile on my face and watch my sisters dance and laugh around me. The pub sectioned off a little area for us, and there's enough room to dance and muck about without knocking into other patrons, which is very much needed with the Cooper sisters and their clan of happy chaos.

Cleo's dancing with Verity and singing along to a song that's shouting out to an ex, with a little bit too much enthusiasm for someone who hasn't had her heart broken before. Interesting. Maybe I need to have a little talk with little Miss Cleopatra about who this ex is that she's singing about. I glance over at Emilia and Juliet, who look like they're in a heated discussion, but I don't want to get into the middle of those two. Especially when they're drunk. As quickly as their arguments start, they finish. And they always make up, so I'm leaving them to duke it out.

I'm reaching for my phone to see if my mum or dad has texted me about Ben, when the barman comes over and places a Vodka cranberry and a shot in front of me.

"I didn't order these," I start to say to him, but he cuts me off.

"There's a guy at the bar who wanted to buy you a birthday drink. Don't worry, I didn't tell him you were on the heavy stuff." He winks at me and nods his head towards the water shot and continues. "He also wanted me to give you this note." He places a napkin in my hands and walks off.

Before I can turn to see who this mystery man is, my sisters and Verity have swooped around me and are very intent on reading the note with me.

"Open it, will you!" Emilia shouts at me over the music. I glare at her a bit but open it anyway, curiosity getting the better of me.

Happy birthday, there was a star danced, and under that was you born.

"Well, what the hell does that mean?" Verity, the non-Shakespeare buff of the group, speaks up. Emilia high fives Cleo whilst looking at the bar.

I frown at them both and turn around to see my admirer. Standing at the bar is the man from this morning. The chocolate brown eyed, beautiful smiled, gorgeous, muscular, stubbled, Shakespeare quoting, flower giving guy from this morning. And he's tipping his drink at me and smiling once again. I shake my head at the fact that the universe seems to be conspiring against me, and get up to talk to this mystery Shakespeare buff, if only to point out that he misquoted. Because, that's what I do.

I notice little flutters in my tummy as I head over to him. Butterflies? I haven't felt those in forever. I tamp down the nerves flitting through me and focus on the excitement instead. I don't know why I'm doing this. This isn't something that I'd normally do, but I have this overwhelming need to speak to this man. It's too coincidental that I saw him this morning and now again in the pub on my birthday, and that he's quoted Shakespeare to me twice now.

I blow out a shaky breath and tell myself, "There's no harm in talking."

He's watching me stalk towards him and there's a twinkle in his eyes. Surprise? Intrigue? Hunger? I don't know, but there's definitely something there. His friend has disappeared and I tilt my head at him slightly as I stand in front of him.

"You're wrong you know." I stare at him boldly, but smile at him smugly.

"How am I wrong?" He asks with the hint of a smirk on his very full and kissable lips.

I avert my gaze from looking at said full lips and my eyes meet his. The heat that surges through my body from his intense stare almost knocks me to my knees. I casually walk around him to lean up against the bar. Hopefully it looks like a cool move to him, when in truth it's a necessity, so I don't fall at this gorgeous guy's feet.

"You misquoted. You replaced 'I' with 'you.'"

He smiles at me and turns his body so he is facing me directly. He licks his lips and grins when he catches my eyes tracking the movement.

"I know. I was going to go with a quote about being old but didn't fancy getting beaten up by you and your entourage over there, so I thought I'd change a word to make it fit. Normally that would have gone unnoticed."

I laugh and we both look over at my 'entourage' to see the girls dancing and laughing with Mr. Shakespeare's friend.

"Is that your friend? Dancing with my sister?" I gawp at Emilia who's singing about being sorry and missing some-one's body. Sambuca and Bieber are not a good combination for the normally controlled and collected Emilia.

"Yeah, that's Marcus. He's a serial flirt and loves to dance, but he's a good guy, and gay, so don't worry about your sister."

I laugh at his concern and gently tell him, "Sweetie, I wasn't worried about my sister. Emilia can handle herself and anyone and everyone else too. I was more worried about your friend."

"Meh, he's a big boy. I'm sure he'll be fine." He shrugs and turns his gaze back to me. "So how come I know your sister's name and not yours?"

I can't help but laugh. "Smooth, Mr. Shakespeare. Smooth. I'm Nell," I tell him and motion to where I was sitting. "My entourage over there is made up of my three sisters and our friend Verity, who's around here somewhere. Just to be clear of who is who, Emilia is the one currently serenading your friend, and Cleopatra is the one grinding on our baby sister Juliet. Your turn?"

He smiles at me and my knees go weak again, but this time I'm already leaning up against the bar, so I don't fall. Ha! Take that Mr. Shakespeare.

Just as he's about to talk, I feel an arm come around my shoulders and hear a familiar voice wishing me a happy birth-day. I turn and come face to face with Connor.

"Oh my God Connor, what are you doing here? I thought you were busy tonight." I give him a quick cuddle and turn back to sneak a peek at Mr. Shakespeare, who, judging by his frowny face and the ticking of his jaw, seems to be quite upset.

I chuckle and lean in closer to Connor, who puts his arm tighter around me, making me laugh more. He's always so protective of us girls. Seeing the glint in Mr. Shakespeare's eyes, I decide to end this now, before they end up squaring off with each other. Even though the idea of Mr. Shakespeare wanting to fight for me is stirring something up inside of me.

"Connor, this is a friend of mine. Mr Shakespeare, meet Connor, my honorary brother. Connor, meet Mr. Shakespeare." He offers his hand up to Connor, who takes it while offering up a rather gruff greeting in return.

I give Connor a look and nod my head over to where the girls are. "The girls are over there if you want to grab a drink. I'll be back up there in a minute." He hesitates but looks at my sisters and then nods his head at me before making his way to the girls.

When I turn back to Mr. Shakespeare with a smirk on my face, he laughs at me and shakes his head. "So, your mum and dad obviously like Shakespeare as much as I do, given your names."

I tilt my head and nod at him. "They're huge fans. Which kind of made it impossible for any of us to avoid his work. Hence me knowing a Shakespeare quote being thrown at me once or twice, even if it is wrong. You genuinely like Shakespeare?"

"I love words, books and English. I'm a massive nerd, Nell." He shrugs when he says that and looks so bloody cute, but all I can focus on is the way my name rolled off his tongue.

How does it make me feel more vulnerable than I've ever felt? And why does it make me want to strip naked, lay on the bar and let him have his wicked way with me? Thankfully I just blush and avert my eyes from his face rather than living out that particular fantasy.

"What's your favourite Shakespeare play?" There's a part of me that knows he isn't lying, but surely he can't be that good looking and a Shakespeare buff as well. The Universe wouldn't be so cruel would it? To throw this beautiful man, who I appear to have a lot in common with, in front of me when I am in no way ready for anything with another man.

"Hmmmm that's a hard one. Favourite play would be *A Midsummer Night's Dream*. It's fun, filled with love, passion and humour. What about you?"

I can't speak. That's my favourite thing ever written. I love Puck, the spirited sprite who plays havoc throughout the play. It's always been my favourite. Steve used to say I was mad because none of it made sense, but it's always made perfect sense to me. It's been my favourite since I saw it at the Globe with my parents when I was eleven.

He gently touches my hand that's resting on the bar, bringing me out of my head, and asks if I'm okay.

"Yeah sorry. You threw me a little bit. I didn't expect you to say that one. It's my favourite too." I pause and look at him curiously. "Who are you?" I whisper.

He laughs as he tells me, "William."

I give him a suspicious look. "If you say your surname is Shakespeare, I'm out of here."

He holds his hands up in surrender and grins that boyish grin at me. "No, my surname isn't Shakespeare. My grandfather was called William and I was named after him. I'm William Blake. It's nice to meet you, Nell. Nell?..." He sticks his hand out as if we're just meeting and I grasp it without a second thought.

"Nell Cooper." God what am I doing? I don't want to flirt with this man, but I can't help it. I love Steve with all my heart, but he isn't here. I want to walk away from William, but I can't.

I look down at my hand and see the gaping emptiness of where my ring should be. I stopped wearing it about a year ago now. It didn't feel right to have it on, like I was clinging to something that didn't exist anymore. It's why I gave him my maiden name. I want him to know Nell Cooper, not Vickers. Steve and I, our marriage, it's gone. I didn't want it to be gone, I still don't, but it is. Just like I don't want to stop talking to William.

I shouldn't be talking to him, I'm encouraging him and I shouldn't be, but I can't walk away. Not yet. There's something I can't explain keeping me here; a need to find out more about him. I'm so confused right now, and I don't know what to do or think.

As if to rescue me from my scurrying brain, my phone vibrates in my pocket and I instinctively reach to get it. "Sorry I have to check this," I tell William. I can't ignore my phone when Ben isn't with me. The screen lights up with a picture of my beautiful boy, fast asleep with his teddy bear. I smile whilst looking at it, but I'm interrupted.

"Wow, I wish I had someone smiling like that when I send them a text," William states. "There was a look of pure love on your face just then. Should I be jealous?" He smiles to show that he's joking, but I can see the nerves in his smile and gently laugh at him. I turn the screen to face him and show him Ben asleep.

"My son Ben. Well, his full name is Benvolio." He smiles down at me, and I roll my eyes and smile back. "My mum just sent me this to let me know he's fine and asleep. You can run in that direction if you want." I don't know why I showed him Ben or even told him about him. I'm normally very private, but there's something telling me this man is trustworthy. Part of me wants him to run a mile now he knows I have a kid, but the other part is begging him to stay.

"He's beautiful, like his mum. I'm not wearing the right shoes for running so I'll have to stay here and keep talking to you, Nell. How old is he?" I look down, suddenly feeling very shy and tell him he's almost four.

"Does he spend a lot of time with his dad?"

I shake my head, still looking down at the bar. I haven't spoken to anyone about Steve except my family, and even that's very rare. To want to tell Mr. Shakespeare about him is odd but feels right. I can't understand it myself. I just know that I want William to know what happened. I want William. I shake my head to get rid of that last thought.

"His dad, Steve, my husband, died when Ben was a year old. He was killed."

I swallow back the lump in my throat as William leans in closer and whispers, "Sorry."

He doesn't say anything else, just lets me gather myself, like he knows how hard it was for me to say. Who is this guy?

I clear my throat and try to get the barman's attention to get a drink of water, when William's hand gently rests over the top of mine and he squeezes it a little. The touch speaks more than any words ever could. That's the second time he's touched my hand and I haven't flinched away or wanted to run. With William, everything feels natural. It's like my body knows him but my mind doesn't. I don't understand any of this. He signals for the barman to come over, and when he looks at me expectantly, I ask for a lemonade.

William's chuckle seems to break the spell. "Something funny, Mr. Shakespeare?" I turn to face him, and I can see pride in his eyes. Is he proud of me? That's ridiculous. Why would he be?

"Back to Mr. Shakespeare eh? I can live with that. Lemonade?" He smiles as the barman brings me my drink and puts a beer down in front of William.

"You didn't order that, and I didn't pay." I state to him and again he's chuckling.

"I have a tab and he knows when I give him the sign that I want a beer. It's a man thing." He smiles whilst saying it and I roll my eyes at him yet again. "What d'you do for fun, Nell?

You clearly don't like drinking that much, so what else do you do to unwind?"

I take a deep breath and sigh out, "Erm, I read a lot." He nods at me and says, 'me too.' and then waits for me to say more.

"I don't know what else to say. I've spent the last three years being a mum, so fun things for me normally involve sand pits, indoor play areas, or cartoons about dogs with really catchy theme tunes. Don't get me wrong, I love being Ben's mum but..."

"You just miss being Nell a bit too. It's okay to admit that, you know. It doesn't mean you love him any less."

I shift from foot to foot, suddenly uncomfortable with where this conversation is heading so I flip it over to him. "What do you do for fun, Mr. Shakespeare?"

"I go to work, work out a lot," he flexes his arm as he grabs his pint, bringing on another eyeroll, but I can't fight the grin that overtakes my mouth. He smiles back at me, making me think he knew I was deflecting, but carries on, "Spend time with my friends, read and watch tv, go on dates, normal stuff."

I look down at the lemonade that I'm now nursing and nod my head sadly.

"Normal stuff." I say quietly, "I used to do normal stuff too."

"You can still do normal stuff, Nell. Why do I think the only person telling you that you can't is you?"

I look up at him suddenly, my mouth gaping open, and realise he's right. What am I doing? I'm moping about not doing 'normal stuff' but I'm the only one stopping me. Everyone I love has told me in the past few months that I need to get out of this rut, but it takes a perfect stranger to get me to listen.

"I've got to go, Mr. Shakespeare. William, sorry. I have to

run. Thank you for everything. Maybe I'll see you around." Before he can respond, I tiptoe up to kiss his cheek and rush out of the pub. Once outside I don't stop to order an uber. I only live five minutes away, so I speed walk towards my house to sort my head and my life out. Thanks to Mr. Shakespeare.

CHAPTER 7

Nell

"And send... It's done, Steve. I know I should've done it a long time ago, but it's the first step to getting me back." I close the laptop and look over to the photo of Steve I keep on the fireplace mantle so Ben can see his daddy.

"I'm sorry if you saw me talking to William. I don't know if you have magical powers up there, where you can read my thoughts, but if you do, I'm sorry for them as well." I bring my legs up onto the sofa and curl them underneath me, getting comfortable for our chat.

"Emilia told me the other day that you'd want me to start dating again, that you wouldn't want me alone. Is that true, Steve? I wish I knew for sure. I know you'd want me back at work. You always told me you didn't want me to quit my job when I was pregnant. You knew how much I loved teaching, so hopefully I'll be able to say that I'm back in the land of the employed soon."

My thoughts turn back to those chocolate eyes. The way his touch didn't send me running, and how nice it was to talk to Mr. Shakespeare.

"I don't know why I felt so at ease with him, Steve. I've only ever felt like that with you. Is it weird to talk to you about this? Shit, it's weird that I talk to you about anything isn't it? It's comforting for me though. I don't know if I'll start doing all the normal stuff that William mentioned, but I'm starting with getting a job. And that's something. Maybe one day I'll look into the other things too. I wish you were here. Come and see me tonight? Please."

I look back over to the picture and blow him a kiss. I used to talk to him like this every day, but recently it's become less and less. I always ask him to come and visit me in my dreams, but he never does. Or maybe I just never remember.

I don't know what came over me in the pub. Everyone has told me that I need to be more than just Mum and be Nell again, but hearing it from William made it so much clearer.

I want to be the woman I used to be. I want to work and go on dates—God I want to go on dates with William—but I can't have those thoughts because I'm not ready to go out with anyone. Am I? I might be. I don't know.

Maybe I want to take these steps so that I'll be ready. For him? Yes. No. I don't know. I just needed to send that email to my old boss as soon as possible. Just taking that step has made me feel like I'm one step closer to my old self again.

Smiling and sipping my tea, the front door slams open and slams shut again and I'm on my feet before anyone has a chance to get into my front room. Stalking into the hallway I see Juliet, swaying slightly and cursing about 'the nerve of some people.'

"Juliet? How did you get home? Did you walk on your own? Where are the others?" I know it's hypocritical of me as I walked home alone, but I wasn't drunk and it's my job as the biggest sister to be hypocritical.

"Oh, stop mithering, I didn't walk home alone. Connor stalked after me the whole way home, the arrogant arsehole."

Slightly taken aback, I tentatively ask her, "Why was he

stalking behind you? Why didn't he walk next to you? And why is he an arsehole?"

"Because he is! All of you think he's this nice guy who is perfect all the time, but he isn't. He is a dick, a massive fucking dick. He kissed me Nell. He shouldn't be kissing me. He knows what I'm, he knows how I... Oh Nell." I wrap my arms around her and stroke her hair and shush her whilst she cries.

"Juliet, did you kiss him back? Is there something more with you and him? Do I need to kick his perfect arse? Cause I will. Sisters before misters all day long!" She laughs a little and wipes her cheeks on my shoulder.

"I did kiss him back, Nell. I don't know what's going on, that's why I didn't want to see him. Please don't say anything to the others or to him, Nell. Please?" Before I can reassure her that her secret is safe with me, the front door opens and the other three girls spill into my front room, drunk as anything, with Emilia screeching questions and demands without giving anyone a chance to answer her.

"Where did you two go? You left without saying bye. What's going on?" She's swaying dangerously in the doorway and Verity and Cleo are near enough sleeping whilst standing up. I laugh at all of them and give Juliet a look that hopefully reassures her that I won't say anything.

"Right. You sorry lot, let's get you to bed and we'll talk in the morning. You two, spare room. Juliet you can come in with me, and Emilia you're on the sofa unless you want to squeeze into Ben's tiny bed. Sorry love." Before I can turn around, Emilia's laying on the sofa half asleep, shoes still on. As Juliet ushers the other two upstairs, I take Emilia's heels off, put a blanket over her, and get a glass of water and some painkillers to leave on the coffee table.

Once everyone's in bed sleeping, I'm heading back down-stairs to get water and painkillers for Verity and Cleo, but

47

stop in the doorway when Emilia sits up and starts speaking to Steve's picture.

"Steve, Nell needs your help. She shouldn't be scared. He's a good guy. Perfect for her. I spoke with him. You know, you saw. I think you sent him, didn't you, Steve? I know you did." She reaches up to her hair and undoes her bun, letting her beautiful locks fall down and around her shoulders. I stand, transfixed, and listen to her talk to my dead husband's picture.

"You agree with me don't you? She doesn't deserve to be alone, none of them do. They don't need to be lonely like me. I can handle it, they deserve love. And you, you sent him. I know you did. I miss you Steve, but I want my sister back. You had her for your time, but she needs to come back to us now. Give her back now Steve. Give her back." She slumps back down onto the sofa and starts lightly snoring.

Tears falling down my cheeks, I absorb everything she said. She wants me back.

"I do too, Sis," I whisper to her, "I do too."

"I'm never drinking again. You're the devil, woman." Cleo points a finger at Verity who's looking as fresh as a daisy compared to Cleo's half dead zombie look.

"Oh sweetie, you should know by now that you should never try to keep up with me." Verity's laughing as she walks around the kitchen island and gives Cleo a kiss on the head. She cuddles me and kisses my cheek, calling over her shoulder, "Toodles girls, I'll see you tomorrow Cleo," and heads to the front door.

I laugh as I look back at Cleo and walk over to the kettle to make a cup of tea. "You want tea, coffee or water with your painkillers?"

She lowers her head onto the counter in front of her and grumbles, "Coffee, black, three sugars please, Sis."

I give her arm a little pat as I place her painkillers in front of her, then shudder as she swallows them down without water.

"I wish I could do that. They always get stuck in my throat when I try." She chuckles at me as I make our tea and coffee.

"Food?" I ask and she nods at me appreciatively. We stay in a comfortable silence as we wait for the bacon and eggs to cook. Once the smells waft through the house we're joined by Emilia and Juliet. I give them painkillers and make tea and coffee for them as well. Plating the food up, I sit on the side and watch my little sisters become more human as the grease eases off their hangovers.

"How come she turns thirty and we have the hangovers?" Cleo asks, pointing her fork at me accusingly. Like I made her try to compete with the ever-impressive Verity, who can out drink everyone.

I laugh as Emilia answers, "Because she and Juliet snuck off early and left us at the pub, remember? What was that about anyway? One minute you were talking to the cute Shakespeare guy, William, and then you were talking with Connor and the next thing I know, you were both gone. And so was Connor. What gives?" Her eyes are darting back and forth between me and Juliet.

Before Juliet can answer, I speak up. "Talking with William made me realise the truth behind what you have all been saying I should do. I needed to come home and send my old boss an email about going back to work. Juliet noticed I left and asked Connor to walk with her to see if I was okay. Once she got home, Connor had to dash off somewhere. I'm sorry I didn't tell you I was...wait, how did you know his name? Did his friend tell you? The one you were serenading all night long?" I give Emilia a suspicious look and she grins at me.

"Don't give me that look," she admonishes me, "Juliet is the one that deserves that look about Marcus, not me." I look at Juliet, confused, but she has her head down like her plate is the most intriguing thing in the world. I make a mental note to talk to her later about Connor, and now Marcus too.

"How did you know his name, Emilia?" I ask her again but I'm met with a grin so wide that I almost smile back at her.

"I may have asked him a few questions after I realised you'd gone. He may have answered. I may also have found out some information about him and possibly threatened him a bit if he'd upset you, which as you have now told me he didn't do, I won't have to fulfil. So stop looking at me like that." I'm frowning at her and I really want to punch her in the throat, but I'm not a teenager anymore and hitting my sister is not allowed.

"Emilia, why…? D'you know what, I don't even care. I decided last night that I'm taking the first step in getting Nell back and doing normal stuff again. Dating isn't one of them..." I look up at them and, at the shock and disappointment on their faces, add, "yet. I'm not ready yet, but hopefully once I get back to having a job the rest will follow. I know you've all told me this for the past six months and I'm sorry I wasn't ready to listen."

I look back down at my slippers, suspended in the air from my seat on the counter top, as Cleo says, "For what it's worth, I liked William. He was gorgeous and I think the Shakespeare quotes were brilliant, especially for you Nell. Just don't write him off completely yet please."

I look up at her and smile. "Too late. We didn't swap numbers or anything, so unless the universe wants me to see him again, I won't be able to even if I wanted to. And that's okay."

I don't miss Emilia's grin when she replies, "I think the universe will definitely set something up between the two of you. You haven't seen the last of him, Sis."

Before I can ask what she knows, my mobile phone starts to ring. I jump down and grab it off the counter and see it's my old boss.

"Shit I didn't expect him to call." I show the screen to my sisters and they silently encourage me to answer.

"Hello, how are you Mr. Rockwell?"

CHAPTER 8

Nell

I can't believe I'm here again. Sitting inside Mr. Rockwell's office, I glance around and realise nothing has changed. His desk is the same dark brown, covered in paperwork and a photograph of his wife and children. The walls are still lined with bookshelves with various texts on them. It feels like I never left.

Everything happened so quickly for me to be here on a Monday morning. The missed call from him on Saturday was to ask if I would consider a temporary position that had just become available. And when he received my email, he called me straight away on Sunday offering me the role.

I barely had time to focus after I got off that call. I called my mum and dad to explain what had happened and find out about childcare for Ben, not that I thought for one second my mother would mind picking him up from nursery. From there I had to find some appropriate work clothes in my wardrobe and make sure they were clean and not musty from sitting there for the last few years unworn.

Once Ben was back at home, I explained to him that mummy was going back to work, and the little smile that lit his face up was everything to me. He was so proud that I was going to be a teacher again, just like his adored Miss Ali. It almost made all the anxiety go away. I had briefly been told about the role by Mr. Rockwell yesterday, but sitting here now, waiting for a full rundown, has all the nerves creeping back in. I cross my legs and sit up straighter just as he comes barrelling into the office.

I make my way to stand but he waves his hand at me. "Sit down Nell, there are no formalities with me. How are you feeling? Sorry to throw this on you."

I smile at him, "I'm a little nervous, I'm not going to lie, but it's the good nerves. I think. If I'm honest with you, I think it's better this way. Gives me less time to panic and change my mind. So, tell me about the team."

I sit back in my chair and relax a bit as he gives me a warm and familiar smile. He looks exactly the same as he did before and I start to get excited by his overzealous attitude as he describes the person that took over for me. I was the head of the English department when I left for my maternity leave with Ben. A little bit of jealousy forms at the idea of someone else running my department, but I put that firmly into a box at the back of my mind, seeing as it isn't my department anymore and I was the one that left.

He speaks very highly of this person, telling me that we're very similar and that he hopes it will create a great working environment. I agree with him, more excited about the opportunity now, and just as I am about to rise to leave, a knock at his door startles me.

"Ah, perfect timing, come in." I keep my eyes focused on Mr. Rockwell as I don't want to seem nosey about who's entering his office, but then he motions to me whilst saying, "Nell, I'd like you to meet the head of the English department and the person you'll be working with closely until you feel confident enough to fly solo. Nell this is William Blake. William, meet Nell Vickers."

I turn my head ever so slowly, hoping that there are two William Blakes out there that can quote Shakespeare as freely as Mr. Shakespeare, but as my eyes meet his, I know that luck isn't with me today. I glance at his face, his expression changing from shock to happiness in a split second, whilst I'm left trying to calm my blazing red cheeks down as I hold my hand out to shake his.

"Mr. Blake, it's nice to meet you again."

He chuckles as he takes my hand. "It certainly is Nell Vickers, welcome aboard."

Mr. Rockwell clears his throat and asks, "Do you two know each other?"

"No."

"Yes."

We both say together and then I give a nervous laugh as William explains, "I ran into Nell at the pub on Saturday night. She was celebrating her birthday and we got to talking about Shakespeare, so yes we know each other but no we don't really."

I smile at Mr. Rockwell who is looking at me rather suspiciously with a smirk on his face. "Ah yes, you both are Shakespeare nuts. You Coopers all are. I told you Nell, very similar." I roll my eyes at him, and fortunately he doesn't see me do it, but William does.

He covers his chuckle with a cough. "Nell, would you like me to give you a tour?"

I smile at William and shake my head. "I'm sure it hasn't changed all that much."

He tilts his head at me and then realisation hits his beautiful face. "You used to be the head of department. Family bereavement, shit, sorry. I should really try thinking before speaking. Mr. Rockwell, Nell, I'm sorry about that."

I smile at him gently as our boss grins at him and slaps

his shoulder, letting him know there are no hard feelings for his swearing.

I glance at the clock on the wall behind William to make sure I'll get to Ben's Nursery in time, and ask if there is any other business for me to do today. When I'm told no, I say goodbye and that I'll see them on Wednesday, gathering my things for a quick escape. I need to get out of there as quickly as I can. My bravado is wearing off.

Walking down the hallways that are so familiar to me I start to panic. What am I doing? I can't work here with him. I don't want to let anyone down, but I'll have to phone Mr. Rockwell tomorrow and let him know I can't come back. What was I thinking? This is all too much too soon. Just seeing his beautiful face again made my body heat up and my knickers wetter than they have ever been in my life, sorry Steve.

I'm nearly to the safety of the parking lot when I hear my name and turn around to see William jogging after me. He's so beautiful it hurts my eyes to look at him.

"Let me walk you to your car and stop that mind of yours from talking you out of doing this." I just stare at him. How does he know? How does he guess that I'm having second thoughts? He holds the door open for me and raises an eyebrow at me, questioning whether I'm going to go with him or not, so I square my shoulders and lead him outside to my car.

Once we're next to it and away from prying ears, I turn around to face him. "I can't do this. I can't come and work here."

"Why?" One simple question that has me squirming, but I have to answer him honestly.

"I feel guilty, William." I look down at the ground.

"For working here again or for liking me?" I frown up at him and catch the glimpse of amusement in his eyes. Infuriating man. Does he think this is all some sort of joke? My feelings are in disarray and he's making a joke about it?

"Cocky, aren't you? Actually, I feel guilty for working and not being there to pick Ben up from Nursery, if you must know. Believe me, I have no feelings for you whatsoever."

The smirk on his face disappears, and I swear there's a trace of hurt in his eyes, but before I can be certain, it's gone. His eyes turn darker as he steps closer to me, backing me up against my car. He licks his lips, and my eyes follow his tongue's movement, giving myself away for my blatant lie a moment ago.

"I think it's time you stopped feeling guilty, Nell Cooper or Vickers, whatever your name is. You have a little boy who should look up to you and be proud of what you're doing, and you have a great opportunity to do that here. You love teaching. The students raved about you when I first started here. I was jealous of you for a long time. You belong here Nell, you know it and so do I. Maybe that's why the universe keeps putting us together. Or maybe it's for... other reasons."

His voice is low and gravelly, and he's standing dangerously close to me. I can smell him. He smells like man and paper and old leather, like books. I can see the pulse jumping in his neck and I can hear his breathing. I look up at his face, hovering inches away from my own, as he licks those full lips again and I bite onto my bottom lip and look down at his feet.

"So why can't you work here, Nell?" He reaches for my chin and lifts my face up to look at him, bringing our lips to within a whisper of each other's, and I want to move ever so slightly so I can feel his mouth on mine. My breath catches in my throat, and I close my eyes ready for his lips to taste me.

"You have no feelings for me whatsoever, remember?" And with that he steps back and turns away from me. I take a few ragged breaths and try to control my heart rate when he turns back to me and says, "'A coward dies a thousand times before his death, but the valiant taste of death but once.' Don't be a coward, Nell."

Rendering me speechless with one of the best-timed Shakespeare quotes ever, he turns back towards the building and is gone within seconds, leaving me feeling like the world's biggest idiot and more confused than ever as I get into my car and head for home.

CHAPTER 9
William

"Shit man, the universe is really playing games with you two. So, she's going to be working with you then?"

It's already six o'clock and I've only been home for an hour. After the most frustrating day I've ever had at work, I spent an hour at the gym trying to clear my mind and then came home to tell Marcus everything.

"I don't know. She bolted from the office pretty quickly. After our little near miss by her car, God knows if she'll turn up on Wednesday."

I'm so mad at myself for letting her rile me in the parking lot. I could see how nervous and flighty she was in the pub on Saturday, and I told myself then that I'd have to go slowly with her. That was before she even told me about her husband being killed. I had no intention of getting in her space like that, or forcing her body to tell me what I already knew, but hearing her say she had no feelings for me was like a challenge. I had to prove her wrong. I was so close to kissing her. I could feel her breath on my mouth; I was practically drooling for her.

I'd gone back to my office and paced around a bit, trying to calm myself down and rid myself of my erection before I had to face a bunch of teenagers and try to teach them. I really didn't need any parents hearing about their kid's teacher and his boner all through class. Maybe I should leave her be, let her run away from this job if she has this kind of effect on me. How could I work next door to her?

The team could really use her though. I wasn't blowing smoke up her arse when I told her I was jealous of her. The kids really looked up to her, and losing her was a massive blow to them. She impacted them and made their learning environment a better place, and when she left, they mourned her. All I heard for the first few months of my position here was 'Mrs. V was amazing' and 'Mrs. V didn't do it like that' or 'Mrs. V wouldn't teach like this.' It drove me mad, but I appreciated a good teacher when I heard about them.

No, I can't let her turn this position down. She needs it and the department needs her. I run my hands through my hair and tug on the ends in frustration. Why didn't I ask Mr. Rockwell for her number to apologise and try to talk her into taking the job? Because he wouldn't fucking give her number out that's why. I should've gotten it on Saturday. Fuck.

Marcus goes into the kitchen and I follow him, hoping to find answers, or at least a distraction from my current thoughts.

"I feel so fucking bad, Marcus. I don't even know if she'll turn up on Wednesday and if she doesn't, she's giving up this amazing opportunity because of me, just when she's finally trying again. I fucked up. I should've kept my fucking distance." I drag my hand over my face and put my head on the counter.

Marcus walks over to me and clears his throat. I look up and see him motioning with his head to a piece of paper next to me. With a frown on my face I stare at the paper and see the name Nell Vickers and a number scribbled on it. I look back up at him and he grins at the confused look on my face.

"Her sister," he answers my silent question. "She gave me this after she finished ripping into you and threatening you within an inch of your life. By the way man, is she fucking scary or what?" I'm too confused to answer him, so he rolls his eyes and carries on instead. "She said to use it in case of an emergency. I don't know what she'd class as an emergency, but I'm going to leave that here, and if you happen to put it into your phone when my back is turned then that's on you. I'll send Emilia here to murder you when she finds out. She terrifies me but I adore her." He grins at me and turns away as I store her details in my phone just as he turns back, picks the paper up and puts it back into his wallet before turning back to the food he's preparing.

"Have I told you recently that I love you, Bro?" He shrugs but his laughter follows me as I walk out of the kitchen and sit on the sofa, ready to compose my text to her and silently pray I haven't blown mine and the school's chances.

Me: Hi Nell, I'm sorry about today...

Nell: Who is this?

Me: Mr. Shakespeare... hi

I wait for the bubbles to appear to indicate she's writing back to me. They start up and then stop, start and then stop, like she's writing something and then deleting it. I jump ten feet in the air when the message chime I'm expecting becomes a full blown ringtone. And when I see Nell's name on the caller ID, I smile as I nervously answer.

"Hi Nell, thank you for calling me." I try to make my heart slow down, but I can't. It's pounding so hard in my chest I'm sure she can hear it through the phone.

"How did you get my number, William? Did Mr. Rockwell give it to you?" She sounds pissed off at that thought.

"No, no he didn't," I quickly stammer out, "he wouldn't do anything like that. Your sister gave it to Marcus actually.

After she threatened to chop my testicles off and wear them as earrings when she thought I'd upset you on Saturday. But she must have deemed me safe if she gave that to him in case of an emergency, though. Right? My testicles are safe aren't they, Nell?" It feels weird referring to them as plural, but she doesn't know that and I'm certainly not about to tell her that story yet.

"Emilia gave you my number in case of an emergency?"

She sounds confused and angry, so I confirm, "Well, she gave it to Marcus, not me. And he didn't give it to me so much as he left it laying around and I found it. Lucky me, hey?" I try to go for a chuckle, but it comes out as a nervous noise and I can practically hear her frowning down the phone at me.

"Emilia shouldn't have done that. She didn't have the right and I'll be dealing with her soon. But, whilst I have you on the phone, I may as well discuss the opportunity I was offered today. I want to let you know..."

I cut her off before she can finish. "Nell please stop. Please don't throw away an amazing opportunity. Something that will help you get a little of the old you back, please. Coming into the school and speaking with Mr. Rockwell took so much bravery, and I never should have compared you to a coward because, if anything Nell, you're the bravest person I've ever met.

I'll keep my distance if you want me to. Back off completely and stop quoting Shakespeare at you if you tell me to. But please Nell, the department needs someone like you. We've been looking for years and the kids would love having you teach them. I would really appreciate the chance to work with the very talented and famous Mrs. V. I'm sorry Nell, I don't normally act like I did in the car park." I sigh and grab the back of my neck nervously and tell her quietly, "You do something to me, something no one else has ever done to me, but I'll learn to control it. Whatever you need. Please."

I whisper the last please and wait.

I hear her take a long breath in, then pull the phone away from her ear and say, "Mummy will be one minute, baby."

It makes my heart ache for her that little bit more.

"I'll see you on Wednesday morning, Mr. Shakespeare. Never stop quoting the big man. And thank you, William, for everything." She ends the call and I stare at my phone, smiling like a looney toon as Marcus walks into the front room.

"Jeez," he groans dramatically and rolls his eyes at me.

"Does Emilia have your number? You might want to answer that next call if she does." I smirk at him.

My humour is short lived, as my phone starts to ring with an unknown number. But Marcus can barely contain his laughter as he snickers, "Ha, jokes on you! I gave her your number instead of mine." That wipes the rest of the smirk right off my face.

I stare at my phone like it might come to life and chew my hand off at my wrist if I answer it. I look at my best friend with a mix of fear and anger, then back at my phone, mostly with fear.

"Shit, Marcus."

He stands up, heads into the kitchen, and leans against the counter where I can see him grinning at me as I answer the phone nervously.

"Hello. Oh, hi Emilia. No, it's William. Yeah, he is. One minute." Marcus looks back at me with shock and fear in his eyes as I laugh and jog over to pass him the phone.

Smirk firmly reaffixed, I walk back into the front room and plonk myself down on the sofa.

Mr. Shakespeare's back, baby.

CHAPTER 10
William

Tuesday morning comes much too soon. Mostly due to not being able to sleep because a certain someone was on my mind all night long.

Every time I close my eyes I see her. Her green cat-like eyes, her dark blonde hair and her little button nose that slightly lifts at the end. I picture her in the street looking down at her phone. I can see her in the pub wearing that ridiculous sash that said 'Birthday Bitch.' Sitting with her legs crossed in Mr. Rockwell's office, and then pressed up against her car, her chest rising rapidly with her short breaths. Her bottom lip between her teeth, her nipples begging for my attention under her blouse, her eyes dark and hooded, looking at me through her lashes.

I only managed to fall asleep after I let my hand drift down to my hard cock and relieved some of the tension that's been building up ever since I saw her on the street that day.

I sleep through my alarm and very nearly don't make it into work on time. The kids would have loved that, Mr. Perfect being late—their name for me, not my own.

The rest of the morning I'm in a foul mood and I'm taking it out on everyone and everything. I decide to sit in my classroom at lunchtime and avoid the teachers' lounge at all costs. I really don't want to snap at any more of my colleagues today.

I'm scrolling through the internet on my phone when a text message comes through from Nell.

Nell: Hi Mr. Shakespeare, I'm having a bit of a panic. If I sent over my lesson plan would you run an eye over it for me please? If not, it's fine. I'm just worried I'm a bit rusty and want to make a good first impression tomorrow. Thanks, Nell.

Me: Of course I will. Send it over. I'm sure it's fine but I'll check it out for you.

Nell: Thank you so much. I've got to go to Ben's Nursery for 'bring your parent to school day' in a bit, so I won't be able to respond. Do you want to call me tonight about it? Or you can send me an email. It's up to you. Nell.

Me: I'll never pass up an opportunity to call you, Nell. What time? I don't want to disturb Ben.

Nell: 7ish? Ben goes to bed at 6:45. I'm outside his class now. I've sent it over, thanks again, Mr. Shakespeare. Nell.

My bad mood has shifted and instead of scowling like I had all morning, I'm smiling. Suddenly I feel like the happiest man on the planet. The mood swings that this woman's causing in me are ridiculous. She's reduced me to a hormonal teenager at this point, but I don't care. Not only is Nell asking me for help, but she reached out first.

I know from the conversations we've had that Nell is going to need space to come to terms with her attraction to me. I know from my encounter with Emilia at the pub, thank you Scary Sister, that Nell has very limited experience with guys and she and her husband were in fact childhood sweethearts. It makes what she's had to endure even more unbearable.

I smile at the memory of Emilia charging towards me,

Marcus following closely behind her, when she realised Nell had left the bar Saturday night...

"Where's my sister? Did you upset her? Do I have to rip your balls off and proudly wear them as earrings?" Emilia may look like a golden-haired pixie, with her tiny stature and long platinum blonde hair, but the anger and fire in those eyes of hers terrify me and make me wonder if she knows how to dispose of a body.

"Hi I'm William. Nell left. She wasn't upset, she just said she had to go. I don't know why. Please don't kill me." I try to give a little laugh, but it just comes out as a nervous chuckle.

She sways a little but maintains eye contact with me the whole time. "Nell isn't as tough as she pretends to be, she's been through a lot. She doesn't need any more grief in her life. If you've upset her…"

I interrupt her when her eyes go from protective to deadly again and I want to stop her murderous thoughts. "I know. She told me about her husband and her little boy too. I don't want to hurt her in the slightest. If anything, I want to protect her. And I know that makes no sense whatsoever because I've only just met her, but I know when someone's special. I know that Nell is."

She's trying her hardest not to sway, but I see it ever so slightly. Her eyes remain fixed on mine and I don't falter in keeping the contact. After what seems like a lifetime, she smiles at me. "I like what I'm hearing. Don't give up, Shakespeare. She's going to put you through the ringer but don't give up." She starts to walk away, but after a few steps she stops and turns back to us. "I know where you work, where you live and now where you drink. I'm watching you." She puts her two fingers up to her eyes and then points them at me, the universal sign that she is indeed watching me, and turns and heads back to her group.

I turn to look at Marcus who has a sheepish look on his

face. "She is like a shark, Bro. She was just asking random questions. I didn't know she was going to store the information in case she needed to whack you at a later date. I'm so scared of her but so in love with her too. I think I've just replaced you as my bestie."

I suppose Emilia liked what I said. She did give Marcus Nell's number so I must have settled her doubts. I just hope after our call tonight I'll be able to settle Nell's a bit as well.

~

It's 7:10pm and I've been pacing my bedroom since 6:45pm. She said Ben goes to bed then, but I didn't want to phone too soon in case he was still up. I mean what does 7ish mean anyway? I look at the phone and see it's 7:11pm and say "fuck it" to no one whilst I dial her number. It rings three times and I'm just about to hang up on the fourth ring when I hear her say, "Hello."

"Hi, hello Nell, it's William." I slap my forehead. Why did I tell her who it was? She knew I'd be calling. Such an idiot. And why is my voice so high pitched? Like I'm just about to enter puberty. This has not started well. I blow out a breath.

"Hi William, sorry it took me so long to answer. I was in the kitchen and left my phone in the front room. You okay?"

I sit down on my bed, her voice instantly calming me down and helping me feel at ease.

"Yeah, I'm absolutely fine. How are you? How's Ben?" I hear a little catch in her throat as she answers me.

"He's absolutely perfect. In love with his nursery teacher, and so excited that Mummy's going to be a teacher like her tomorrow." I chuckle at that and let her carry on, content to listen to her all night long if she wants me to. "Did you get a chance to look at my lesson plan?"

I sigh, a little disheartened that she's gotten straight to the point. I wanted to pretend we were talking just because and not for work, but she's shattered that pretence.

"I did. It's really good, I wouldn't change anything. The only advice I'd offer would be to go in there as you, not a stuffy teacher. I mean, not that I think you'd ever be a stuffy teacher, but you know. Jeez, I used to be able to talk a lot better than this, Nell, I promise." I groan as she laughs at me.

"I'm nervous too." She quietly tells me. "This is all new for me, Mr. Shakespeare. I don't understand why you're so tongue tied though."

I want to tell her it's because I crave her. I want to tell her that I think I fell in love with her the second I saw her. I want to tell her that she's the most beautiful woman I've ever seen and that if she'd let me, I'd worship her every day of our lives together. That life's too short, and we should jump in with both feet and take the risk.

I can't tell her any of this though. She isn't ready to hear it, and, if I'm honest, I'm not ready to say it out loud. I am feeling it, but I know how crazy it sounds to tell a woman I've just met that it was love at first sight for me, even though it was. I can't risk scaring Nell off; she's been through too much. I know I have to show patience, I know I have to play the long game with her.

"You make me nervous, Nell. You're beautiful, smart and did my job a lot better than I do now. That's enough to tongue tie any man."

She sighs and I swear I can hear her rolling her eyes through the phone at me. "Yeah, of course I did. You're not called Mr. Shakespeare for no reason, William. According to Mr. Rockwell, you're amazing at your job. I'm not after it, if that's what you think. Or are you just fishing for compliments?" I smile to myself at her quick wit.

"Ah you got me. My ego was in need of some inflation."

67

She laughs and we go silent for a second. "I'm sorry if I came on too strong yesterday, Nell. It wasn't my intention."

I can hear her take a deep breath and when she replies she slowly lets it out. "I think it was the right strength. I kind of like that you call me out on my bullshit, if I'm honest."

I catch a glimpse of myself in the mirror, grinning like the Cheshire cat. "Well, I'll be certain to keep doing so. Persistence is key after all, my lady."

"Hmmm my lady. I quite like that. Makes me sound like a dignified lady instead of a mummy/teacher." She pauses and I know she's biting her lip, thinking before speaking. "I agree. Persistence is key, but so is patience. *Maxima enim, patientia virtus*. And on that note, I'll bid you goodnight, Mr. Shakespeare."

She hangs up before I can ask what she just said or even say goodnight to her. I Google what I remember quickly, hoping I remembered it all correctly. I know it's Latin but I'm not sure what it means. The nerd in me is doing a happy jig that my lady knows how to speak Latin. The results shoot up onto the page "patience is the greatest virtue." I rub my hand over my face and smirk, bringing up my messages and quickly typing out a text to Nell.

Me: So, you speak Latin as well. I'm impressed. Goodnight my lady.

I don't expect a response back from her. I just needed her to know that I heard her loud and clear. She needs time, and I'm prepared to give her that, whilst also letting her know that I'm what she wants. She doesn't know it yet, but she's stuck with me. Not only is she beautiful, intelligent, sassy and vulnerable, but this lady knows Shakespeare and can speak Latin. Yeah, I'm not going anywhere.

CHAPTER 11

Nell

Sitting in the driver's seat of my car, staring out the windshield, not thinking, I'm just breathing and trying to keep the nerves at bay.

"Mummy, why are we staying in da car? I don't wanna be late for Miss Ali." I unclip my seat belt and turn in my seat so that I can face my boy.

"Mummy's feeling a little bit nervous about going back to school, baby, so I was just taking a second to breathe through it." He smiles at me and instantly all my worries and fears go away. I take a second to stare into my boy's beautiful eyes and before I can say or do anything, he breaks the moment with a huge fart.

"Oops, s'cuse me, Mumma."

I clutch at my throat and pretend that I'm choking. "Oh Ben, that's nasty. Quick, open the windows! I can't breathe. Your farts are deadly, boy." He's howling with laughter at my amateur dramatics, and I'm pretty sure there are other parents looking at me like I'm crazy, but I don't care. The sound of Ben's laughter has me at ease, putting a huge smile on my face.

I jump out of the car and hurry around to get Ben out of

his seat too. Holding hands whilst walking into his nursery, I feel him give me a gentle tug."What's up, my boy?"

"I maded you dis for luck, Mumma." He holds his hands out and I see a macaroni bracelet. My eyes mist over a bit as I bend down and examine my gift without correcting him.

"Ben, it's beautiful. It's perfect. Can I put it on?" He nods his head at me, and when I place the colour pasta bracelet onto my wrist, his face is beaming with pride.

He jumps into my arms and I kiss the top of his head. "Ben, I love you so so much. More than all the stars in the sky..."

"More dan all da dinosaurs and more dan chocolate cake," he finishes for me.

I laugh, kiss him one more time and have a little sniff of his head too. I used to do that a lot when he was a baby, but he doesn't let me as much now.

We're outside of his class and Miss Ali is at the door to greet us. "Morning Ben, how are you? I see you gave Mummy her present." Miss Ali motions her head at my wrist.

I smile up at her. "Did you help him do this?"

"Ben asked me if he could make something for you to wish you luck for today, so we did it yesterday before you came in."

I'm back on my knees cuddling Ben, so I mouth "Thank you" at her and she gives me a little smile. She sees me; she sees my struggles with leaving Ben, she isn't judging me, she understands. At least that's what I get from her look. I pat Ben on the bum as he runs inside and thank Miss Ali again.

"Go get 'em Nell. You got this."

I tilt my head and smile my thanks back to her as she moves on to greet another child. My nerves are completely gone now. I look down at my bracelet. How did my boy know that I'd need a visual today? I silently thank Steve for giving me Ben, like I do a million times a day, and jump back into my car to head to my first day at my new job.

$$\sim$$

The morning flew by, and I must admit it didn't go too badly. A few kids tried the normal tactics with a substitute teacher, which lasted all of ten seconds. Telling them I wasn't afraid to give the whole class detention during breaktime because 'I've better things to do with my time after school than babysit a bunch of teenagers who should really know better' seemed to do the trick. Once they knew I wasn't going to back down they started to listen.

It's so exhilarating to be back, not only in my old school, but teaching what I love again. The two year nine classes this morning have been learning 'A Midsummer Night's Dream' which I love to teach. I let them know it wasn't important whether they understood the dialogue or not right now, as it's my job to help with that. I also told them it's better to let me know what they do and don't understand so I can help them fill in any gaps they might have. It seemed to work, and when they left, they were engaged and talking about the scenes we'd read through.

I sit back in my desk chair, looking around at the now empty classroom, and let out a contented sigh. I've checked in on Ben, even though I didn't need to. Now I need to eat some lunch and prepare for my year ten classes that I have this afternoon.

My eyes flit to the white rose I found on my desk when I got into class this morning. No note, but I knew who it was from. William. A smile spreads across my face and a tingling sensation erupts over my skin.

I shake my head to stop all thoughts of him and take out my lunch. The moment I take a bite out of my sandwich there's a knock on the door. I roll my eyes and chew as quickly as I can but still have to mumble, "Come in," around a mouthful of ham and cheese.

"Hey, how did it go? Sorry, I didn't mean to interrupt." Those chocolate eyes are twinkling at me from the doorway. The butterflies in my stomach start to flutter around as I try to smile with a half full mouth.

I put my finger up to motion for William to wait a second whilst I swallow my food, and laugh as I tell him, "It's always the way. It was good, I think. They seemed engaged as they left, but I don't know. Thank you for checking in on me, Mr. Shakespeare." He grins a lopsided grin at me and bows his head as heat flames through my body. It's just a grin, Nell, I tell myself as I try to cool my internal inferno.

"Anything for my lady. Seriously though, I overheard a couple of kids talking about you earlier." There's a glint in his eyes and my mouth is suddenly dry.

"What were they saying?" I ask him tentatively.

"Nell, don't worry, it wasn't anything bad. A couple of the boys said you were fit. I had to refrain from high fiving them on their awareness." He winks at me and my stomach does a somersault, but I roll my eyes at him and smile to try to hide the feelings inside of me as he continues, "Do you remember a girl called Jen in your class?"

I frown as I try to place her in my mind. "Brown hair, braces and freckles?" I ask him, and see I've hit the nail on the head when he nods and smiles before carrying on with his story.

"She said she never really understood anything of Shakespeare's with Miss Neb, but after reading just a couple of scenes with you she understood what was going on in them." He's smiling at me proudly and I know I'm beaming back at him with the same look of pride on my face.

That's what this is all about. If I can just help one mind to see things differently then I will have succeeded at my job.

"Nicely done Nell."

I tip my head at him in thanks and pick my sandwich back up, only to put it back down again. "I'm really not hungry anymore. Do you want a cup of tea?"

He nods yes, and when I stand up and stretch I don't miss the way William's eyes greedily graze over my body. He starts at my feet, his gaze roaming up further and further, until it pauses momentarily on my breasts before travelling upwards to meet mine. His eyes are darker than normal, almost black, burning with desire. I can feel my face flush and my knickers are damp, but I try to keep my composure and raise an eyebrow at him instead of jumping him and riding him like a cowgirl.

What is happening to me?

He smiles that sexy lopsided grin and shrugs his shoulders. I roll my eyes at him and head over towards the door so that we can head to the teachers' lounge. Maybe in a more public space I'll be less inclined to dream private things.

I can feel my heart beating faster the closer I get to him. I'm just about to reach for the handle when he catches my hand, links our fingers and gives a little squeeze. I peer at our joined hands, slowly lifting my eyes to his as he smiles at me, winks, lets go of my hand, opens the door and steps out into the hallway.

CHAPTER 12
Nell

"The teachers' lounge is still down there. I take my tea with two sugars and lots of milk. Just nipping to the gents, I'll see you in a minute, Nell." With a swift turn on his heels, he strides down the hallway in the opposite direction, leaving me feeling very confused and a little turned on.

Stunned and bewildered, I head forward. And whilst my feet carry me in the familiar direction, my mind is whirring. Why do I keep having these reactions to him? I don't want to react to him, do I? It's been such a long time since I've been with a man. Yes, I miss sex, God I really miss sex, but it's more than that. I miss intimacy, hand holding, cuddles, and just being comfortable with someone.

I miss Steve, but I'm also yearning for William. Holding his hand felt so right that when he took it away, I missed it. What ifs are buzzing in the back of my mind, but they flit by so fast I don't have the time or energy to grab hold of them.

Before I know it, I'm standing outside the teachers' lounge feeling nervous about venturing in. There are a few people still here that I know. Some I like, and others, like Jeff the sleaze, I don't. He earned the nickname honestly when he kept touching me and asking me out after Steve died, despite me telling him I wasn't interested. He would see me in the supermarket, in a restaurant with Ben, everywhere and anywhere, and start in again. The man didn't take the hint.

I know most of my colleagues know about Steve, and it's making me want to turn around and dive into the sanctuary of my classroom. Away from the sympathetic faces, the head tilts and smiles. The pity. I don't want to be known as the poor, widowed, single mum who bravely returned to work. I just want my colleagues to see me for me. A bad arse teacher who rocks teaching Shakespeare.

"Come on Nell, you can do this. Who gives a fuck what they think!" I whisper encouragement to myself and channel my inner Emilia and Cleo as I open the door to go inside.

Standing in the doorway looking around, I notice that not much has changed. There's a round coffee table in the corner, various magazines and newspapers from tube stations stacked haphazardly on it, tucked nicely next to the little brown sofa someone donated when they got a new one. The hot drink station, set up next to the sink on the opposite side, consists of a kettle, tea, coffee and sugar nestled beneath a cupboard filled with mugs. There's a fridge for teachers to stash their lunches. The walls are still a boring cream colour, and the carpet is still the bog standard school carpet, dark grey, threadbare.

I finally notice a few of my colleagues are looking at me, and I'm not sure if that's because I've been staring at the lounge for a while or because I'm the old newbie whose husband was killed. I smile at them, my eyes locking on someone I know and like, Lucy. She's a science teacher and was a close friend when I worked here before. She made such an effort after Steve died, but I wasn't very receptive. My smile starts to waver as I wonder if she'll even want to talk to me.

I start to avert my gaze, but she smiles at me and waves

whilst taking a few steps towards me. "Well, aren't you a sight for sore eyes, Mrs? I heard you were back. How are you?" She reaches out her arms and hugs me.

I beam at her. "I'm doing really well, how are you? I'm so glad to see a familiar face. I'm sorry we lost contact. I was in a weird space..."

She cuts me off with a wave of her hand and motions for me to follow her over to the kettle. "Nell, don't even. Especially not here, woman." I laugh as I remember how bad the gossiping is within the teacher's lounge.

"Nothing's changed then?" I ask as I flick the switch and grab two mugs from the cupboard. She shakes her head to answer my question but then motions to her coffee in her hand. She gives me a questioning look, then glances at the two mugs I'm filling with sugar and tea bags.

"Oh, I just bumped into William a minute ago and said I'd make him a cup."

She wiggles her eyebrows at me. I smirk back shaking my head, about to explain that we're nothing but friends, when I feel a hand at the bottom of my back, dangerously close to my arse. I flinch away and look behind me to see Jeff, the sleaze himself, smiling like the cat who got the cream.

"Nelly, you're back. I'm very happy to see you here. Finally, something decent to look at." He laughs at his own comment and licks his lips at me, and I see Lucy shudder in disgust at him.

"It's good to be back Jeff. I have something I'd like to talk to you about..." I smile sweetly at him and watch as his sleazy little eyes light up. "Please don't touch me again. I don't particularly like your hands on me. I've told you before, on numerous occasions, and I really won't ask you again. I would hate to have to speak to Mr. Rockwell about this, Jeff." I drop my tone, giving him a warning look to not mess with me, and he smirks a nervous smirk before walking away, muttering something under his breath about me being frigid.

I shudder but ignore it, not wanting any drama on my first day back, but as I turn back to Lucy I see William standing in the doorway, watching me with a face like thunder. For a split second I panic, worried he might think I encouraged or, yuck, enjoyed him being that close to me. But as Jeff walks past him, William's eyes follow him with a murderous look that sends chills through my body.

I quickly turn my head to Lucy, who's watching me very carefully. "That guy is a sleaze. Way to put him in his place, girl. Now this guy is the opposite of a sleaze. Hi Will. How are you?" she asks as I feel him stop next to me.

His arm brushes mine and a sharp zing, the feeling you get from a static electricity shock, goes through my body. I lift my arm to run my hand through my hair, making sure there's no contact between us, and go back to making the tea whilst William chats with Lucy.

"I'm good Luce. How's that husband treating you? You need me to kick his arse yet?"

She laughs at him and I note the friendly affection in her tone. "He's perfect, thank you. And no, I don't need you yet, but I'll have you on standby."

She laughs as I hand William his tea, and I notice how comfortable and cosy it feels. Almost like we're in our own kitchen and I've done this a hundred times with him before. I steal a quick glance at his eyes, noting that the anger has gone. As I look away, Lucy catches me, grins a knowing grin at me, and because I'm very grateful she doesn't say anything, I smile back at her.

"Lucy, I'm so sorry. I heard you got married last year. I know it's a bit late but congratulations. If this one falls through on the arse kicking, give me a call and I'll send Emilia around. You remember my sister, right?" She laughs, as does William, and they both nod at me. Emilia's reputation precedes her.

"I'm going to head back. I want to prepare a bit before the next class. I'll see you later Lucy. And, thank you." I grasp her hand and squeeze it a bit. Catching up has been nice, but a bit overwhelming.

As I head towards the door, I feel a hand on my shoulder and note that I don't flinch. "Nell, I want to talk to you about your next class, so I'll walk with you." I nod my head, knowing from that simple touch that it's William's hand resting on my shoulder.

I walk out into the hallway quickly, and take a few steps at high speed to reach my class in record time. I haven't given William a chance to say anything. I know the halls have ears in this school, and I've a feeling it isn't just my next class he wants to discuss. I open the door and head straight inside as he follows me.

"Are you okay?" He asks me, concern lacing his tone. "I saw your disagreement with Jeff and wanted to check you were alright."

I nod my head at him, trying to appear nonchalant. "It was nothing. It's not the first time he's touched me without me asking him too, but I want it to be the last, so I told him. I'm not looking to start trouble on my first day, but I don't want him to think he can just come over and put his hands on me, or any other woman in here for that matter. Maybe I didn't handle it in the right way, in front of everyone. I'm sorry for doing that on my first day back."

"Nell please don't apologise. And don't think for one minute I was implying you shouldn't have put him in his place. I genuinely wanted to see if you were okay. That was it. Not as a colleague, but as your friend. You looked really nervous when he touched you."

I look up at him with shock written all over my face. "Oh,

I didn't realise. Sorry. Erm… since Steve, I haven't really liked it when a man touches me, innocently or not. I, erm, flinch and try to get away from them, as you saw. I didn't want to have to deal with him doing it again, so I told him off."

He's looking at me intently, his brow furrowed, and then he looks down at the floor. "Well, I'm glad you did." He hesitates before continuing. "Nell. I'm sorry if I've ever touched you when you didn't want me to. I'll be more conscious around you now."

My eyes snap to him in a panic. I want him to touch me. I liked it when he touched my hand in the bar, and when he held it before. I step closer to him and place my hand on his shoulder. When he drags his gaze away from the floor, I look straight into his eyes.

"It's different with you, Mr. Shakespeare. I don't flinch and I don't mind you touching me, so please don't change because of this conversation. I like it when you touch me, William." My eyes plead with him, and in return I'm treated to a slow, sexy, cocky smile. I roll my eyes and laugh, "Don't get a big head now, will you? This doesn't mean anything."

"Oh, my lady," he chuckles at me, "you really are clueless, aren't you?"

Confusion sweeps over my face, and he chuckles as a teenage boy sweeps into the class and greets him. The boy eyes me up and down and then smirks at me. For a split second I'm shocked at the brazenness of this young man, but William's cough to cover his laugh snaps me out of my awe. I raise my eyebrow at the boy and give him my best teacher glare. Turning my back to both of them, I walk behind my desk as rest of the class files in and William leaves the classroom.

Just before the bell sounds to indicate that lessons have started, I feel my phone vibrate in my pocket. I pull it out, checking it quickly in case it's Ben's nursery, and see a text from William.

William: You realise that hot 'don't make me punish you' look was perfect spank bank material for him, don't you?

Me: And how would you know, Mr. Shakespeare?

William: Because I was once a 15-year-old boy. And if that look made me want to be very naughty around you, I can guarantee it did something for him too. By the way, you can discipline me anytime you want too, my lady X

The bell makes me jump and I hastily shove my phone back into my pocket, looking up to a sea of curious teenage eyes. I'm blushing and flustered at William's words. But he put a X at the end of his text too. He hasn't done that before.

The young man who started all of this is smirking at me and nudging the boy next to him. I square my shoulders, tell the class to take out their texts and let them know we'll be doing some reading out loud. They all groan, and as I look the boy in the eyes, his smirk wavers as I address the class. "As you should all know, Shakespeare used males to play the female characters in his plays so you," I look at the boy again to indicate I'm talking to him, "will read Desdemona and the person next to you will read her love interest, Othello." I notice the slump in his shoulders, and the smirk disappears from his face as he starts to read. Ha! One situation resolved.

Now, how do I punish Mr. Shakespeare?!

CHAPTER 13
William

The best things about being the head of a department are having your own office and having dedicated time throughout the working day free, so that when you're feeling angry, happy or turned on you can escape to it. Having time off during the day from teaching so that you can do 'planning' or 'figure out the budgets for the term' makes it easier to calm yourself down when you're feeling the aforementioned feelings, and make sure you don't do something rash that could jeopardise your job or your future with Nell as well.

Sitting behind my desk, I don't know which I want more; to punch Jeff in the fucking face or grab Nell and watch her come on my dick. He had his fucking hand on my lady. I wanted to walk over there and snap every finger off his hand. I was close to stepping in when I saw her flinch away from him, but I was so proud and impressed when she handled it by herself. I knew she could.

It's one of the reasons I didn't go into the teachers' lounge with her, pretending I needed the loo first instead. She has to prove to herself that she can do these things on her own. I didn't want to walk in there hypothetically holding her hand in front of everyone. I wanted her to go in there and own it, be the confident, sassy woman I've come to adore. I see it in her. I know she's there. And slowly, slowly, I can see her coming out of her grief-induced shell more and more.

When she walked back to her class, well when she practically ran back to her class, I could feel her retreating. I needed to do something to stop it from happening. I wanted to know what had happened with her and Jeff as well. I wasn't happy when she told me she didn't like being touched, innocently or not. My mind flashed through every meeting we'd had, every time I'd touched her. The idea that she was uncomfortable because of me made me feel sick. When she told me she didn't feel uncomfortable with me, it took everything in me not to grab her, kiss her and fist punch the air.

I see snippets of her liking me, of how it could be with us together, and I really fucking like it. But, I've got to force myself to keep going at the slowest pace ever in order to not startle her. I need her to come to terms with everything she's lost and everything she has to gain. She isn't ready for Steve to be in the past yet, and I can accept that. I don't want to replace him. I want to honour him. Share this beautiful woman and his son with him. I just need to convince her that it's okay for us to do that. And in time, I will.

I dig my phone out of my pocket and read the texts between us. I laugh as I picture the look of shock on her face when AJ looked her up and down and showed an interest in her. The kid has good taste, but I need to remind him that he shouldn't be eye fucking his English teacher at the age of fifteen. Hypocritical I know, seeing as I want to do so much more than eye fuck her, but hey, he doesn't need to know that. And I'm a grown arse man, not a student.

That look she gave him gave me a rock-hard dick, and sporting that in the middle of a secondary school is not an ideal situation to be in. Jeez, that look. The raised eyebrow, hand on hip, glare in her eye that said, 'fuck around and find out!' Shit, I can feel myself getting hard again and I close my eyes, counting down from one hundred and trying to recall the opening scene of King Lear in my head.

I've managed to calm down when I get to about thirty-six, and apart from a massive case of blue ball that I've got going on, I'm back to my normal self. I just can't think about Nell or I might actually need to lock myself in the bathroom to relieve myself, and that's a level I definitely do not want to stoop to. Well not at school anyway.

I text Marcus to distract myself more.

Me: Bro, what are we doing for dinner tonight?

Marcus: Erm new number who dis?

Me: Dick. Who else opens a text with Bro to you? And if it's a new number how do I have it?

Marcus: Jeez somebody's in a grouchy mood. Take it you haven't got laid yet?

Me: I was in an okay mood until you started your shit. Anyway, dinner tonight, what you making?

Marcus: Well, I actually have something planned tonight.

Me: What like a date? What the fuck. With who?

Marcus: Most people just put WTF. Why do you write like that in texts. It's so ducking annoying.

Marcus: Ducking

Marcus: DUCKING

Marcus: F-U-C-K-I-N-G. Stupid motherducking phone.

Marcus: I give up. Phone gods you win. It's now ducking forever.

Me: Are you finished arguing with your autocorrect? Who's the date with?

Me:?????????

Me: Ignorant ducking dick

≈

Being alone in my house is something so rare, that when it does happen, I don't really know what to do. I couldn't be bothered to cook so I decided to stop off to grab some Chinese food on the way home.

As I sit in the kitchen eating, I find my mind wondering what Nell is doing right now. Probably having dinner with Ben or giving him a bath, getting ready for his bedtime. I sigh as longing fills me and roll my eyes at myself.

Scraping the leftover food that's on my plate into the bin and placing the still half full containers in the fridge for Marcus later, because I'm that considerate, I head into the front room to call my mum. As I listen to the rings of the phone and wait to hear her voice, I smile knowing exactly what she's going to want to talk about.

"Hello, my baby boy. How are you? Did you read it?"

I chuckle and lay my head back on the head rest of the sofa. "Hey Ma, I'm okay. Feeling good, apart from the one ball business. Of course, I read it. Did you read it?" I hear my mum tut when I mention my one ball.

I smile when she admonishes me, "William, you're not defined by how many balls you have. Your dad had two, and he was a giant pussy, so you know."

I laugh harder than I have in a long time. "Woman, you are the best thing in this whole damn world. I have no idea why anyone would want to leave you." Before she can chime in and tell me I left her, I continue, "Well apart from a son that had to take an amazing job, but you know I'm not really gone. I also left you in the very capable hands of Frank, so I don't count."

I love my mum. I know everyone does, but my mum is something else. I hate that my biological dad left her for another woman when I was four, but I love that she moved on and found an amazing partner for herself and stepdad for me. I was seven when Frank came into our lives, and he just fit in

84

like the missing puzzle piece that we needed. I mean Mum and I were fine alone, but we were better with him.

"Hmmmm I still think you could have gotten a job closer to home, William, but I don't want to get into that with you." This was a constant battle between my mum and me. Without Frank's support, I don't think I would have ever left my mum's house. She wants me close, and I understand why— she almost lost me— but sometimes it's stifling. Especially when I was going through treatment.

When I found the lump in my testicle, I was terrified, but I knew I was strong enough to fight whatever it was. I was more scared about telling my mum than the treatment or the fight to beat it. That's why I kept her in the dark until it had been diagnosed and I knew what the plan was.

Of course, she went ballistic at me, told me I was a selfish arsehole, but I knew she didn't mean it. Once she was over the initial shock of it all she apologised. I did too. Explained my reasons for doing it that way, and she understood. She didn't like it, but she understood—thank you Frank.

It didn't stop her from insisting that I move back in with her whilst I went through treatment. And it didn't stop me from accepting her offer. I felt obligated after upsetting her so much, and I knew how ill I was going to be. But, it's also the reason why I'm currently living in a house with Marcus about 80 miles away from her.

"How's Frank doing, Mum? How's the florist shop?" My mum and Frank are joint owners of a florist. Contrary to what most people assume when they hear that, Frank does the flower arrangements, whilst Mum deals with the business side of things like accounts and taxes.

"It's going okay, making a good turnover. Frank's the same as he always is." I can hear the smile in her voice, and it makes me smile at how happy they both are.

But it creates that pang of longing in my chest again. I

close my eyes and see Nell. She's smiling, relaxed, her long dark blonde hair is loose around her shoulders and her beautiful, kissable mouth is so inviting. Begging me to taste her. The more I picture her the stronger the urge gets.

"William, did you?" My mum's voice brings me out of my daydream, and I grunt 'huh' at her and she tuts again.

"Honestly the men in my life never bloody listen. I asked if you read the book and if you enjoyed this one, seeing as you didn't like the last one I picked."

"Mum," I say through a chuckle, "I didn't like the last one as it was full-on erotica bordering on porn, and discussing that with my mother just didn't sit right with me."

She huffs down the phone. "It wasn't that bad. Marcus enjoyed it." She pauses and I guffaw at her. "Alright it was. This one was better though. Made me laugh so much I woke Frank up." She laughs as she recounts the situation and her laugh is so infectious it makes me laugh along with her.

"It was funny, I'll give you that, especially the first scene. Coconut boobs, very ingenious. I like Pippa's books." She hums her agreement and when I hear Frank say something in the background, my mum fiddles about with the phone, putting it on speaker.

"You're on loudspeaker my boy, go back to pretending to like Frank." I chuckle at my mother's sense of humour and say hi to Frank.

"She still making you read those girly books?"

"Yeah, but it's your fault. If you read them with her, she'd leave me alone." Frank doesn't really think they're girly books, but he likes to annoy my mother by saying that. We all know he reads them in secret, we just don't say anything about that as he finds it more fun to wind her up about them instead. They seem happy so who am I to judge, eh?

"And if you weren't reading these and talking to me, your mother, the woman who gave birth to you, what would you be doing eh? It's not like you have a nice girl to settle down with and give me grandbabies is it?" And that's my cue to end the conversation. Words like this lead to her mentioning setting me up with a friend of a friend's daughter or such. No thank you.

"You know William, my friend's daughter has just gotten out of a relationship. She's very pretty, I could always..." And there it is.

I cut her off quickly. "Actually Mum, I'm kind of interested in someone at the minute."

"WHAT!" She screams in my ear, making me nearly drop the phone.

"Jeez Mum, I think I'm deaf. Calm the fudge down."

"Calm down? Are you mad? My baby boy has just openly admitted to liking someone. I need details NOW William. Who is she? Why aren't you dating? How old is she? What does she look like? What's going on? William?"

I wait for my mum's incessant questions to stop before very calmly telling her as little as I can get away with about Nell.

"I saw her on the street after my latest check-up and thought she was beautiful, but I didn't talk to her as she was in a hurry and was with a big group of women. That night, Marcus and I went to the pub, and she was there. We spoke for a while, then she left."

"What? What d'you mean she left? Why didn't you ask her out? What is wrong with you? Is this because of the one ball crap again?" My mother is brutal, but I fucking love her.

"No, Mum. Nell has some things to work through, so I need to move slowly."

"Like what?" She asks me without missing a beat. I don't particularly want to, but I know I have to tell her about Steve and Ben.

"She's a widow, Mum. She has a little boy too. Her

87

husband was killed a few years ago when her son, Ben, was a year old. She kind of retreated into herself and focussed everything on Ben and is only now starting to try to get herself back. I took her old job actually. She was on maternity leave when her husband died, and she couldn't come back." I hold my breath whilst I wait for my mum and Frank's reactions.

"That's... wow. That poor girl." Frank always was a man of few words. The fact my mother hasn't spoken yet worries me.

"Mum?" I ask hesitantly.

"William, be careful with her. She's fragile. She doesn't deserve anymore hurt, intentional or unintentional. Make sure you are very sure about what you want before you pursue anything with her. You have to be sure you want her. You can't leave her after a little bit after all she's been through."

I take a deep breath to calm the anger that's risen inside of me. Does my own mother think so little of me? Does she think I'm like the deadbeat who left her alone? The scumbag who left not only her, but his four year old kid, for some other woman? Does she think I'd do that to Nell after all she's been through? She can't think that, can she?

"I know Mum, but what do you think I'm going to do? Shag her and then dump her in the morning?" I can't help the scathing tone in my voice. Normally I'd never speak to her like this, but why would she instantly think I'd hurt Nell? Didn't she hear me when I said I was taking things slowly? My defences are up and I can't seem to shake the idea that my mum thinks I'm like him. The sperm donor.

"William, I didn't mean that. I know you wouldn't treat her badly on purpose. I just want you to be sure before you do anything, that's all." She has that mother tone in her voice. The one that says, 'I know you're behaving like a brat, but I'm going to be patient with you here.' I know she's being practical. I know what she's saying is right. But this isn't the reaction I was expecting, and it's pissing me off. She's comparing me to him, and I can't even begin to deal with that.

"Okay, Mum. I've got to go. Speak to you both later." Before they get a chance to reply, I hang up.

I know I shouldn't be acting like a petulant child, but she's hurt me. I'd never hurt Nell. I've been nothing but patient and kind towards her, and you'd think that my own mother would know what kind of man I am. The hurt and doubts are bubbling up in me. I'd never take advantage of a woman. Especially one as vulnerable as Nell. I'm not like him. She should know that, but the apple doesn't fall far from the tree does it?

My thoughts mock me. I always vowed I'd never be anything like him, but I am. I left my mum too. I took a job that was deliberately away from her. What would stop me from hurting Nell? Leaving her and breaking her heart? It's in my DNA after all.

That thought tips me over the edge and I yell in frustration as I grab the remote control from the coffee table and throw it at the wall.

CHAPTER 14

William

The remote smashes to pieces as Marcus walks into the front room.

"Woah, what the duck, Bro? What's going on?" He's standing in the doorway with his arms raised and his shoulders hunched, clearly confused about my little temper tantrum, and I hang my head and cover my face with my hands.

What the hell am I doing? Maybe my mum's right and I should stay the hell away from Nell. Maybe I should give up on this whole thing I have going on with her. Fuck, I don't even know what to call it. A flirtation? A friendship? God knows what it is. All I know is I'm confused as hell and now I need to replace the fucking remote control.

I'm pacing around the front room like a caged tiger whilst Marcus picks up the bits from the remote. "Sit down." Marcus demands. "Do you want to explain what's going on?"

"I'm sorry. My mum got in my head about Nell. She implied that I needed to be careful and that I could hurt her." Marcus looks at me with his head tilted and his brow furrowed, but he remains silent.

"WHAT?" I shout at him.

"Calm the duck down, Bro. Don't shout at me and just… Calm. The. Duck. Down!"

He punctuates every word and I turn away from him, regulating my breathing, trying to get my shit together. For as much of a joker as he is, he's never not had my back, or given it to me straight when I can't see things outside the narrow window of my thoughts.

I sit down on the sofa and apologise again. He comes and sits next to me, placing the remote bits on the coffee table. I wince at the visual it represents.

"Will, your mum isn't wrong though, is she? You do need to be careful, and you could hurt Nell, she's incredibly vulnerable..." I'm just about to bite his head off, but he places his hand over my mouth to silence me.

"BUT that's why you're going slowly and taking your time, which I bet you failed to mention to your mum. She was just telling you to be careful, that was it. What else riled you?"

I shake my head and curse out loud as I realise that Marcus is right, and she didn't really say anything that I hadn't already thought myself. Hearing it from her, though, it made it more real, more of a possibility. A possibility I didn't like acknowledging.

"Shit. I was really rude to her man. I'll phone her tomorrow. Shit." I run my hand through my hair and tug on the ends of it. "Once she said that, my insecurities got the better of me and I started comparing myself to my waste of space dad. I convinced myself that she thought I was like him, and that's why she was warning me off Nell."

Marcus rolls his eyes and snorts at me. "Ducking idiot. Your mum thinks the world of you. I'm sure she thinks you're the best thing since sliced bread. She'd never think you were anything like the sperm donor. You have to know that man. The only person that ever compares you both is you."

I nod my head slowly at him. "Yeah, I know. It's hard not to. I don't want to be anything like him, Bro."

Marcus drapes his arm over my shoulder, bringing me in closer to him, and I drop my head on his shoulder. "You're nothing like him, Will. And if I ever catch you acting like him, I'll kick your ducking arse."

Laughing, I raise my head from his shoulder. "I'll apologise to her tomorrow. So, you're sticking with ducking then?"

It's his turn to laugh at me. "Yeah, I think it suits me better. How are things with Nell going?"

I shrug my shoulders at him. "Today was good. She did an amazing job with her classes, put a teenager in his place for ogling her, and a teacher too." He eyes me suspiciously with an eyebrow raised and I laugh as I tell him, "Not me, a maths teacher named Jeff. He's a little too touchy feely for Nell, and me for that matter. She told him not to touch her again. But Marcus, when I saw her flinch away from him, I've never wanted to hurt someone as much as I wanted to hurt him. I got a little panicky afterwards." I lean forwards and put my elbows on my knees and sigh loudly.

"We were back in her classroom, and she told me she doesn't like being touched. I apologised for all of the times I've touched her without an invitation. To be honest, the idea of not touching her was driving me fucking mad, but the idea of making her uncomfortable was worse." Marcus nods his head at me as I continue. "But when she told me that she liked me touching her, that I didn't make her uncomfortable and she didn't want me to change, the relief. Shit. I let out a breath I don't think I even knew I was holding."

I smile at him and he smirks back at me. "She's there Will, she's just buried beneath the layers. Take your time removing them, be patient, but I'm with your mum here, be careful. For as long as I've known you, you've wanted to be in love, in a relationship and happy, like Frank and your mum."

Darkness clouds his face, and I know where he's going, but I don't stop him. "You were devastated the last time. You were with her for years, and I don't think you even liked her half as much as you do Nell. If this doesn't work out with you two, it scares me how it will affect you." I look down at the floor and take a deep breath. We don't talk about her—ever— but he's not wrong.

I lift my head up and give Marcus a tight smile. "I get you, I really do. But you don't need to worry about me. I'll be fine. I'm going upstairs to have a bath and relax." I stand and point at the pieces of the remote control. "I'll replace those tomorrow. Night." Before he has a chance to respond I'm halfway up the stairs.

The beauty of living with Marcus is he knows me inside out. He knows when I need space, so he doesn't follow me as I head straight to the bathroom and turn the taps on. I feel like I just ran an emotional marathon. Why did he have to mention her? On top of all the shit with my mum, now I have this on my mind too.

He is right, though. I didn't like her half as much as I do Nell. The only reason we stayed together for so long was because of the cancer, which, ironically, was the same reason we broke up as well.

Stepping into the bath I rest my head on the side and lean back. Fucking Nora. I started dating her just before I was diagnosed, and she stayed with me for the two years that I was having treatment. We shouldn't have stayed together. I think she felt too guilty to leave the cancer patient and, self-ishly on my part, I liked having someone besides my family and Marcus caring about me whilst going through treatment.

It wasn't a love story—we didn't even mention love to each other, which should have been a red flag—but I was desperate to have someone by my side, and she didn't want to be the girl who dumped the cancer patient. I convinced myself that she was my love story and put the doubts to the back of my mind, until I found her in her apartment, fucking another bloke.

To top it off, I'd just shaved all my hair off as it had started to fall out, and this dude was sporting a magnificent man bun. It was so thick and luxuriously glossy. Looking back, I think I was more upset about his glorious mane of hair, and my lack thereof, than his dick being inside my fucking girlfriend.

I can hear her words now as clearly as if she is standing in this bathroom.

"It's not my fault Will, it's the cancer's fault. You never have any time for me, and you never want to have sex anymore. When I try to start something, you turn away from me. Is it any wonder I had to go somewhere else to have my needs met?"

I shake my head to myself, but her words keep going.

"I mean, I've paid my dues Will. I've stuck it out for as long as I could and, let's be real, I want to have kids someday and, well, you know..." And with that final blow she had pointedly looked at my crotch and grimaced.

I took it badly. I had one ball, less chance of having kids naturally, and I felt like less of a man. Didn't help that I couldn't keep my girlfriend satisfied. That cut deep, but she wasn't the reason I was broken.

I couldn't say out loud what the real reason was. I couldn't let people know how terrified I was of losing my fight and dying. I hated seeing the pain and fear in my mum's eyes. Marcus's too. I didn't want to watch them watch me fade away. I was scared I was going to die before I'd really lived, but I didn't want to tell anyone because that would have scared them too. They already had so much fear in them, they didn't need mine too.

I was weak, ill, vulnerable and lost. So, I pretended it was a broken heart. People know how to act around that better than a man afraid of dying from cancer. It was my coping mechanism.

I dunk my head under the water to rid my mind of these thoughts, and when I pop my head back up, I remind myself, "You are healthy, you are alive, you are happy, and you can grow a fucking man bun if you want one."

Stepping out of the bath, I hold onto the sink and blow out a weary breath as I look at my reflection in the mirror. Tired eyes stare back at me. Maybe I should take a break from all this Nell stuff. Let her figure out her issues and then once she's done, see where we are. I mean what if, once she rediscovers her old self, she realises she doesn't want to be with a one balled guy who may or may not be able to have kids and may have to fight cancer again one day? She'd have to face losing someone again. I can't put her through that.

I shake my head at my reflection. "Not much of a catch, am I?" I say out loud with a slight, uncomfortable chuckle. Nell deserves so much more, and I'm going to make sure she gets it. Even if it isn't with me.

CHAPTER 15

Moody Margaret - send help!
Group texts

Three weeks later...

Juliet: Daily update guys. She is still in the worst mood ever. I should have stayed at Mum's. I forgot to put the recycling out and I feared for my life... HELP!!!

Cleo: Why is she so pissed off? It's getting on my nerves not knowing.

Emilia: I don't know. Has anyone heard her talking about Will recently? Or have you heard Shakespeare talking about her, Marcus?

Marcus: No nothing. Like Juliet, I fear for my life most nights around him.

Juliet: They're both pissed off? Something must have happened between them.

Cleo: Well duh sherlock.

Juliet: Whatever bitch.

Emilia: You really need to work on your comebacks kiddo.

Juliet: You call us bitches all the time.

Cleo: It's different.

Juliet: Whatever!

Marcus: God it's like having kids being in this group chat with you lot. I think I know what's going on between these two moody bastards anyway.

Juliet: ???????

Emilia: Trust you to drag out the suspense…

Juliet: Tell us, bitch.

Emilia: Still no!

Juliet: (Sad emoji)

Cleo: Marcus you going to fill us in or what?

Marcus: Well I was waiting for the witches of London to shut up so I could get a word in...

Emilia: Cute, now spill or maybe some of your secrets will be revealed.

Marcus: LOL okay. So, while you were having the impressive Cooper collective clap back, I went and braved the beast and asked what was going on. Turns out he's been avoiding Nell for weeks now. He's into her still, but he freaked himself out and convinced himself that she wouldn't want him. My guy is complex, that's all I can say without telling you *his* secrets. And you know, bros before hoes.

Marcus: Shit, sorry, I wasn't saying you were hoes.

Marcus: Duck, please don't throat punch me.

Emilia: What are his secrets?

Cleo: So, we're just skipping over us being hoes hey? Just asking for clarification so you know...

Marcus: Shit, you just made me send my cousin a text about hoes and throat punches. Damn, being popular needs so much attention.

Marcus: I can't tell you his secrets boo. It's not fair on him. Plus, Nell should be the one that knows first.

Marcus: Trust me when I say that Will is the best guy I've ever met and ANY girl would be lucky to date him.

Emilia: Okay. I trust you. How do we fix this?

Juliet: I think we should set them up.

Cleo: Oh it just got interesting. But still, we're all okay with being called hoes?

Emilia: How?

Juliet: We plan a night out in a couple of weeks. In London. We organise the babysitting and make out that we're going out for dinner and to a bar afterwards. Say Emilia got promoted or landed a big client or Cleo landed a big client or we could say that I, oh wait, I'm broke, unemployed and bored AF (eyeroll emoji)

Marcus: And me and Will turn up at the same place, coincidentally of course.

Emilia: *Will and I* not me and Will.

Marcus: Oh duck off woman. I have enough of Will correcting me, I don't need you doing it as well.

Emilia: LOL okay, so we all end up in the same restaurant. Then what? We have a nice dinner together and go to a bar, how is that going to get them together?

Cleo: We leave them alone together. Duh. Connor can take Juliet home because she's 'sick' and he has a car. Nell doesn't have to leave with her then. That's two down. Emilia and I can say there's a problem with the building, another two down. And Marcus you can pretend to go to the gents and sneak out and meet us around the corner in another bar. Leaving them all alone. They'll have to talk.

Juliet: Why does Connor have to be involved and why does he have to take me home? Can't I meet you guys in the bar like Marcus? BTW not okay with being a hoe MARCUS!

Juliet: Cleo?

Juliet: HELLO...

Connor has been added to this group chat

Connor: Who's here? What's going on? Are we planning a surprise for your mum or dad?

Cleo: Cliff notes version for you, Connor. We figured out why Nell is being Moody Margaret and why Will is pissed off too. They like each other and won't get their heads out of their arses for long enough to do something about it.

Connor: Ohh. Kay. What does that have to do with us?

Emilia: We're going to give them a push to get them together.

Connor: WHAT?

Marcus: They're both crazy about each other, it makes sense.

Connor: New number, who this?

Marcus: Marcus… Hi

Connor: Why is HE in this group?

Cleo: Don't be rude Coop-hay. He's Will's best friend. Juliet shouldn't have tried to kiss him that night. Marcus actually did nothing wrong except tell her to stop. He didn't mean to upset her. She was drunk.

Connor: Whatever. Princess can do what she wants obviously.

Juliet: DON'T CALL ME THAT.

Connor: Fine, JULES. I won't call you Princess (Eye roll emoji)

Marcus: I didn't mean to upset her that night. I'm gay, I would have preferred you kissing me than Juliet. Just felt like you should know that.

Connor: LOL okay, I like you a bit more now. You've obviously got excellent taste in men (winking emoji) So why hasn't your friend made a move on Nell?

Marcus: (Blushing emoji)

Juliet: (Eyeroll emoji)

Marcus: Sorry Princess. He knows what Nell's been through and he started off giving her space at work but now he has it in his head that he shouldn't even try with her.

Juliet: FFS MY NAME IS JULIET!

Marcus: Whoops. Sorry JULIET

Connor: So this dude is a decent guy. He knows about Steve and Ben and they work together?

Emilia: Yep. Will's an English teacher who just happens to love Shakespeare.

Connor: Wow he sounds perfect. What do we need to do to get these two their happily ever after?

Cleo: We'll give you a few seconds to read over the above messages to catch up Coop-hay.

A few minutes later...

Connor: I don't think Princess is on board with your idea, Cleo.

Juliet: And I'm out.

Juliet has left the group.

Connor: Was it something I said?

Marcus: Well shit... someone's in the doghouse

Connor: Nah, she loves me really, they all do.

Emilia: Unfortunately, he's right we do, maybe some more than others. So can we finalise these plans please?

Cleo: Somewhere better to be?

Emilia: Open your fucking door bitch.

Marcus: On that note...

Connor: LMFAO

CHAPTER 16

Nell

"Oh, come on Nell, it'll be fun. Since I moved in here, we've done nothing but drink wine and moan about how bored we are. This is exactly what we need."

I look over at Juliet who is perched on the side of the bath applying her makeup, because apparently 'the light is better in here,' and a stab of guilt hits me. This past month or so I've been pretty brutal to live with. If I'm not biting her head off about nothing, I'm moaning about my lack of social and sex life. She's taken it all on the chin and hasn't once snapped back at me. Or told me to shut up. Or said I should tell William that I want to jump his bones. I know she moved in here to gain some independence back from Mum, but she didn't sign up to live with Moody Margaret. I can't even be angry with her for the little nickname she gave me; it's scarily appropriate. I've tried not to be so bloody angsty, but I can't help it. I'm confused and I feel out of control.

William has barely spoken to me at work, and the times he has it's only because I've initiated the conversation. And he can't get away from me fast enough. He always has a convenient excuse to leave, and I'm left standing there gaping like a fish out of water.

I don't know what happened. The last full conversation we had was after my run in with Mr. Sleaze and my aversion to being touched. I know he felt bad about the innocent touches he'd initiated between us, but thought I assured him it was different with him, basically begged him not to stop.

Maybe he realised I'm not worth the effort. That I'm too broken and need too much work and time. I can't blame him really.

I just wish it didn't upset me so much. I wish I didn't *want* William to put the effort in, but I do. I want him to want me. Even though I don't know what I could offer him, relationship wise. How selfish is that? He deserves someone who will give him everything, and I don't know if I can even if I want to.

The scary part is I do, I do want to, but I can't. When I think about us together I get a pang of guilt over Steve and sadness envelops me. How can I want someone else? I know Steve isn't here—if he was I wouldn't be feeling like this over William—but he's not and I am, and it's hard to argue with myself every day. It's why I haven't confronted him. I've typed out a text to him a thousand times in the past few weeks, but I haven't sent any of them.

How can I be upset and angry when I don't even know what I'm asking of him?

I feel lost again. I hate that feeling. I like being in control. I like plans and structure. William going distant on me isn't in my plan at all. I thought we would build a friendship, a really good friendship, and maybe one day it could lead to more. Obviously, he has other ideas.

"Nell? You okay, Sis?" My head snaps to the left and I see a worried looking Juliet frowning at me.

"Yeah, I'm fine Princess. Just in my head too much. Help me pick a damn outfit before I change my mind."

Juliet squeals in delight and jumps up and down clapping

like a cheerleader. When she finally composes herself, she flings her arms around my neck and hugs me tightly whilst whispering into my ear, "Never give up hope, Nell." She kisses me on the cheek, grabs my hand and drags me into my bedroom.

I squeeze her hand in thanks and my heart warms a little more when she smiles at me. She turns back to my opened wardrobe, looking through my clothes for the perfect outfit, and I give a silent thank you for my sisters, once again.

"Why did I listen to you?" I groan as I climb out of the taxi across the busy road from the restaurant. I glance down at my barely covered breasts then at Juliet with mild annoyance. She wasn't impressed at my 'boring ensembles' and refused to let me wear any of them for a night out in London. Instead, she's somehow managed to get me into a romper of hers. It's a little bit tighter than what I'd normally wear and shows way too much cleavage for me but, I must admit, I do look good, albeit very exposed.

I try to pull the romper up to cover my breasts a bit more and she slaps my hand away. "Will you leave it alone, Nell. For God's sake. You look fricking hot. The more you pull it the more out of shape it will get, and then you'll really be exposed, if you get my drift."

She gives me a pointed look, and I stick my tongue out at her. "Fine, just so you know I'm really uncomfortable."

She sighs and I'm sure I hear her say something like *you will be* under her breath. Before I can ask her, I hear someone call my name.

"Nell, you look amazing! It's about time you let the girls out to play." Cleo wraps me into a hug, but not before she waggles her eyebrows at my exposed cleavage.

I hug her tightly back and take in her outfit. Her jet black, dead straight hair is flowing down past her waist and her brown eyes are twinkling. She looks bloody hot in her little black jumper dress and thigh high red boots. "Cleo, I love those boots."

She kicks up one leg, waggling her boot at me. "What? These old things?" I laugh as she turns to Juliet, her light blonde hair in a high ponytail, and a pair of tight leather trousers and intricately detailed white corset style top accentuating her every curve, and takes a step back. "Wow Princess, just wow."

I nod my head in agreement. "Tell me about it, Cleo. Isn't she absolutely stunning? The lace on the top makes it look like it belongs on a wedding dress, doesn't it?" Juliet blushes and does a little curtsey at her big sisters. "Where's Emilia? She's always on time."

Cleo looks at her phone and lets us know Emilia is waiting inside for us, so we walk across the busy road carefully and enter the restaurant.

They've chosen a quiet little Italian place on a side road in Piccadilly. I glance around, taking in the rustic brick walls and dimmed lighting, and notice there's only a handful of tables, creating quite a romantic setting. It makes me wonder which of my sisters picked this particular place as this isn't where we'd usually go to eat. I gaze over to the only occupied table and smile as I see Emilia and Connor there.

Instinctively, I shoot a look at Juliet who is worrying her bottom lip with her teeth. I reach back to grab her hand and she smiles a little at me. She hasn't mentioned him since her little drunken outburst, and I haven't pushed her because, selfishly, I've had my mind occupied with William. When I look back at Connor, his mouth is gaping open, a look of longing on his face.

Cleo steps in front of me to say hi to them, and when I

look past her at Connor, his face is guarded and filled with rage. Following his glare, I find Juliet smiling at the waiter politely and I smirk to myself. So Connor has the hots for my baby sister. I really need to find out what's going on here.

"Well, it's about time you bitches got here," Emilia says and bursts out laughing. Juliet and Cleo join in and I notice Connor has a smirk on his lips too.

"What's so funny and why are you calling us bitches?" I ask, feeling completely left out. This just makes Emilia laugh harder.

Cleo ushers us into our seats. I step forward to take the seat next to Connor and Cleo screeches *no* at me. Shocked, my hand frozen on the back of the chair to pull it out, I raise my eyebrow at her.

"Let Juliet sit there, and you sit on the end. That way if you need to get up to call Mum about Ben, you'll be able to easily." She gives a weird little laugh and Emilia smacks her forehead, murmuring *idiot* under her breath.

"Guys, what is going on?" I ask, taking the end seat to avoid Cleo screeching at me again. I give Juliet a sorry look and she just grins and shrugs her shoulders at me. Cleo goes around the table and sits next to Emilia, directly opposite Juliet, which makes me curious.

"Are you guys expecting someone else? Is Verity coming?" I ask, nodding my head at the empty space opposite me and next to Cleo, but she shakes her head vehemently.

"No, she's with her boyfriend tonight. So, Nell, how's work going?" Her voice is too high pitched, and she keeps squirming. Something is going on, I just don't know what.

I eye her suspiciously and offer, "It's fine, but shouldn't we be talking about your work? You're the one who landed a big client. Why are you acting so shifty?" I ask as I catch her glancing out the window for what seems like the hundredth time since we sat down.

"I'm not, am I?" She asks and giggles as she looks at the rest of our group. They all say no and shake their heads, but as none of them are making eye contact with me I'm getting very suspicious that they're all up to something. Emilia changes the subject, deflecting my curiosity away from Cleo by talking about one of her clients, and I relax a bit.

I'm sipping the wine that Emilia ordered for us when the hairs on the back of my neck stand up. My hand instinctively goes to smooth them down, and when I look around to see what's behind me I'm met with shocked, big, beautiful, brown eyes.

They were definitely up to something.

"Wow small world, eh?" Marcus laughs nervously next to William, who's giving him daggers, and Emilia smacks her forehead again. Obviously, she expected them to be more subtle about this little set up.

"Hmm, so it appears, Marcus," I reply coolly, turning back to the table, my stare boring into all of my sisters and Connor, who are all looking in another direction. Funny that.

Emilia clears her throat. "Special reason for you two to be out in London?"

Sounding very robotic and rehearsed, Marcus chimes in first. "Yes. I just clinched a big deal and we thought it would be nice to celebrate away from our usual haunts." I can hear shuffling and turn my head slightly to see William standing with his arms crossed over his chest, staring intently at Marcus. He clears his throat, clearly nervous as he shoots a panicked look at Emilia.

It takes her a second before she realises her error and asks, "Would you guys like to join us? We're celebrating Cleo getting a new client."

Marcus jumps into the vacant chair opposite me with a very enthusiastic, "Yeah, why not. We're all friends here aren't we?" and looks up at William who hasn't budged an inch since he spotted me. "Waiter, could you bring another chair please. Will, you don't mind sitting at the end, do you?"

I can feel the anger vibrating off him as Marcus smiles sweetly up at him. "That's fine," he says through gritted teeth. The waiter brings over a chair, placing it at the end of the table, and as he sits his knee grazes mine.

A shot of heat goes up through my body and my knickers are instantly wet. I try to move my leg away, but with the close proximity of how we're seated, I can't. I shift uncomfortably in my chair and give Marcus my best mum glare as he looks down at his cutlery.

"How are you Nell?" William's voice is barely audible.

I tilt my head towards him and give him a raised eyebrow look. "Oh you want to talk to me now? The whole avoidance system is just for school then?"

He sighs and looks down at the table where his hands are clasped tightly together. "I wasn't avoiding you. I was just trying to give you some space."

I look at him, but he doesn't meet my gaze. "Space for what? I told you I didn't want you to act differently around me."

When he doesn't answer or even look at me, I blow a breath out, agitated.

"Just forget it, William. I thought we were friends. I thought... never mind. It's... *I'm* all too much effort, I get it."

I stand up, telling the table I'm going to the ladies, and walk away quickly before anyone can ask me anything or follow me.

Closing the door of the lady's bathroom, I turn to look at myself in the mirror. Biting hard on my lip, I force the tears that are threatening to spill from my eyes away, take some deep breaths, and after a few minutes I manage to calm down. I look at my reflection again and tell myself, "Come on, Nell, you were fine before William's attention, and you'll be fine without it."

I mean, it is a lot to ask of any guy. Taking on a woman with a child is a lot anyway, but taking on a woman who doesn't even know what she has to offer is too much. It's not his fault. I need to just go back, smile, laugh and then I can go home and let all the disappointment out.

Oh, and bloody murder my sisters too.

I straighten my shoulders, run my fingers through my hair and open the door to find William standing outside.

CHAPTER 17

Nell

"What do you want?" I ask wearily. His eyes finally meet mine and I can see the anguish in them. It takes me by surprise, and I find myself taking a step closer.

"I'm sorry, my lady. I never meant to upset you." He reaches his hand out and strokes my cheek.

"William, don't. I understand. It's okay. It's too much. I'm too much. I have too many scars and too many issues for you to want to pursue a... friendship with me." I pause and take a breath before continuing. "I won't hold it against you. You deserve someone who can give you everything, not something, maybe, sometime. I get it." I squeeze his arm to try to hit my point home and turn to walk away, but he grabs my hand and spins me back around. Pushing the bathroom door open, he walks inside, dragging me in behind him.

"William, what are you doing?" I ask him as he closes the door and locks it.

"I need to talk to you, and I need you to not walk or run away. Please, Nell." The urgency in his tone makes my voice falter so I nod my head and wait.

He runs his hands through his hair and breathes deeply. "Nell, you are worth every effort in the world. I would wait for you forever. I don't want you to doubt you're worth that, because you are. You're right about me deserving someone else though."

My heart sinks and I step closer and reach around him to unlock the door so I can escape. Even though I know he's right, it still hurts, and I don't want him to see that. Before I can pull the door open, he grabs my hands and holds them, entwining our fingers together. I look up into those chocolate eyes with confusion.

"I deserve someone else because *I'm* not good enough for *you* Nell. You deserve the world. The best man there is. And there are things that I can't give you. Things that I know you'll want, and that I want for you, and even though it kills me to say it, I'm not the right man for you." He lets go of my hands, strokes the side of my face, and turns and leaves the bathroom.

After a few minutes, clarity begins to overpower the confusion swirling around in my head. He isn't good enough for me? That's ridiculous. He can't give me things he knows that I'll want? But how can he know I'll want them if I haven't told him? He can't just assume to know what I want and need in my life. Why does he get to decide he isn't the right man for me? No, this stops here. I open the door and storm back to the table.

I take my seat next to Will as everyone eyes me suspiciously, but instead of causing a scene I ask sweetly, "So, what's everyone getting?"

"Actually, I'm not feeling too good, Nell," Juliet tells me. She's looking away from me and keeps twiddling with her hair, a clear sign she's lying. It's always been her tell.

"Oh no, you poor thing," I say with mock empathy in my voice.

"Connor is going to drive me home so you can stay and enjoy your night." She eventually looks up at me with an apologetic look in her eyes and I can't help but feel sorry for her. Knowing how uncomfortable she'll be in the car with him, I decide not to give her a hard time about her part in this 'well thought out' plan.

"Oh, are you sure? Feel better Princess." I grin as she walks past me and catch the little smirk that Connor gives to the waiter as they leave.

Next up is Cleo. "Oh no, Verity's just had a big bust up with her boyfriend. I have to go and see if she's okay." She jumps up and runs out the door before I can say anything.

I bite the inside of my cheek to stop myself from laughing at the sheer stupidity of my sisters to think they could get away with this.

I look at Emilia who gives me a smirk and stands up. "Come on, Marcus. They know what we did." She looks pointedly at William and I and implores us, "Talk. It. Out." Then she tugs on Marcus's arm, who's giving William an apologetic smile and shrug whilst mouthing 'scary as fuck,' and pulls him towards the door.

I chuckle as they leave and turn my head to William. "Do you think we've been set up by any chance?"

He rolls his eyes and laughs. "Could they be any more obvious?"

My eyes bulge out of my head. "Did you just make a Chandler Bing reference?"

He smirks at me and nods his head. "How you doin?" he asks, and we both burst out laughing.

"I love that show. Steve used to hate it. He'd always moan about me watching it on repeat." He gives me an incredulous look and I nod at him with a sad but amused expression on my face. We both laugh a little and silence falls on the table.

I take a deep breath and tell him, "You have no right, you know?"

He tilts his head at me and raises an eyebrow. He looks so

damn sexy like that, and it's taking everything I have not to jump on top of him and kiss the living daylights out of him.

Instead of having his lips pressed up against mine, I carry on with what I was saying. "You can't choose what I want or what I need before I've decided it myself. You also can't assume that I want things you can't give me. We decide that together."

He blows out a breath and nods his head at me. "You're right. But I know what my scars are and what my limits are, and you don't."

He looks down at the table and I reach over and place my hand on top of his. "Then tell me. I've shared my scars with you, share yours with me. Trust me."

He looks down at our hands clasped tightly together and meets my eyes with his beautiful, but sad ones. "I had cancer, Nell. Four years ago, I was diagnosed with stage one testicular cancer. I caught it early, before it spread anywhere. They removed my testicle, and I went through extensive chemotherapy. I had a recent check-up and there are no cancerous cells in my body, but who knows how long that will last for. I can't give you forever when I don't know how long my forever is, and I won't put you through losing someone else."

He diverts his gaze and looks around the restaurant, trying to look anywhere but at me. My heart is pounding and my mouth is dry. My poor, beautiful Mr. Shakespeare. He's been through hell too, and instead of shutting himself off he's out there living his life to the fullest.

My mind is racing. I want to go home and do extensive research on stage one testicular cancer so I have all the facts about it, so I can feel in control of this. I feel his hand twitch underneath mine and realise he's just borne his soul to me, and I haven't said anything.

"Will, I don't know what to say." I clear my throat, "I was going to say I'm sorry you had to go through that, but I know you've probably heard that a million times already. Were you alone? When you were fighting?"

My question shocks him as his eyebrows shoot up towards his hairline and he smirks at me. "No, I wasn't. I had a girlfriend, Marcus, my stepdad and my mum. I moved in with my mum during my treatment, and then out again and into an apartment with Marcus as fast as I could once the treatment was finished."

I nod my head and try to shake away the jealousy at the mention of his ex-girlfriend. I know it's ridiculous, as I'm always bringing Steve up, but the idea of him with someone else makes me feel sick to my stomach. "And your girlfriend? What happened to her?"

He squeezes my hand and reaches over to tip my chin up so I'm looking at him. "I walked into her apartment and caught her fucking another man, who had glorious hair by the way. She blamed me for her cheating. Apparently, I didn't have enough time for her."

I give him an incredulous look and then anger takes over. "Are you for real? You had cancer! What an absolute bitch." My temper is raging and heat surges to my face in anger. "Oh my, I'm fuming right now. Tell me her name and address and I'll go kick her arse for you. Even better I'll send Emilia."

He laughs and threads our fingers together. "In all fairness, I was more upset about the man's hair than I was about him being with her."

I frown trying to understand.

"Because I lost mine."

The penny drops and realisation sinks in. "Right. I get you." I laugh uncomfortably and then ask, "Why weren't you more upset with her? How long were you together?"

He smirks at me, very smugly. "You seem to be more curious about my ex-girlfriend than me having cancer and

113

only having one ball now." He tilts his head at me, and I feel my face blush.

I take a deep breath and decide to be brave. "I don't care about how many balls you have, William." I roll my eyes at his grin and continue, "I know about cancer, and what I don't know I can research on my own. I can't research your ex-girlfriend without asking you the questions now, can I?" I stare at him, a flash of defiance on my face.

I notice his eyes darken as he licks his lips and holds my gaze with his. "I never loved her. I stayed with her because it was nice knowing someone other than my family cared about me. When she cheated, I acted like it gutted me, but it wasn't that I was upset about."

I stare at him intently, willing him to go on whilst my head wraps around the fact that he didn't love her. I can't help but do a happy dance in my head. How fucked up am I? I have a dead husband who I adored, adore, but I'm glad that my 'could be more than a friend' just told me he didn't love his ex-girlfriend.

I stay quiet, hoping he continues what he was telling me, but he doesn't. His eyes never leave mine and our hands stay entwined on the table. When he reaches over and cups my cheek, I nuzzle into his hand. I lean closer, wanting desperately to kiss him, but the waiter interrupts us and asks to take our orders. He releases my hand and I sit back in my chair, feeling disappointed and frustrated.

After mumbling my order to the waiter, I look over to see amusement in William's eyes. "What's so funny, Mr. Shakespeare?"

He chuckles and shrugs his shoulders at me, his eyes twinkling mischievously.

"Okay, we've established that you've been ill in the past. That you're not ill now. That you had a bitch of an ex and were jealous of a man's hair. And that you're worried about me losing you after losing Steve. Is that it?" He nods at me, but I know there's something else from the way his eyes are shifting about.

"Nobody can promise forever William, and I don't want that promise. It's already been made to me and broken. I don't want promises like that, okay. So, what is it you think I want that you can't give me, William?" I watch him closely, his eyes dart about and his tongue flicks over his bottom lip.

He looks down and whispers, "Kids. I can't have children."

I quickly reach over and tip his chin up, so he's looking at me this time. "Who said I want more kids? Like I said before, that's something we decide together if or when this, whatever we are, gets to that point. You can't make decisions for me." He looks up at me and nods just as our food is brought out.

After a companionable silence William says, "I have to ask Nell, what are we? I don't want to rush you or pressure you but..."

I wipe my mouth on my napkin and smile at him. "Honestly, I have no idea. I didn't like not speaking with you and having you avoid me. I've been a moody cow to be around." I take a deep breath and continue, mustering up all my courage. "I want to explore what this is. I want to get to know you. I want you William, but I'm terrified. I feel guilty but I don't want to stop what this is. We have this pull, something that draws us together, and that realisation makes me feel bad about Steve. We promised each other forever." I look down at the table and blow out a shaky breath. "I meant it when I made that promise to him, but he isn't here for me to fulfil it. I'm so confused and I don't want to lead you on. But, I can't ignore this, what we have here, and I don't think I should."

He licks his lips and takes my hand again. "Nell, I'm not beating around the bush here. I shouldn't have avoided you. It was stupid but I did it because I fucking want you. I want

115

everything with you. I want you to be mine. You feel like mine and I know you're not ready for that just yet.

I don't want to replace Steve in your heart, ever, but I would love to share it with him eventually. Just because he isn't here with you doesn't mean that he won't have a piece of your heart forever. You're fulfilling your promise to him every day. You both are. You have a piece of his heart too. You always will." He leans over and wipes away the errant tears that have spilled from my eyes and rests his palm on my cheek again.

"I know you're scared, Nell, so I'll be patient and take my time. Let you get to know me properly, let me woo you a bit." I smile at him and nod my head. He squeezes my hand and smiles back at me.

"Why me William?" I ask him, not in a self-deprecating way but just out of curiosity.

"I don't know. The first time I saw you on the street, before you'd even looked up at me, I was transfixed. Then I saw your eyes and I was lost. The quote, 'She is woman, and therefore to be won' came to mind and I knew I had to win you. I can't explain it. I've never felt like this before, Nell. I just need you to be mine. No matter how long it takes, my lady."

Without hesitation, I lean over, my hand cupping his cheek, and place my lips onto his. The kiss is soft yet filled with so many emotions. There's an urgency there, a need from him, but he keeps the kiss slow and soft. I break away from him and smile.

"Let the wooing begin."

CHAPTER 18
William

This night started out as one of the worst and now it's one of the best.

My lips finally landed on my lady's, and she tasted exquisite. What makes it even better is that *she* kissed *me*. She opened up to me. She wants me just as much as I want her, and she let me know that. That's a huge fucking step. I know I still have to go slow with her, but she's on board with me wooing her now. Who knew that baring my soul would get me here?

Apparently, Emilia and Marcus knew, the fuckers. Marcus has been telling me for weeks to just sit and talk with her, but it turns out I'm an idiot who doesn't listen. So he took things into his own hands, prompted by Emilia no doubt. I must remember to thank him later. After I've made him sweat a bit first.

"So, Mr. Shakespeare, what now? What does wooing me look like?" She smiles at me, but I see her nerves there.

I take my time in answering, not wanting to scare her away. "I'd like to take you out. On a proper date, not a forced one like this. Even though I'm grateful for them for doing this, I want it to be on my terms."

She lowers her eyes and nods at me shyly. "I agree to that."

"I want to buy you flowers, spoil you, kiss you, introduce you to my world," I start, but when I see the panic rising in her eyes, add, "but only when you're ready." I breathe a little easier when she relaxes a touch at that caveat.

"I want that, William. I really do. The thing is, I have to be cautious about telling people I'm dating. I have to think about Ben. He's never seen me with anyone, not even Steve really. And then there's his grandparents, my parents as well, and I don't know how they'll take it. Plus, we work together. Mr. Rockwell might not be impressed with the idea either. What if we fail spectacularly and can't even bear to be in the same place together?"

I can see her trepidation resurfacing and her mind spiralling. I can't lie, the idea of not shouting that we're dating from the rooftops makes me a little crazy, but she's raised some valid points. I know she's panicking and I want to make her feel better, but she's biting down on her bottom lip which is making my dick rise and my concentration levels plummet.

"Nell, slow down, my lady. Take a breath and look at me. And please, for all that is holy, stop biting on your lip or I'm going to do things to you that I certainly won't regret." I give her a look that tells her just how much she's turning me on with it and she stops instantly, trying to hide a tiny grin.

She whispers "Sorry" to me but the twinkle in her eyes tells me she isn't sorry at all.

"I understand your concerns. We can keep it quiet, Nell. I won't tell anyone at work. When you feel comfortable enough for me to meet Ben and your parents, I will. Although I don't think we'll be able to hide it from Marcus and your sisters. It seems they know us better than we know ourselves."

I watch as she breathes out a sigh of relief and a smile comes back on her face. "Thank you. I'm sorry. It's just, this is a big deal for me, especially with Ben. He's already lost too much in his little life."

I reach over, grasp her hand and look into those beautiful green eyes of hers, and tell her, "I understand, so no more about it. I'm looking forward to meeting him eventually. It doesn't have to be as your boyfriend, maybe I can be his friend first. I'd love for you to tell me about him. Please don't think you can't talk about him with me."

She beams at me, and her smile is the widest and most genuine I've ever seen on her face. "Thank you for that. He's amazing. He loves his nursery teacher now, like I've told you before, but I mean really obsessed by her. I'm a little jealous if I'm honest. He's spent the last three years obsessed with me and I'm not sure I'm ready to share him with another woman." She laughs an uneasy laugh and I chuckle at her. "You think I'm crazy, don't you? Being jealous of his nursery teacher."

I shake my head at her and smile as I link our fingers together again. I don't know what it is but I can't stop touching her. It's like I'm making sure she's real and I'm not making this night up in my head.

"I think it's beautiful actually. He's your world and of course you don't want to share him, but he'll never be able to replace his mum. I'm a grown man and my mum's still the one I go to when I've had a bad day or need advice. I speak to her all the time. I'm even in a romance book club with her." I grimace as I realise what I've just said and close my eyes in embarrassment, but not before I watch her eyes widen and she claps her hands in glee.

"No, freaking way. You read romance books? Oh, this is too good. Mr. Shakespeare reads good old fashioned romance books. I love this so much. I have so many questions. How did this come about? What ones have you read? Do you have favourite authors?"

I open one eye and look at her, clearly abashed at her gleeful face. "You promise to keep this a secret? Only Marcus knows, and that's only because she makes him read the ones I can't, or won't."

"Why won't you read them?"

I shake my head at her and mumble about a certain book being too explicit for me to talk about with my mum. I shouldn't have said anything, because now she's even more curious.

"What book was it?"

I shake my head no again and mutter, "never going to happen."

She thinks for a second and then her face lights up with an idea. "Okay, okay let me guess what it was about? Erm, grouchy boss trope?"

Another shake of my head has her scrunching her nose up in concentration and she looks bloody adorable.

"Hmmm, brother's best friend? No, too meek. Ha, I have it. BDSM."

I close my eyes and nod my head at her, completely embarrassed.

"Don't be embarrassed, Mr. Shakespeare, your mum is a badass. From the sounds of it, our mums would probably get on really well. Mum got a book like that, and she ordered copies for me and my sisters. After we all finished reading, we had a night in discussing it. Wine was consumed, food was eaten and my bond with my mum took on a whole new level. It was different, talking about that kind of stuff with Mum, but it was so much fun."

"So, what did you think of it then?" I look at her with amusement on my face, wondering what her reaction will be to my question. She brings her gaze up to me, her cheeks turning a pretty shade of pink, but the flash of defiance that streaks through her eyes makes me smirk.

And she smirks right back.

"I enjoyed it. I liked the romance, and the fact that they loved each other and trusted each other enough to do that sort of thing together. Would I want someone inflicting pain on me? I don't think so. But I do think there's something appealing about letting your man take complete control in the bedroom, provided he knows what he's doing." She tilts her head, looks me straight in the eyes and smiles sweetly at me.

My body is on fire with a desperate need to feel her underneath me, writhing as I put my tongue all over her, showing her exactly what it feels like to have her man take control. My dick is as hard as steel, and I almost flip the table and throw her over my shoulder in true alpha style when she bites her bottom lip and shyly lowers her eyes. I shift in my seat and reach over to her, rubbing my thumb over her bottom lip and tugging it free from her teeth.

In a low voice I tell her, "I thought I told you about doing that, my lady. Wooing you doesn't include me dragging you out of here, fucking you in an alley and making you come so hard that you scream my name out for all of London to hear... yet." My breath is ragged as I drag my gaze from her mouth where my thumb rests and look at her face.

Her lips are parted slightly, her eyes focused on my mouth, and when I lick my bottom lip, her eyes track the movement. Her breaths quicken as we stare at each other for what seems like an eternity, until we're abruptly brought back to our surroundings by the waiter clearing his throat right next to us.

She blinks several times and I watch as a red blush replaces the pink on her cheeks and down her beautiful neck, and I wonder to myself where else that glorious colour goes when she's flustered. The waiter clears his throat again and asks if we'd like dessert, to which we both say no and I ask for the check.

I pay for our meal quickly and help her up from the table as we politely say goodbye to the staff in the restaurant and step outside onto the busy London street. I'm thankful for the cool air as I try to get my dick to behave, and silently remind him that we're taking things slowly with our lady.

As I reach out for her hand, my phone rings in my pocket. I dig it out and smile at her. "It's Marcus, want to screw with him a bit?"

Her eyes light up with mischief and she smirks at me. "Oh yeah."

I answer the phone on speaker, grumpily and aggressively. "What?" Nell puts her hand over her mouth to keep quiet as we hear Marcus's sharp inhale.

"Shit. It didn't go well after we left?"

"No, Bro, it did not. She kept going on about how she doesn't need someone in her life, especially not someone who's hot and cold. Wouldn't even let me explain." I grin at her as she's shaking her head at me, whilst smirking.

"For real? I thought for sure once you were alone you would sort things out. I'm sorry man."

I hear muffles from his end like he's putting his hand over the speaker before he tells whoever's with him, "No, she wouldn't listen to him. Apparently she doesn't need anyone in her life." We pause for a second trying to hear the response from the other person and Nell giggles when we hear Emilia say, "Idiot," in the distance. Stifling our laughter, we hear Marcus reply, "Yeah, she is. Will is the best guy I know."

Nell mouths 'aww' at me and I shrug my shoulders at her, touched at my friend's words.

"Listen, boo," we hear Emilia tell him, "I can call her an idiot all I want to, she's my sister. When you do it, it makes my blood boil and makes me want to rip your balls off and wear them as earrings. Do you get me?"

My eyes go wide, and I mouth, "Oh shit," at her, to which she raises an eyebrow and shoulder in a proud way.

Marcus stutters something that sounds like *whatever* and I roll my eyes at his comeback. He's obviously no match for Emilia.

"Will, where are you and Nell now?" He asks me carefully.

I put the authority back in my voice and ground out, "I don't know where she is, I left her in the restaurant. Like fuck am I getting spoken to like a piece of shit and staying there for it."

I can hear what sounds like a scuffle on the other end of the phone and then Emilia's voice comes through as clear as day. "Shakespeare, if you're telling me you left MY sister in a restaurant in the middle of London on her own, I am going to kidnap your bestie and send you pieces of his body through the post. Where. Is. Nell?"

I look at Nell, panic in my eyes as she giggles next to me. I hear Marcus whimper and Nell steps closer to me and says, "Sis, stop being mean and tell me where you are. Will and I are going to come to wherever you lot are and slap you all silly. Then we're going to do some shots. Sound good?"

Emilia laughs so loud she snorts.

Marcus shouts, "Oh, thank the ducking gods! I didn't want to die."

They give us the address to a little bar around the corner and we head over to them, holding hands and smiling at each other. This is turning out to be a great night.

CHAPTER 19
William

"Mr. Black top is eye fucking you, Em." Cleo shouts loudly to Emilia who looks over her shoulder at the huge guy in a black t-shirt.

She brings her gaze back to us and shrugs nonchalantly. "Not feeling him," she replies coolly to Cleo who isn't buying her answer.

"Are you sure? He fits your type down to the tattoos on his arm." Cleo grins.

Once again Emilia calmy replies, "I didn't notice."

I'm intrigued by their little back and forth and lean over to ask them, "Just out of curiosity, what's going on here? I feel like I'm missing something. I don't have siblings, so I find this fascinating." I grin at both of them, but they miss it as they eye each other up, maybe sharing some sort of sibling telepathy.

Cleo finally breaks their staring contest. "Emilia is normally about the hook ups, no feelings involved, just getting her needs met. It's the best way after all." I look at them confused and raise my eyebrows to press them further. Cleo smirks and Emilia blows a frustrated breath out as Cleo carries on, "Except she hasn't had her 'needs met' by anyone for a long time. I'm suspicious she's getting some on the regular and won't tell me who it is. Which leads me to two conclusions. Either he's ugly and she's embarrassed of him, or she really likes him."

Even though she scares the hell out of me, the flash of vulnerability in Emilia's eyes makes me want to protect her. "Maybe she got a really good vibrator and is taking care of her own needs."

Cleo laughs loudly as Emilia brings her glass up, tips it at me in a silent thank you, and drinks.

I sit back with a sigh of relief and turn my head to see Nell has been watching me the whole time. She leans over to talk into my ear so I can hear her over the music and her scent consumes me. It's like I can feel her unique fragrance inside my body as if it's a potion casting a spell. It drives me crazy and makes me want it more and more at the same time.

"Are you some sort of miracle worker? Normally a conversation like that about Emilia in front of people she doesn't know would have resulted in a big argument, but you diffused it. Thank you." She places her hand on my chest as she speaks to me, and as she starts to lean away and move her hand I grab it, holding it back where it was, directly over my heart.

I lean into her and quietly ask her, "Can you feel what you do to my heart, my lady?" She nods her reply and her eyes darken as she licks her lips. I chuckle close to her ear, my breath tickling her. "I want to kiss you, Nell."

She straightens in her seat and thinks for a second. A glimmer of that mischief twinkles in her eyes again and she leans into me. "Then come kiss me, sweet and twenty."

She's just quoted Shakespeare at me.

I growl at her and press my lips against hers. My hand cups her cheek and then slides around to her nape where I hold her firmly and bring her even closer. I kiss her hard and fast, a possessiveness to it, wanting to brand those lips as mine. I sweep my tongue against hers and she moans into my mouth. Her hands are gripping my shirt as she meets my tongue's pace stroke for stroke.

She breaks away from me but rests her forehead on mine as she tries to catch her breath. "You kiss by th' book, Mr. Shakespeare."

I groan at her, and she grins, knowing exactly what she's doing. "I like it when you quote the big man to me, my lady." She grins again and I want to lay her down on this sofa and fuck her ten ways to Sunday. But wooing first, I remind myself.

"I know, I could tell by that kiss."

I laugh, cup her cheek and kiss her on the head. "It wasn't just the quote, Nell. That's been building up since I saw you that first time on the street." She rolls her eyes at me, but I see the little smile that's hinting at her lips. Lips that I smugly notice are swollen by my kisses.

"Hey lovebirds, we're taking this little soiree back to ours. You coming?" Cleo is standing in front of us with Marcus and Emilia, grinning at us like Cheshire cats, and we both nod.

"Can I have a, er, I need erm..."

I look at Marcus who suddenly understands my situation. "Oh yeah, just let me finish my drink here and we will be up, I mean, ready to leave in a bit."

I smack my hand on my forehead and the girls cackle around me.

"We'll take a quick bathroom break to… give you a, er, a minute," Nell tells me, trying to stifle a giggle.

"Woman don't you laugh at me, this is your damn fault."

She smirks as they walk away, and I send daggers to Marcus.

"Bro, cut me some slack. I got you the girl."

I laugh at him and take a second to go through everything unsexy that I can think of. My mum and dad, Marcus, football, maths equations. Yeah, that does it.

Once I'm fully calmed down, I stand up and join Marcus just as the girls make their way back to us.

As we head outside Emilia says, "Oh, it's so cold out here, it's enough to make me all stiff." She giggles and waggles her eyebrows at me.

"It really is, it's a good job you have a jacket, Em. We don't want you getting all frozen and hard." Cleo of course has to get her two cents in.

And, of course Marcus has to join the fray, "Oh, girls be nice. It's not easy to get rid of, you know." At least he is defending me. I think.

Nell laughs as she says, "We know, it must be really hard." And even though they're all laughing at my expense, seeing Nell so comfortable and happy, I just can't be mad.

Emilia grabs her in a cuddle headlock hug and through wheezing laughter says, "Rock fucking solid sister. Mazel tov."

I shake my head and chuckle at them all bent over and laughing their heads off. "Right ladies, enough about my dick please. We need to grab a black cab."

Cleo sticks her leg out into the road and shouts, "Yoo hoo, cabby cabby, cabby come get us."

Still laughing, I pull her back and stick my hand out as I see one with its lights on. I gather the rowdy lot into the back as Emilia tells him her address.

Sitting opposite Nell, who's next to Marcus, I watch as he puts his arm around her and she leans into him. I raise my eyebrow at her and flatten my lips into a tight line. She smirks at me and puts her head on his shoulder as her eyes flash defiance. My warning look to her doesn't remove her smirk as she mouths at me, "He is gay," and rolls her eyes.

I lean forward and mouth, "I don't care. You. Are. Mine."
I see the little shiver that rolls through her and she raises her head but is still leaning into him.

Marcus looks over at me and rolls his eyes too. "Bro, she should be more worried about me living with you than you should be about my arm being around her." He laughs and gives me a 'come on, Will' look.

I shake my head and look out the window. I know he isn't into girls, and even if he was he would never go after one that I was with, but seeing his arm around her is doing something to me. I want to rip it away and claim her in the back of the cab. I won't, because it's completely irrational and ridiculous. And because, well, we wouldn't have enough time for what I want to do to her.

When I glance back at her, she's studying me carefully. Can she see the ridiculous feelings of jealousy flashing through my eyes? Does she know what she's doing to me?

I blow out a confused breath and watch as she removes Marcus's arm from her shoulders and turns her body away from him so her legs are facing him and her back is against the inside of the door. Striking up a conversation, she asks him what he does for a living, making out like she moved because she wanted to talk rather than because I was acting like a twat. That little gesture makes me appreciate her even more.

I give Marcus an 'I'm sorry' look and he rolls his eyes and answers Nells question. I settle back watching her and thank all the gods above she's decided to give me a chance.

Marcus whistles his approval as we pull up outside Emilia's building. "Damn woman, you live here?"

Emilia nods, holding her head high.

"She lives on the top floor and doesn't rent, she owns that bad boy." Cleo puts her arm around her sister and kisses her on the cheek, clearly extremely proud of her big sister.

"I pay a mortgage, Cleopatra. I don't own it yet," Emilia retorts back looking embarrassed.

"That's still impressive, Emilia. Sports agents get paid a hell of a lot more than us teachers, eh Nell?" I nudge her as I say it.

Nell nods her head at me as she replies, "I couldn't afford to live in the bush outside this place, let alone on the top floor."

I put my arm around her shoulders and kiss her temple, mainly because I can but also because I feel like she needs it. I can sense a sadness in her, so as the others walk inside ahead of us, we take our time at the back.

"Thank you for that. I'm so proud of Emilia. She works her arse off to be the best and have the best, but," she stands in front of me and tucks her hair behind her ear, "sometimes I feel like, as the big sister, I should be more successful. Rather than jump starting my career again at the ripe old age of thirty."

I reach over to her and grab her around the shoulders, squeezing her tightly and bringing her closer to me so she's snug at my side. She fits there perfectly, like she was made just for me. "Nell, you're perfect the way you are. You've achieved other things in your life that Emilia hasn't yet." I turn her to look at me and grasp her face in my hands. "There's no comparison. And it's not a competition. Don't be so hard on yourself." She beams with happiness at my words and nuzzles into my hands which makes me smile back.

"If you two don't stop with the lovey dovey looks I will throw up in this bloody lift." Cleo brings us back to our surroundings and makes us all laugh.

"Don't mind Cleo here. She is anti-romance. Has been

ever since her first year in Uni. She's against all forms of romance, love, PDA's, she's a real grinch when it comes to it all," Nell informs us as we join them in the waiting lift and turn to look at Cleo who's scowling with her arms folded over her chest.

"I'm not the grinch of romance. I'm happy for you and anyone else that wants and finds love. I just don't believe in the bullshit hype about it that certain movie and book franchises portray. Not everyone gets a happy ever after, and I think that's important to remember."

She looks pointedly at Nell, and I can feel my temper start to rise. Is she trying to ruin this for us? Does she not realise her words could make Nell retreat into her bubble again?

Before I can speak, Marcus pipes up again. "Sounds to me like someone had her heart broken and has never gotten over it."

My eyes dart to Nell and Emilia, who are flicking nervous looks at each other, and then to Cleo who looks furious and sad at the same time. I actually fear for my friend's life around these Cooper women.

"For your information, Marcus, I've never had my heart broken because I've never been stupid enough to give it out to anyone. My point is simply that I think people focus too much on what they *should* have rather than what they want. If you want to be in a relationship and in love, good for you. But if you don't, you shouldn't be questioned about it and called a grinch. Simple really."

The tension in the lift is stifling, and I look around trying to get eye contact with one of them to make a joke or say anything that will help shift it. I'm just about to speak, when the doors open and we all trudge out into the hallway.

As we enter Emilia's home, all thoughts of the tense lift ride are forgotten as my eyes take in the most beautiful apartment. The floor to ceiling windows offer a stunning view of

London, and I find myself gravitating towards them without waiting for an invitation. Just as I utter a single, "wow," I hear a giggle behind me and turn around to find Nell standing close by.

"Beautiful isn't it?"

I can't speak so I just nod my head. My eyes swoop around the rest of the open space and see a sparkling white kitchen to the left of me. Everything in here screams expensive but tasteful. I gaze at her living room and notice the huge bookcase in the corner behind her white leather sofas. There is a lot of white, but it doesn't feel clinical as you'd expect, the pictures and knick knacks scattered around making it feel homey and lived in.

Nell walks over to the kitchen and I find myself in front of the sideboard next to the bookcase, taking in the pictures that are scattered on the shelves. The sisters, a picture of their mum and dad I'm presuming, and a picture of a little boy. I pick it up and study it. This must be Ben. He has blonde hair like Nell but lighter, more like Emilia and Juliet's. His eyes are the same shade of green as his mum's though. He has a different smile. I wonder if it's the same as Steve's. I run my finger over the picture of his sweet smiling face and my heart breaks a little for him, Steve, and Nell. For what they've all lost.

I look over to the next picture, Nell in a beautiful white wedding dress, and my heart skips a beat. She's stunning. Her green eyes are alive with happiness. I focus on her for a second and then force myself to look to her side. There is Steve, blonde hair the same as Ben's and smiling his smile too. I can see their love and happiness emanating from the picture and it breaks my heart. Sadness consumes me. She had that happiness and love before me. I'm sad that she lost it, I'm sad that she's had to face such heartbreak, and I'm terrified that she might never feel that way with me.

Looking at the two pictures in my hands that show pieces of a beautiful, happy family, I can't imagine the pain she must have felt at losing him and then having to keep it all together for Ben. She's so much stronger than I gave her credit for.

I glance back at Nell on her wedding day and can't help the onslaught of questions that fly through my mind. Will I ever be able to make her that happy? Or will she always compare what we have to what she had with Steve? Will I be her consolation prize? The thought pops into my head quickly and takes root, and I struggle to shake it off as I notice someone behind me. I turn my head slightly and see Emilia.

I quickly put the pictures down, but not before she notices. "He's cute, isn't he?" She motions to the picture of Ben and smiles. My eyes follow hers and I find myself staring at the beautiful little boy again. "Takes after his favourite auntie of course."

I give a little half-hearted chuckle and look back at the picture of Nell and Steve.

Emilia sighs loudly. "Steve's gone, Shakespeare, Nell isn't. Yes, she loved him fiercely and he did her too, but they were only meant to be for a short time." She places her hand on my arm and gently pulls on it.

As I turn to face her, her eyes lock onto mine, desperately trying to drum her point home. "Maybe you two are meant to be for the rest of time. Don't let her past affect your future. And don't compare what you guys have with what they had. It's not comparable. People change and the way they love does as well."

Stunned at her words, I manage a small smile and put my hand over the one on my arm and squeeze a little, words failing me.

She clears her throat and moves her hand off my arm. When she looks over my shoulder, I follow her gaze and watch as Nell walks over with a concerned look in her eyes.

"You two okay?" She glances between me and Emilia before her gaze flicks down to the pictures, and I watch as her eyes study the one of her and Steve. She looks away quickly and her eyes bore into mine, questions flying through them. Worry, fear and confusion etched on her face.

I smile at her to show her that I don't care about her past. "You looked so beautiful and Steve was a handsome chap, wasn't he? You were definitely punching, my lady."

Emilia snort-laughs as Nell's mouth gapes open like a fish, my ploy of distraction through humour working beautifully.

"I was most definitely not punching, you cheeky sod. I was the better looking out of us two. Emilia back me up."

Still laughing, Emilia shakes her head. "Sorry, Sis, Steve was hot." She looks at me and I motion punching and point at Nell.

She punches me in the arm. "That's bloody punching, you twat."

I laugh as I pull her into my chest and kiss her head. I motion to the picture of Ben and tell her, "I've never seen a cuter kid. He's the perfect combination of the both of you."

She smiles up at me and the look in her eyes is one I couldn't walk away from if I tried. "Really? You see me in him? I only see Steve," she tells me, hesitating on his name.

I look down at her and try to convey with my eyes that I'm okay with all of this, because in honesty, I am. Yes, I had a wobble, but Emilia kicked me right up the arse and sorted that out. She's right. The past is over, and the future is everything.

"He has his smile and hair colour, but his nose and eyes are all you. He's a beautiful little boy."

"Beautiful like his auntie, Shakespeare." Emilia calls from in front of the sofa.

Cleo, who's fixing drinks in the kitchen with Marcus, shouts back, "Aw Em, thanks, he is beautiful like me."

"Seriously? Little blonde haired, green eyed Mr. Adorable looks like Miss jet black haired, brown eyed, Cleo? Get real love..."

They bicker back and forth, but it turns into white noise as I have Nell in my arms still.

I'm inhaling her scent, committing it to memory, just in case.

"William? Are you okay, with seeing the pictures? Especially me in my wedding dress." She grimaces a little and buries her face into my chest.

I kiss her on the head again and hold her tighter. "Yes, Nell. Of course I am. I'll be honest, I was a little jealous of him, seeing you in that dress looking stunning and so happy. But I'm glad you got to have that with him."

She sighs and hugs me tighter, and I let all the doubt and insecurities go. She's with me now, and I'll share her with Steve for as long as she wants me to.

CHAPTER 20

Nell

"Ow, what was that for?"

"Ow, Sis why are you hitting us?" It's the first time that I've been alone with my sisters since they set up their little ambush on me and William, and although I know all's well that ends well, they still deserve a little pop to their arms for getting involved in my life.

"Hmm I wonder why I could possibly want to punch my sisters. What have they done recently that would warrant an assault on them from me?" I feign a look of wonder as Emilia and Cleo both scowl at me whilst rubbing their arms.

"Yeah okay, okay, genius sister. We aren't that dumb that we don't get your, 'not so subtle' sarcasm." Emilia is the first to challenge me, been that way since she first started talking.

Cleo rubs her arm some more, looking at me like a hurt puppy. "We were only helping. Look around, it got you what you wanted." She motions over to where William and Marcus are standing and frowns back at me.

"I know, Cleo. It could have gone very differently though. I have to work with him, and I still don't know how this will pan out in the long run. I would've liked to have done things my way."

She gives me the puppy dog eyes again, making me feel bad for hitting her. I swing my arm around her shoulder giving her a side hug.

I always felt bad for arguing or hitting the youngest two. Not Emilia, though. She shared a room with me. She was always annoying me, always with me and my friends, never leaving me and Steve alone. She took the brunt of my obnoxious teen years. As there's less than two years between us, we bickered the most but were also the closest. We became best friends as well as sisters.

It took longer for that relationship to develop with the younger two as they were four and six years younger than me. I always felt more protective over them than I did Emilia.

As I finish hugging Cleo, I catch Emilia throwing me some wicked side-eye. "You're such a sucker for the 'babies.'" She air quotes on the word babies as that's what Mum and Dad have always called them.

"I'm madder at you. You instigated the whole thing, didn't you? You're always sticking your big nose into my business. You never could let me have my own life, could you?"

She scoffs at me and shakes her head, surprising me by looking a little wounded. Emilia is usually as tough as old boots. "Actually, it was 'the babies' that came up with it. Juliet was sick of you being a moody bitch to her all the time. She and Cleo came up with the whole outing to London. Don't believe me? Read the texts for yourself."

She looks furiously at me and then continues her tirade. "Yeah, I went along with it because I care about you and I want you to get your head out of your arse, so sue me for messing up your fucking life, Sis." She slides her phone over the counter at me, picks up three drinks, then walks back over to the guys, leaving me standing there slack jawed and a little shocked. Where did that come from?

I look from Emilia's phone to Cleo and she shrugs her shoulders at me, disappointment etched on her face. "She's not wrong, Nell. Princess came up with the idea of going to London and I planned the rest. Juliet wasn't happy with all of the ideas but we decided to go through with it anyway."

I frown at Cleo and ask, "What wasn't she happy about?"

She blows out a frustrated breath, confiding, "She didn't want Connor to drive her home, she wanted to come with us. She was supposed to meet us around the corner after fifteen minutes but texted me saying she really did feel ill and wanted to go home. So, Connor drove her." My frown deepens as I wonder yet again what is really going on with Juliet and Connor.

Cleo must interpret it as anger at her as she starts to justify her actions again. "You were so sad and miserable, and we just wanted you happy. We want the old Nell back. The one who didn't think twice about having fun and enjoying her life. Not the shell of her. Sorry."

She looks over to Emilia and then squares her shoulders and hits me with a frown. "Emilia didn't deserve what you just said. She's always got your back, you should try having hers." She takes another two drinks and stomps into the living room too.

I stand in the kitchen feeling like an utter bitch. Emilia was right. I do cut the girls a lot more slack than I do her. They aren't babies, they're adults. I know I was being a bitch to Juliet and anyone else around me when William wasn't talking to me. I did need the push when it came to him.

Thinking back to six months ago, Emilia was the one telling me that I should email my old boss. I just brushed her off, ignoring her and carrying on with my new normal. But when William mentioned going back to work, I jumped at the idea.

I paid more attention to a stranger than I did to my sister.

What an idiot I am. Since Steve died she's been my constant. All of my family have, but her more so. She is always there when I need her, most times before I even know I need her. Memories of her drunk on my sofa, talking to Steve's picture, flash through my mind.

"I want my sister back. Give her back."

Brushing away the memory, and the emotions threatening to overtake me, I take a deep breath and walk into the front room.

Emilia doesn't look at me or flinch when I plop myself down beside her. I put my legs over hers, which are propped up on her coffee table, and cuddle into her like a kid with its mum.

"Emilia, I love you. I shouldn't have said that to you. I'm sorry. Thank you for always being there for me. Even when I don't know I need you, you're there. You're not just my sister, you're my bestie too."

I snuggle into her neck and I can feel her rigidness subside as she starts to giggle at me nuzzling her. "Okay you're forgiven, but you can stop. You have a man to nuzzle now. Leave me alone."

She pushes my head away from her neck, holding me back with her palm on my forehead. "And Nell, bestie? Really? You're better than that." She gives me a look of scorn and shakes her head at me as I laugh uproariously. I knew that word would irk her.

Marcus yawns loudly, drawing everyone's attention. "What? Between texting these hellions and trying to get through this knobhead's thick skull, I haven't been sleeping well. And alcohol makes me sleepy. We need to get on a train to go home. Can I sleep on your shoulder?"

He directs his question to William who sighs heavily. "Of course, you can. When have I ever stopped you before?" Marcus gazes adoringly at William with his hands under his chin and sighs deeply, which just makes me giggle and William roll his eyes.

"We do need to head out though. It's going to take us ages to get home, and he drools." He points at Marcus who is now scowling at William. The man gives me whiplash with his facial expressions.

"You two can stay here. We can crash at Cleo's." I swivel my head to stare at Emilia with wide eyes and a gaping mouth. She normally likes her space from people, especially ones she doesn't know very well.

"It's okay, we honestly don't mind going home. We don't want to make you leave and go all the way to Cleo's. Thank you though," William bats back to her, and I stifle a giggle when he says 'all the way to Cleo's,' as if she lives in Newquay instead of a couple of floors below Emilia.

"What's so funny? All of you have this amused look on your faces."

Cleo takes pity on him and decides to put him out of his misery. "I live downstairs, Will. I don't own like Emilia, my room-mate's family are super rich and own my apartment and let us live there for free. She's with her boyfriend most of the time and won't mind if we use her room. It's fine. You guys stay here, and we'll be downstairs."

Will stands in front of us looking uncomfortable and inde-cisive so I stand up and take his hand. "Honestly, it's fine. Emilia wouldn't have offered if she didn't want you staying here, believe me. She's normally quite fussy with people being in her space."

I smile up at him and he links our fingers together as he turns to Emilia."If you're sure?"

She nods at him. "Do you mind sharing the guest room

though? I don't really want either of you in my bedroom, no offence."

We all laugh, and they shrug their shoulders as Marcus informs us, "It's not the first time we've shared a bed, and I'm sure it won't be the last. That's right Nell, I've slept with your man." He clicks his fingers at me three times whilst waving his hand in front of his face, making me giggle.

"Oh no, you didn't..." I say back shaking my head from side to side and adapting a really bad fake American accent. My sisters shake their heads at me, groaning as they walk away. Marcus grimaces at me too.

"Jeez I knew my accent was bad but I didn't think it'd clear the room," I declare as my sisters and Marcus start taking the empty glasses to the kitchen. William wraps his arms around me and I don't care that the room is emptying because of me anymore. All I care about is being cocooned in his scent.

"How am I supposed to sleep knowing you're only a few floors away? It was hard enough knowing we lived near each other, but being in the same building is going to be torture."

He kisses the top of my head and I smirk, cheekily telling him, "You'll have Marcus to snuggle up to. Will you be the big spoon or the little spoon, Mr. Shakespeare?"

He chuckles, squeezing me tighter. "Always the big spoon with Marcus, he gets grabby in his sleep."

Laughing, I hug him harder and sigh. This night has been perfect, and I feel the vice I've had around my heart since Steve died loosen a little more. It seems to do that a bit more with every encounter I have with William. And I realise that makes me really happy.

CHAPTER 21

Nell

I feel sick with anticipation. William and I have been dating for a month now and he's definitely come through on his promise to woo me.

Little did I know that his idea of wooing me meant he would hold off on the more intimate areas of dating as well. He calls it romantic and gentlemanly; I call it annoying and frustrating. We've seen each other nearly every weekend, plus many evenings after Ben has gone to sleep. Having Juliet on tap to babysit has been a blessing. Every time we've gone out he's been the perfect gentleman and hasn't tried to make a move on me. We've kissed a lot, and we've fooled around, but whenever it starts to get really good, he pulls away.

I'm frustrated, horny and irritated. So tonight, I have a plan that will make resisting me impossible.

It's our sixth date and I'm pulling out all the stops. Mum and dad are looking after Ben overnight. Juliet is staying with Cleo and they're going out clubbing with Marcus and Emilia. Both mine and William's houses are empty, and William is under the impression that we're going bowling. I smirk when I think about his potential reactions to my actual plans.

After padding into my kitchen to grab the picnic hamper that I've packed with a smorgasbord of food and wine I prepared earlier, I walk out into the hallway and stop at the full-length mirror to check my appearance again. My dirty blonde hair is straight, hanging down past my shoulders. My makeup is natural and minimal, and thankfully the eyeliner gods were kind to me today and I was able to do those little flicks to make my green eyes even more cat-like. I tilt my head to the side and consider my emerald green wrap dress again. The style makes my boobs look good and my legs look amazing, if I do say so myself.

I hesitate, wondering if I'm coming on too strong and should wait for him to make the first move, but as quickly as the self-doubt starts to form I shake it out of my head. William has made the first move with everything. He's been the perfect person; patient and so understanding. It's my turn to take the lead.

My gaze wanders through the front room door to the picture of Steve on the mantle, and I freeze as I look into his smiling eyes. I take a step towards him and stop, my mind at war with itself. Shaking my head, I turn away from the picture. That's all it is. A picture.

Steve isn't here anymore, but William is. I close my eyes and see his beautiful smile and deep brown eyes. Taking a deep breath, I square my shoulders then head out the door without a look back or hesitation in my step.

"I thought I was picking you up?" William's eyes are wide in shock as I stand outside his door. His gaze sweeps over me, and I can see a flash of desire in his dark eyes as they land on mine.

"Change of plans. I didn't feel like bowling. I thought we

could stay in and have a carpet picnic instead." He hasn't moved from the doorway since he opened it to me, so I hold up the basket and ask hesitantly, "Can I come in?"

He blinks rapidly at me, shock apparent on his face. "Uh yeah. Sorry. Yeah. Of course you can." He blows out a frustrated breath and starts again. "Sorry. You threw me a bit. Erm, what if Marcus comes home? You sure you wouldn't prefer to eat out?"

He finally moves out of the way, and as I head into his hallway I turn and face him. "Marcus is out in London with my sisters for the night. We have the place to ourselves." I smile up at him and take a step closer, but stop when I see the panic in his eyes.

I've read this all wrong. He doesn't want me like that. That's why he hasn't made a move.

I put my head down, step back around him and reach out for the front door, embarrassment flooding through me. "Don't worry, William. I'll see you on Monday at school." My hand is shaking as I finally reach the handle and open the door, but before I can get it all the way open William slams it shut and growls at me.

"What are you doing, Nell? You're not leaving."

Anger rushes through me as I spin around and yell, "Can you make up your fucking mind. I'm getting whiplash from this back and forth. One minute you're all over me and then when I try to take it further you push me away." Gathering speed with my tirade, I put my hands on my hips and glare at him. "You never want to be alone with me and always insist on dates in public. You kiss me senseless and then pull away. You want to date me, to woo me, but you don't want to fuck me? Do I just not do it enough for you, William?

"I know I'm not as young as I was and I've had a kid, so I understand if you're not attracted to me like that, but you have to stop with the back and forth. I'm dizzy and I don't like it." Running out of steam, I look away from him, frustrated and exhausted by the emotions of it all, nervously chewing on my bottom lip, waiting for him to say something.

A deep growl from William is the only warning I get, and with my next breath I'm pushed up against the street door, his body as close as it can get to mine, trapping me against him, his hands on either side of my head, caging me in.

His face is so close to mine that I can feel his breath on my lips. "Woman, you are infuriating. How you could ever doubt I want you is beyond ridiculous. Nell, can you feel how much I want you? Feel how hard you make me? And that's before you've even touched me." I can feel his erection digging into me. I gasp in shock as he pushes against me even more.

He chuckles and nudges my nose with his, so I'm looking straight into his eyes. "My lady, I've had to fight every caveman instinct I have in me every time I've been with you. The reason I see you in public is because if we're alone, I won't be able to resist you. And I have to resist you, Nell. If I don't, I won't be able to keep my fucking hands off you."

Breathless, I whisper, "Why do you have to? I want your hands on me, William."

He groans, and as he strokes his thumb over my bottom lip, my tongue reaches out to taste him. His eyes turn black and he puts his forehead to mine. "You still want to keep this quiet, Nell? Once I've been inside you, claimed you, made you mine, I'm going to want it again and again and again. I won't be able to stop touching you, even at school. It's so hard already."

I grin up at him. "That's what she said."

He chuckles at me, but his eyes remain serious. "Nell, please don't ever think like that about yourself again. You're the most beautiful woman I've ever seen. You're the sexiest little wench too. I want you so badly, it hurts. I literally have a blue ball."

A smirk plays on my lips as I put my hands on his chest. "We can do something about that right now, William. Listen to me, please. I want you, Mr. Shakespeare. I've waited far too long now. I hear your concerns and yeah, they're kind of valid, but I think we can make this work. I never said you couldn't touch me at work, just that we can't get caught."

I wink up at him and slowly run my tongue over my bottom lip, knowing it will drive him mad. He growls again and kisses me, his lips hard and powerful, dominating my mouth, demanding I follow his lead. I moan into him as he presses his body harder against mine. He brings one hand up to the back of my neck and holds me in place whilst he continues his onslaught of a kiss.

Everything is gone around me and all I can think about is him. His scent, his taste, his touch, everything that makes up my Mr. Shakespeare. My William.

He breaks away from my lips and I groan in frustration.

"This is your call, my lady. What do you want, Nell?" His breathing is laboured and I know that holding back is killing him. I was stupid to ever doubt how much he wants me.

I look up into his almost black eyes and lick my lips as I tell him, "I want you. Naked. Upstairs in your bed. Now."

I'm thrown over William's shoulder, bobbing up and down as he takes the steps two at a time in his rush to get me upstairs.

A mixture of excitement and nerves takes root in the pit of my stomach, and desire rips through me as I watch in awe as his spectacular bum strides up the stairs. I want to take a bite out of it, but instead bite on my lip as I run my hands over the muscles in his back. This teacher's physique is seriously impressive. I feel my body heating up from the inside.

I'm so turned on, but I'm also wondering whether this is the right move or not. Is it too late to chicken out? I can fake a call from Mum about Ben.

He puts me down as we enter his room. His eyes are blazing at me, and as his tongue slides across his bottom lip I clench my thighs together to try and tamp down the wetness. My mouth is dry, and my heart is thumping in my chest. No, I'm not backing out now. I'm so ready for him. I can feel my orgasm forming just from looking at his gorgeous face.

I watch as his gaze sweeps up my body, lingers on my breasts and then travels up to my lips. I feel completely naked, even though I'm fully clothed.

He growls when I dart my tongue out and sweep it over my bottom lip, and I moan as he grabs my face and holds me in front of him. "You are fucking gorgeous, my lady, and I'm going to devour every inch of you. You'll be screaming my name and begging me to make you come, Nell."

I'm loving this alpha version of him. As my body vibrates with need, all my nerves and doubts are eviscerated by my desire for him. "I want you too, William. I want you to make me come. No begging necessary."

He smirks as he dips his head to me, and just as our lips are about to meet, he moves to the left and starts to nibble on my ear instead. I whimper with frustration but he just chuckles at me. "What do you want, my lady? Do you want me to kiss you?" He moves his hands from my cheeks and slowly trails them down my jaw to my neck. I nod my head at him, unable to speak.

He places his mouth on my collar bone, kissing me there. "Where else do you want me to kiss you, Nell?" he asks as his hands hover over my breasts, my nipples straining against the fabric covering them to get to his touch.

146

"William, please, everywhere." My voice comes out half whimper, half moan, and he smiles smugly as he crashes our mouths together.

A jolt of electricity scorches through my body. Heat is curling from my lips down to my toes. "William." I moan as his hand dips inside my dress and rolls my nipple through my bra. A zing of heat shoots down to my pussy and my hands grip his shoulders tighter.

"William." I shout his name, the only word I can form coherently. His hands untie the ribbon at the side of my dress and it falls open to reveal my lacy white bra and knickers.

He stops all movement for a second and inhales sharply before moaning and bringing his head down to my nipple. His hands cup my arse, and he digs his fingers into my cheeks as he lifts me up.

I wrap my legs around him and push my hands into his silky, dark blonde hair, tugging on it a little and drawing a moan from his throat. Pleasure flows through me knowing I made that sound come out of him, but it's soon replaced with my own cry of pleasure as he takes my other nipple into his mouth and sucks on it hard.

"Yes, William, yes!" I shout out and pull his hair harder. Lips fused together again, we move across the room. I shrug my shoulders so my dress falls to the floor. He places me gently on the bed, my legs hanging off the side, then steps back and breaks all contact with me, leaving me panting as I look up at him.

"Nell, you're a fucking goddess. I want you like this all the time."

He reaches up to his shirt and starts to unbutton it as I slide my heels off. I watch as his shirt falls to the floor, and moan my approval at his sculpted bare chest. His abs are delicious looking, blowing my mind with that tantalising V pointing into his waistband, like an arrow to the good stuff.

"You like what you see, my lady?"

I can't take my eyes off him, so I just nod my head. I seem to have lost all ability to speak in the presence of this man. In the blink of an eye, his trousers join his shirt and my dress. My jaw drops as I look at him standing naked and glorious in front of me, and I reach out to touch his rock-hard abs. My hand dances over the ridges and down past his happy trail to that incredible V.

He hisses out his approval when my hand wraps around his rock hard cock, but as I bring my mouth closer to him he takes a step back. "Nell, not before I've tasted you."

He smirks at my frown and bends down in front of me. Picking up my foot, he slowly glides his mouth across the inside of my ankle. Gentle, hot kisses trail up my leg, whilst his hand skims the inside of my other leg at the same time. The anticipation is unreal, and I prop myself up on my elbows so I can watch him. The image of him heading to my most sensitive area is so erotic.

I can feel his breath on me and I moan his name as he licks me through the lacy thong I'm still wearing. "Is that good, my lady? Or would you like me to take these off now?"

He digs his thumbs into the sides of the skimpy material and toys with pulling them down, but instead pulls them up until they're pressed tightly against me, making me yell out in pleasure. He chuckles, swipes them down my legs and without hesitation has his mouth on my pussy.

He flattens his tongue, takes a long slow swipe at my centre, and I almost combust. "William." I shout out loud as he moans against my clit, sending electricity surging through my body. I'm on the edge, one more touch and I'll topple over.

"William..." I beg and he moves away from me, leaving

me panting in frustration. "What are you doing?" I almost scream at him.

He looks up at me, a smirk on his wet lips. "What do you want, Nell? Tell me what you need, my lady." I gyrate my hips towards him to try to get some friction, anything to give me the release that I desperately need, but he moves further away.

My eyes flash with anger and I bring my hand towards my clit, determined one way or another to find my release. "Fine. I'll do it myself th..."

Before I can finish my sentence and get my hand on myself, he has both of them pinned above my head. "Nell, from now on, the only person who's going to give you pleasure is me. Do you understand that?" He holds both of my hands above my head. His other hand presses hard on my clit and he pushes his finger inside of me, making me shout out, "Yes!"

He looks me in the eyes and continues, "This pussy is mine now. Mine to fuck. Mine to bring pleasure to. These..." he moves his mouth to my nipple and sucks on it through the lacy material causing me to shout out again. The words he's saying, the feel of his mouth on my breast, of his hand fucking me, are too much. I shout out something incoherent whilst he finishes his sentence. "Are mine too, Nell. You are mine. I'm yours as well but you, my lady, are all mine. Say it back to me, Nell. Whose pussy is this?" I lick my lips, the delicious feeling of soaring is building higher, higher. I'm going. I'm right there, right at the edge.

"Nell, answer me. Whose pussy is this?"

He stops moving his hand and I pound on the bed with my head and scream at him, "Yours. It's yours, William. My pussy belongs to you. Now please for the love of God, make me fucking come!"

He leans over me and kisses me hard on the lips.

Smirking against my mouth, he tells me, "Whatever you want, my lady. All you had to do was ask."

I'm just about to shout at him for being so damn frustrating, when he bends back down, takes my nipple in his mouth and thrusts two fingers into me, curling them against my G spot. And I shatter, shouting his name as the white noise engulfs me.

CHAPTER 22
William

She looks up at me, fully sated, and I smile. "You okay?"

She nods her head and bites on her lip then reaches her hand up to touch my throbbing cock. "That was amazing, William, but I want this inside me. Do I need to beg again?"

She smirks at me and I can't hold back my grin. "No, I think you did enough of that. Take that off whilst I get a condom." I motion to her bra as I reach over to my bedside table and grab a foil packet. I sheathe myself and turn my attention back to the beautiful goddess waiting for me. My breath catches when I see that she's completely naked and sitting up on her knees on my bed. I tilt my head whilst looking at her body appreciatively and then growl when her hand reaches up towards her nipple. I lunge for her and we fall back onto the bed with me on top of her.

I pin her hands above her head. "You aren't very good at listening, are you, my lady? Do I have to tie these hands up?" Her eyes look at me in shock, but I can see curiosity in them as well. My lady has a little kink to her. "Those are mine. I get to touch, bite, kiss and lick them, whenever I want. Understand?" She nods at me with hooded eyes.

I part her legs with my thigh and line myself up so that

I'm just brushing her entrance. I smile when she gasps as I slowly enter her. She is so ready for me it's taking every bit of restraint to tease her like this, but she needs to understand that in the bedroom I'm the boss. She groans as I move away from her hot wet pussy, and I chuckle at her frown.

"If you don't want me to punish you, you need to remember the rules. What are they again, my lady?" I ask her as my lips roam over her body. I kiss her collarbone, down her arm, onto her stomach. Her creamy white skin is covered in goosebumps as I lick over her belly button. She thrusts her hips towards me, seeking friction for another release. I'm fucking dying to drive into her and feel her pussy squeeze around my cock, but I also need to make sure she understands that now, her pleasure belongs to me.

My hands are at the tops of her thighs and my mouth moves up towards her breasts. I hover above her beautiful pink nipple. "The rules, my lady?"

Her eyes fly open and she holds my gaze with a touch of annoyance. "You are the only one to bring me pleasure, William. Now bring me some fucking pleasure with your dick inside me. Please."

Hearing her talk like that tips me over the edge and I bite down on her nipple as I thrust my cock into her. She feels too good. Her pussy is wrapped around me and I don't dare move. I stay as still as I can, just feeling her tight heat and taking her in.

She holds my gaze again and I can't help the words from spilling out of my mouth. "You feel amazing, Nell. So fucking good. You're so tight. I just need a second. I don't want this to be over too soon."

She runs her hands up and down my arms and over my shoulders, over my back and down to my arse. "You feel good too, William. Please move now. I need you, Mr. Shakespeare."

Her big green eyes burn into mine and I can't hold back any longer. She whimpers when I pull out of her, then screams my name as I slam back inside.

"Are you okay, Nell?" I grit out through my thrusts, not knowing what I'll do if she says no because I don't think I can stop right now.

"Yes, William, yes! Harder, William! Just like that."

I roar like a lion who has finally found his mate, and throw her legs up and over my shoulders. I grip her hips and slam into her again, the new angle allowing me to go even deeper. I can feel her gratitude as she tightens around me, gripping onto me for dear life. She's close and so am I. "Come for me, my lady."

I pound into her twice more and watch as her climax takes over. She looks so beautiful, her face showing pure bliss. I bellow her name as her pussy milks my release and makes me come harder than I ever have before. I collapse on top of her for a minute, careful not to crush her, place a quick kiss on her lips, and roll to the side to take care of the condom.

Climbing back on top of her, I kiss her little button nose, the freckles that are scattered over her cheeks, and when I reach her beautiful pink swollen lips, I envelop her in our kiss.

Reluctantly, I pull away from her because I need to ask, "Nell, are you okay? Do you want me to get you anything?" She chuckles, shaking her head, and I reach up and tuck her hair behind her ear. "What's so funny?"

She looks up at me and her eyes lock onto mine. "You are, Mr. Shakespeare. You were all alpha, dominating man one minute and then the next, all soft and attentive. The juxta-position amused me, that's all."

I chuckle with her and dip my head to kiss her mouth again. I'll never get enough of this woman. "Are you complaining about my alpha side? You seemed to fucking

153

enjoy yourself with him. Especially when you begged me to make you come and screamed for me to fuck you harder."

Her hands come up to cover her pink face as she groans into her palms. Panic surges through me. Fuck. I've just embarrassed her after we had the most intense, mind-blowing sex ever. Shit, what if she runs?

"Nell, I'm sorry. I shouldn't have said that... Shit. Are you crying?" I lift myself up a little more and try to move her hands away from her face. Panic and anxiety grip my heart and constrict my throat, but she lowers her hands slowly and I see her smiling. Confusion surges through me and when she catches my expression she laughs harder. I hold myself up on my hands, hovering over her.

"William, I'm sorry. I got all embarrassed and then couldn't help but giggle about it. It's ridiculous. I'm embarrassed talking about what we did, whilst laying naked with you in bed. That was the most intense sex I've ever experienced. The irony was too much and I couldn't keep the giggles at bay. Then when I saw your face when you thought I was crying, it was too much. Why would I be crying anyway?" She asks as her laughter subsides.

I swallow a little too hard and she frowns up at me. My heart is racing, and I know I can't lie to her. "I was worried that when I teased you about before when we were, er, you know, that you were embarrassed and upset and would retreat back into yourself and leave."

I lower my gaze so she can't see the vulnerability in my eyes and shift nervously on the bed, sitting up with my back against the headboard and pulling the duvet over myself. The bed dips as she moves, probably to get dressed to go home. Disappointment runs through me and my heart breaks a little at knowing how close we were to making this work. I close my eyes and run my hand through my hair.

I feel her touch my arm and then the covers are pulled off

as she straddles me, still naked. I look up at her with confused eyes while she strokes her palm on my face.

"Are you always worried that if you upset me I'll retreat inside myself again?"

I look away from her eyes as they try to bore into my soul. I shrug my shoulders, words eluding me, which only seems to happen around her.

She sighs and lays her other hand on my chest over my heart. "William, talk to me. Please?" She pleads with me, and I lean my cheek into her hand and kiss her open palm.

Knowing that I'm going to have to tell her the truth about my fear, and knowing she won't like it, scares the life out of me. But I can't refuse her anything, so I take a deep breath and put my insecurities out there for her to see, letting my vulnerability be free.

"I'm not going to lie to you, Nell, not after what we just experienced together. In case you couldn't tell, I like you. I really fucking like you, Nell. More than I've ever liked anyone. But I'm conscious of everything that you've been through. I don't want to rush you into anything, and I'm only mentioning this because you asked. I was holding back on you before because I know what I feel, what I want and who I want. But for you, it's different."

She doesn't move a muscle as she listens intently to what I have to say. "You were in a long-term relationship for so long, and the time you weren't you were grieving. You've never been just you and you haven't dated before. Well, not really, as you and Steve got together as kids. You might decide that this, me, what we have, isn't what you want. I don't want to do or say anything that might push you to come to that conclusion any quicker than I think you already will. I hope that makes sense. My knowledge of words is still coming back to me after what we just did." I wink at her and grin, but I know she can tell it's forced.

Fear grips me as I wait to hear what she thinks about my worries.

She brings her beautiful eyes to meet mine and sighs. "I don't want you walking around on eggshells with me, William. Just because I spent a long time with Steve, and then grieving his loss, doesn't mean I don't know what I want now. Yes, I was confused at the beginning, but that was more about whether it was the right thing to do by Steve and Ben. Guilt was a major factor of my confusion too. I wanted you from the beginning, William. I was just scared. When I saw you outside on the street, you evoked emotions in me that I thought were dead. You sparked them back to life, William. And do you know why? Because I like you too. Really. Fucking. Like. You."

I go to respond but she places her hand over my mouth.

"I want to explore this, and I *choose* to do that with you. I know I have issues. I still have a lot of guilt over Steve, and I don't know if it will ever go away, but it's getting better. Please try to relax a bit, Mr. Shakespeare. I'm not going anywhere. Especially when you can make me come like that. Twice." She looks at me and moves her hand from my mouth, but before she can take it too far away from me, I grab it and bring it back to my lips. I kiss the palm of her hand and lace our fingers together.

I look up at her and smile. "Let's go hand in hand, not one before another."

She smiles at me, and the fact that she understands what that means, means the world to me. My words might struggle to form, but I can always rely on Shakespeare to convey what I need to with her.

"So, I take it by that quote you understand you have to stop making decisions for us when we should be making them together. Do you feel better and more at ease now?" She grins as she asks me but I don't fail to notice the little inflection in her voice that tells me she means business.

"You've made me a very happy man, my lady. I'm more than happy to walk side by side with you as we navigate our way through this. I promise I'll try to stop making decisions or basing my actions on what I think is right or what I think you're feeling without talking to you first."

She leans in and kisses me, her lips grazing softly against my own. Her pussy brushes against my cock, waking him up, and I'm hard and ready to go again with her.

I turn my head and whisper in her ear. "By the way, Nell, I wanted you the moment I saw you too, but not more than I want you now. Hold on, you're in for one hell of a ride, my lady." I flip her over so she's beneath me and she shakes her head at me.

"Oh no, Mr Shakespeare, you were on top last time. Now it's my turn." She grabs my thighs and tries her hardest to move us around, but I don't budge. She frowns up at me, pouting. "William..."

When she raises her eyebrow and gives me what I assume is her 'mum' look, a rush of blood surges to my cock and before I can react, she's managed to knock me off her and is now straddling me again.

"Hey now that's unfair, I was distrac...FUCK YEAH!" Before I can finish whining about being distracted, she's sunk down onto my dick and is rocking back and forth. I reach up and cup her breasts as she tightens around me and everything else disappears.

"Fuck, Nell. You feel so fucking good like this." I thrust up as she bounces back down on me and her eyes fly open as she shouts my name. She might be on top but I'm still in control. I hold onto her hips, guiding her in time with my thrusts, and before long I can feel the inevitable tensing of her pussy as she shouts my name out loud.

I flip her over, her legs wrapping around my waist. "I can't last much longer, Nell."

She opens her eyes, looks straight into mine and whispers, "Then come, William." I surge inside of her harder and harder. I can feel the pressure start in my ball and on my next thrust, my climax takes over and I roar her name.

Completely spent, I flop down beside her. She snakes her arm over my chest and rests her head in the crook of my neck. I squeeze her tightly, kiss the top of her head, and fall into a blissful sleep.

CHAPTER 23
William

As the sun streams through the blinds that I forgot to close last night, I squint my eyes against the onslaught of light hitting them. I'm still tired, and a grin plays on the corners of my mouth as I remember why.

Nell.

I stretch over to reach out for her and my hand brushes the cool pillow. Sitting up quickly, I scan the room and relief washes over me when I see her clothes on the floor. Panic averted. She hasn't left. She's still here. Just not in bed.

I throw on a pair of light grey tracksuit bottoms and pad out of my bedroom, heading for the noise coming from the kitchen downstairs. When I get to the doorway, I watch as she stands at the counter making a cup of tea, dressed in one of my shirts and nothing else. Every time she reaches for something the hem of the shirt skims the bottom of her arse and I feel my dick stirring again.

"Couldn't sleep?"

She jumps and twirls around to face me with her hand on her chest. "Jeez William, you scared the hell out of me. Don't creep up on people. What's wrong with you?"

Laughing, I stalk towards her. "I'm sorry, my lady. I

didn't mean to scare you. You look damn sexy in my shirt, though. I needed a minute to take it all in."

I bite on my lip and go to grab her around the waist when she puts her hands on my chest.

"Stop right there, mister. Do you wear those outside?" She glances down at my bottoms and I shrug.

"Yeah, sometimes. Why?" Confused, I take a step back and look at them again.

"You shouldn't. In fact, don't again." She steps around me and heads towards the table as I frown at her.

I look down once more and start laughing as realisation dawns on me. "Grey trackies. I get it now. If it makes you happy, I won't." I sit next to her and kiss her cheek, feeling pretty good about giving in to her so easily.

"Good. I don't want other women looking at your junk. Oh, hang on, does that mean men know about the magic of grey tracksuit bottoms then? Do we have nothing sacred anymore?" She shakes her head sadly and I chuckle again.

"Only because I live with a gay guy and Marcus is obsessed with TikTok. They've been mentioned in a few of the books I read with Mum as well." She rolls her eyes and smirks.

But when a frown furrows her brow, my panic rises, even after what she told me last night. "Are you okay, Nell? Talk to me."

She takes a deep breath and anxiety fills my stomach when she says, "We need to talk, William."

I nod my head at her, my anxiety turning into dread. "Okay, about what?" I force myself to stare at the table, not wanting her to see the hurt in my eyes with what she's going to say.

"Last night William, it was amazing..." I nod my head waiting for that little word *but*. "But... we didn't use a condom the second time. It's my fault, I didn't think about it.

I'm not used to using them. I was on the pill, and after I had Ben I went back on it as it helps with my irregular periods. I've always suffered with them. Was a nightmare trying to conceive Ben.

"Oh shit! I'm sorry William, you don't want to think of me and St... Fuck why can't I stop fucking talking? I'm going now."

Her face is flushed with embarrassment, but as she goes to stand up, I grab her hand and force her to stay where she is. Her rambling was fucking adorable, but she's biting that bottom lip again and I want to bend her over the kitchen table and fuck her. I shake my head and try to calm my dick down, reminding him she needs reassurance first.

"Nell, it's okay. Calm down, it's alright. If you're worried about an STD, I had a test when I had my cancer check-up, all results negative, and I haven't been with anyone since before then. It's okay. It does explain why I couldn't last as long that time though," I say, trying to inject a bit of humour.

She looks up at me, her eyes wide. "You're not angry? I swear I didn't do it on purpose. I didn't use them with Steve and... Oh shit, sorry, again."

"Nell, you can talk about him. I know you two had sex. I mean I don't want to know the comparisons or anything. But honestly it's okay. I didn't realise either. We don't need to worry about...pregnancy or anything so it's fine." I take a deep breath and force the idea of her being so worked up about being pregnant with my baby into a box and lock it with a key, not wanting to delve into what that means about us and me.

"Oh William, I wasn't worried about that. I thought... I was scared you'd think badly of me to be honest. I didn't want you to think I did it on purpose. I just got carried away."

She looks down at the table and I reach over and tilt her chin up so she's forced to look at me. "My lady, it's okay. I'm perfectly comfortable with not using them if you are. You just jumped ahead a couple of steps, but I'm fine with that. If you're not there yet, we'll put this down as an oversight, a result of going with the flow in the heat of the moment, and can use them again. There will be an again, right Nell?" I ask her gently, refusing to take my eyes off hers. I exhale a breath I didn't realise I was holding when she nods at me.

"I want there to be lots of agains, William. I don't care about condoms. You feel better without them, but it's your decision."

I smirk as I lean over and kiss her. "No condoms then. Nell, can we have another again now?"

She smiles at me and bites her lip, on purpose this time. "Well, you are wearing those tracksuit bottoms, and I can see every inch of you through them, so I'd say most definitely, Mr. Shakespeare."

I smirk as she stands up and takes my hand, leading me towards my bedroom, and I can't help but reach out under the hem of my shirt to stroke her glorious bum as she walks up the stairs. Every agonizing step she takes is like torture, so I sweep her into my arms with her squealing in delight as I tell her, "You're taking too long," and all but run to my room.

Casually flipping through the TV stations whilst laying on the sofa in the front room, I hear the door open and close.

Marcus walks into the doorway with his hands over his eyes shouting, "I'm home, everyone better be wearing clothes. If not, you better run upstairs, Nell."

I chuckle and he peeks through his fingers and mouths

'oh,' clearly disappointed that he didn't catch us in a compromising position of some kind.

"You on your own?" He asks as he flops down on the sofa, pushing my feet from his seat.

"I was laying there, Bro. You couldn't have sat over there?" I point towards the kitchen and he tsks at me and shakes his head.

"Now why would I want to go over there when you so desperately want to tell me what happened with little Nelly-poo yesterday? Where is she anyway? How did it go? I assumed you two would be bumping uglies still."

I shake my head at his terminology but chuckle at it as well. "Nelly-poo? Bumping uglies, seriously? You couldn't have used a better nickname or phrase than those, Marcus?"

"Oh sorry, would one have preferred if one said that you and Nell were having coitus instead?"

I shudder at him. "No, don't say that. Yuck." I hate the word coitus and he knows it. I don't know why, I just hate it. It sounds like a hospital term or something.

"Where have you been, by the way? Were you really out with her sisters in London?"

He smirks at me slowly and nods his head. "Yep." He makes the p pop and says no more.

"Well, did you have fun?" I ask, curious as to what they got up to and to stop him questioning me over Nell anymore. I don't want to tell him yet. I like having everything to myself for a change. Marcus has known every detail of my life for as long as I can remember, and I love him like my brother, but I just want to keep this for Nell and me, just for a bit.

"Yep, it was fun." He shrugs his shoulders and turns towards the TV, blocking me with his back.

I switch the TV off and tap him on the shoulder. When he finally turns to look at me, I raise my eyebrows, silently asking *what the fuck* as he feigns innocence dramatically in true Marcus style. "Oh, did you want to talk to me now? Because I'm sure I asked you some questions and you ignored them. Kind of got the impression you didn't want to talk to me."

I dismiss his antics with a heavy sigh. "Don't be a dick, Marcus. I don't want to get into details." I wave my hand in his face to silence his protests and continue. "I know I have before, with other girls, but Nell's different. I respect her. I want a future with her and I just want to keep this side of us between us. I'm sorry, Bro."

He smiles at me and shrugs his shoulders. "Nah, I get it. She's your lobster, Bro." I shake my head at him but grin at the reference. The fucker makes me watch those shows back to back still.

"Just tell me one thing, Will?" I raise an eyebrow at him and tip my chin to motion for him to continue. "Was it worth the wait?"

I smile and nod my head at him. "Hell yeah!" He stretches his hand up and I high five him like we're teenagers again.

"So, you going to tell me what you got up to with her sisters or what? How did that come about?"

I sit back as Marcus explains that Nell arranged for the whole thing to happen so she could finally get me alone. Knowing she wanted me so badly she'd arrange for her sisters to take Marcus out for the night fills me with a euphoric happiness I've never experienced before.

"Anyway, I think you've lost the rights as my best mate after last night. They go to Emilia now, soz."

I follow after him when he stands up and heads into the kitchen, a little hurt to have been tossed aside so easily. "Erm excuse me. Firstly, *soz*? Come on dude. What happened to bros before... shit I can't say that. Well you know, boys before... nah that doesn't work either. I've known you my whole life and you're choosing a woman over me? Damn that feels weird saying to you of all people."

His shoulders shake from his laughter as he opens the fridge and grabs two waters. "What can I say? That woman is amazing! If I wasn't gay, I swear I would wife her. Screw that, I'll still wife her even being gay, she's that good." The look I give him says it all and he holds his hands up in a surrender gesture. "Okay sorry, I'm not a teenager anymore. I shouldn't try to talk like one, I get it. Seriously though, she's fucking amazing. She can out-drink anyone, her sense of humour is on point and she is drop dead gorgeous. Between her, Cleo and Juliet, every man's eyes were on us last night. I was a little out of my depth until Connor showed up. FYI there is something going on there with him and Juliet, you mark my words."

I splutter as I take a sip of my water and laugh at him. "Shows what you know. Cleo told me she hates his guts. She doesn't know why though. There's nothing between them, well not on her part."

He smirks and shakes his head at me. "It's a good job we convinced Nell to give you a go because you're completely clueless when it comes to the fairer sex. You going to the gym tonight?"

I sit down at the little table and tell him, "Nah, can't be bothered. I'm knackered. I'm going to call my mum, talk about the book and go to bed."

He frowns at me and asks, "What book? I didn't get the memo on this one." I laugh at the hurt in his voice. Only Marcus would be upset that my mother didn't ask him to read a romance book and then discuss it with her.

"It's called *Not my Romeo* by Ilsa Madden Mills. She thought it was funny because it mentions Romeo and Juliet in the last scene. It was really good, one of my favourites, but I'm going with the 'it was crap line' just to annoy her."

He frowns at me and shakes his head. "You should be nicer to your mother. She's another amazing woman." I smirk at him. I love the way he loves her as if she was his own mother, but sometimes it winds me up that he always sides with her.

"Oh, look out Frank, Marcus is going to wife my mum," I say whilst rolling my eyes as he mutters 'wanker' under his breath and leaves the kitchen to my laughter.

CHAPTER 24

Cooper Sisters group texts

Juliet: Ben is in bed and she's sitting next to me with a cup of tea...

Nell: She's also a part of this group chat, you twat.

Juliet: Oh yeah (woman slapping her forehead emoji)

Nell: No, Juliet. No emojis or I go upstairs and lock my door and block you all!

Juliet: Alright, jeez, no emojis. Emilia, Cleopatra, are you there? If not I can just talk face to face with her...

Nell: Again, I'm here you know.

Juliet: She has her frowny face on. I would insert the right emoji but she said no more :'(

Juliet: She threw a pillow at me... GUYS!

Emilia: Alright, alright, you know some of us have work to do, Princess.

Nell: It's Sunday!

Juliet: Rub it in why don't you and don't call me that!

Emilia: No rest for the wicked, Sis. Juliet, I distinctly recall Connor calling you Princess a lot last night. Didn't hear you complaining that much ;)

Nell: Emilia, please reference my earlier text, it stands for you too.

Juliet: Ha! You must have been drunker than you realised then because I told him every damn time.

Emilia: Nell, noted *eyeroll* Juliet, that must have been what you were whispering into his ear all night, or was that your tongue in there.

Juliet: I will throat punch you. I don't like him enough to even want to talk to him let alone kiss him. Fuck off, Emilia.

Nell: Emilia, stop it. NOW!

Emilia: Jeez what crawled up your butt? I thought you would have been on cloud nine after your little sexcation at Shakespeare's house.

Cleo: What did I miss? I can't be bothered to scroll up, there's too many to read.

Emilia: Nell is pissy. Juliet is pissy and I'm fine.

Cleo: Nell is pissy? What happened? D not big enough?

Emilia: Don't know. She hasn't mentioned last night. That would be disappointing and would explain the pissy mood though.

Cleo: Nell, it's not about the size of the boat, it's the motion in the ocean babe.

Nell: What the actual fuck, Cleopatra? I'm pissy because YOUR sisters are infuriating.

Cleo: MY sisters, ouch, what did you do, Em?

Emilia: Oh the irony... Juliet, I'm sorry.

Juliet: It's fine. Nell, tell us how last night was please?

Nell: Well now you two have stopped acting like little brats, I'll tell you. It was amazing.

Cleo: Yeah baby...

Emilia: Care to elaborate, Sis?

Nell: Nope, night sisters. I love you xxxx

Cleo:?

Emilia: Nell???

Emilia: Juliet, where is she?

Juliet: Gone to bed (monkey covering its eyes emoji, laughing face with tears emoji)

CHAPTER 25

Nell

"Are you really going to ignore them and not tell them anything?" Juliet looks over at me, her beautiful green eyes shining at me expectantly. I know she's waiting for me to spill the beans to her, but I'm not going to.

I smile at her and bring my legs up to curl them underneath myself on the sofa. "Yes, and I'm not telling you anything either."

She pouts at me and crosses her arms, it reminds me of when she was younger and would get in a huff.

I laugh at her petulance and shake my head at her as she smiles up at me. "Have you ever had something that you wanted to keep just for you, Princess?" I ask her.

She bites her lip and nods her head at me even as her body language changes. She sits up straighter, her legs cross in front of her and her hands wring together in her lap as she avoids my gaze. I want to ask her so many questions. What is she hiding? Is it to do with Connor? Did it happen when she was away? Is she okay? I don't though, because that would step all over the point I'm trying to make.

"So, you'll understand when I say that this thing between us has involved everyone from the beginning and I kind of want last night to be for William and me. Just us. I appreciate all of you interfering..."

"Hey! We helped, and you know it!"

I chuckle at her indignant outburst and continue, "Okay. I appreciate all of you 'helping' at the beginning, but right now I just want to focus on Nell and William for a bit."

She nods her head at me and smiles, but it's a sad one and I hate not knowing what happened to her. "I get it, Nell. If you do want to talk or say anything you know I'm here. I can keep it a secret too. I think I'd enjoy that, knowing there was something I knew that Emilia didn't. You two are so close, I would love to have one over on her about you."

She laughs, but what she's just said hits me straight in my heart. "Juliet, you know I love all of you the same, right? I know I was closer to Emilia growing up, mostly because I had no choice as she took over my bedroom, but you and Cleo are just as important to me as Emilia is. She's always, I don't know, needed me more than you guys did. Cleo went off to Uni on her own and I was just kicking off married life. You were enjoying yourself being a carefree teen, I figured you didn't want your oldest sister butting in. Plus, you had Cleo and Connor." I stop when I see her flinch and wait a second to see if she says anything.

"Nell, I know you love me, and since I've been back it's been nice getting one-on-one time with you. Emilia is your go to, and that's okay. Cleo's mine, but there are things I keep even from her. I get you wanting to keep it for you and Will. I just wanted you to know if you wanted to, you could tell me anything."

I look at my baby sister and I see pain flash through her eyes, but I know not to push it. She's very cleverly and clearly told me she's keeping her secret, and if she hasn't even told Cleo about it, I have no chance.

"I will tell you this, he wore grey sweatpants."

She giggles at me and wags her eyebrows. "Was everything as it should be and appropriately sized?"

I nod my head at her. "Oh yeah. So much so that I forbade him from wearing them outside. Ever."

She gasps and blushes and I can't help my laugh at her reaction.

This Wednesday morning is shaping up to be quite possibly the worst day I've had in a long time. Ben woke me up throughout the night with horrible nightmares, making me grumpy and irritated before the day even started. So, when Ben's nursery called at 7:45am, fifteen minutes before we were due to leave, to tell me that their heating system had broken down and they wouldn't be allowed to open today, I wasn't in the best space for a reasonable reaction.

Normally a little hiccup like this wouldn't be a problem, but Mum, Dad and Juliet decided to take an impromptu trip to London to go shopping at the West End, have lunch in a posh restaurant and be carefree for the day—my mother's description. When I phoned her frantically at 7:49am to ask her to watch Ben for me, she offered to reschedule her trip. But as she was already heading out the door to get the train, I felt bad and told her not to worry. Ben is, after all, my responsibility and I'll deal with this like every other working mum out there.

With a frustrated sigh, and after a call to my boss, I reach for my phone, bring William's information up on the screen and hit call.

"Hey, my lady. Are you okay? You never phone this early." He sounds so sexy on the phone, sleepy and caring. I wonder if he's had time to do his hair yet or if it's all messy and dishevelled?

I shake my head to clear those thoughts and focus on my crisis. "Hi William. I'm sorry to call you first thing, but Ben's nursery is closed today and there isn't anyone to watch him for me. I'm going to have to stay home with him I'm afraid." I blow out a sigh and give Ben a small smile to make sure he doesn't think I'm frustrated about him.

"Erm, Nell, I'm sorry, but you can't. The Ofsted agent is coming to assess your class today, remember? 2:00-3:00. If you're not there, it'll reflect badly on the school and on you as well. I'm sorry, my lady."

I let out a groan and whine, "What am I going to do? I can't leave him here alone, and I can't bring him to school. What should I do?"

There's a brief silence on his end before he says, "Calm down, my lady. I got you covered. No, you can't leave him alone at home, he's way too young to party without me." I know he's trying to make me laugh but my silence speaks volumes, so he continues, "Wow, tough crowd, wench. You can bring him to school though. No one will mind. Set him up on one of the desks in your class with his tablet, headphones, pen and paper and he'll be okay. I can take him to my office or to the teachers' lounge when the agent is there for your assessment. But only if you want me to, of course. I mean, I get it if you don't."

He mumbles that last bit and my heart flutters in my chest. This man is helping me. He's trying to find a solution to my problems, and he wants to help with Ben.

I'm taken aback for a few seconds. Of course, I'm nervous to take Ben to school with me and to let William watch him for an hour. Only my family has ever watched him. I know I can trust William, but is it all too soon? He's never met Ben before, doesn't know his quirks, but I have to be in this assessment, and this is the perfect setting for them to meet. No labels, just work colleagues.

I look over to the picture of Steve on the mantel, like I might get some assurance of what to do from him, and shake my head at myself. Come on Nell, this is William. You trusted him enough to sleep with him. You're forging a relationship with him. It's an hour tops and he's a teacher for god's sake.

"Nell, are you still there? Listen if you're not comfortable with that I can..."

"NO!" I shout into the phone, a bit too loudly. "Sorry William, I didn't mean to shout at you. I'll be honest, your suggestion freaked me out a little bit. Only my family has ever looked after him." I take a deep breath and continue. "I would like to bring him to school though, and if your offer still stands, I would love it if he could sit with you whilst my assessment is happening please." I hold my breath waiting for his response.

"Anything for you, Nell. I'll see you in a bit."

I'm smiling like a maniac as I hang up and turn to Ben. "Guess you're coming to work with me today, mister. You can stay in class with me, but you have to be good. Then you can sit with my friend William for a bit, if that's okay with you?"

He shrugs at me and nods his head. "Can I bring my tablet?"

I nod at him and smile at the turn of events as I usher him towards the street door. With my hand on the door, ready to open it, a message beeps through on my phone.

William: Don't worry, my lady. I won't tell Ben you're my girlfriend ;) xxx

Me: I don't think we ever agreed on that terminology, Mr. Shakespeare. NO EMOJIS PLEASE. Xxx

William: Woman, you're my girlfriend whether you like it or not. Keep up that attitude and you'll be sorry. That's not an emoji, it's punctuation marks strategically placed xxx

Me: Oh, I like that. All alpha on me again. Makes me think of other times your alpha has come out to play. Mr. Shakespeare, I need to get to work or else I would continue this xxx

Me: No strategically placed punctuation marks either please (it's a pet peeve of mine) Thank you again xxx

Before he can respond I pop my phone back into my bag, jog out to the car and strap Ben into his carseat. One way or another, I think today will be an eye opener for me when my two worlds collide.

CHAPTER 26
Nell

I glance at the clock hanging on the wall over the door. It's 1:30pm and William's on his way to get Ben from me. My palms are sweating, my breathing is shallow, my nerves are shot, and I haven't had a minute to think about the assessor that's coming to judge me whilst I teach my class. I can't think about that or I'll crumble with the pressure of it all.

Ben has been a superstar all day. He sat at his desk with his tablet and a phonics app and just got on with it. He hasn't complained about being stuck here, and loved every minute of the older girls fawning over him whilst the boys mucked about with him.

I look over at him, the classroom empty for lunch, and can't help but smile. His bright, blonde hair is mussed up, his green eyes are staring at his screen in concentration and his little tongue is poking out of his mouth. He looks up, catching me watching him, and when he beams at me it makes my heart beat a little faster. Sometimes I like to think it's Steve smiling through him, telling me I'm doing the right things. Silly, I know.

"Right, cheeky monkey, do you remember I said you would need to go with mummy's work friend William?" He puts his tablet down and nods up at me. "He'll be here in a minute. He is really nice and funny. I hope you like him. Oh and he is lots of fun."

He tilts his head and grins at me. "I will like him Mummy. If you like him, I'll like him." I ruffle his hair and bend down to scoop him into my arms, noting that he's a little bit bigger every time I do it. He doesn't fit as snugly as he once did.

I breathe in his scent and kiss his head as he squirms and squeals. "Mummy, stop smelling me, it's gross." I turn as I hear the deep chuckle from behind me and give William a look with narrowed eyes, wondering how long he's been watching us.

"It's not gross. I've been smelling you since you were a baby, and I'll always smell you, mister." I tickle my son and he wriggles out of my arms.

"I'm not a baby endymore."

"Anymore bud, not endymore, anymore. Sorry, I'm Will." I slow blink at William and stare up at him. He just corrected Ben instead of cooing over how cute it is when he says things wrong. My heart beats a little faster again and I smile at him.

I watch as Ben smiles and waves and then puts his hands on his hips and tells me in a very matter of fact tone, "I'm not a baby *anymore,* Mummy. I'mma big boy now. I go to nursery and I'mma play wiv Will on my own. See?"

I roll my eyes at the giggles that I hear from William behind me. Putting my hands on my hips to mirror Ben and show him I mean business too, I tell him, "Well mister, you are MY baby. You always will be, no matter how big you get. Get it?"

He grins and shakes his head at me, then walks over to William and shrugs his shoulders. I watch closely as William bends down and tells him, "Don't worry, bud. I know how you feel. I'm old and my mum still calls me her baby. It's best to just let them get on with it." Ben chuckles and nods his head. I raise an eyebrow at William, but he just winks and blows me a kiss over Ben's head so he can't see.

"Right, you ready to go, bud? I've got some playing cards in my office, thought we could practise your numbers in a fun way. What d'you say?" Ben nods and holds out his hand. I watch as William reaches down, enveloping it with his large one, and the look of contentment that washes over his face causes a lump to form in my throat.

I try to stem the emotion in my voice as I wave goodbye and tell them to have fun. Seeing them together makes me so happy, and a little sad too, but I force myself to cling to the happiness. I've been sad for too long.

I sit back at my desk and just smile. I smile picturing my beautiful, kind, little boy, making another friend and again not realising his importance in this world. I smile at William holding hands with Ben, his eyes shining with happiness and a smile on his face that could eclipse the sun. I don't know how I managed it, but I'm so thankful that William chose me. And that I let him.

"Knock, knock. How are we doing in here?"

When I go to get Ben after my assessment, he's sitting on William's desk, facing William who's sitting across from him in his chair. They both grin up at me as I stand in the doorway, and I can't stop the laugh from bubbling up and out of my mouth at just how cheeky they both look.

"We're good Mummy. I just beated Will again."

I'm just about to correct him when William jumps in. "It's beat, remember bud? And you did not beat me, you cheated."

"Oh, yeah, I forgot." Ben giggles and my heart skips a

178

beat. "I did beat him, Mummy. And I didn't cheat. I got a full house."

I frown over at William. "He got a what now? Have you been teaching him poker? William?" I'm in full on mum mode and I'm scowling at them both as they break into the biggest smiles and start to laugh. I shift on my feet with my arms folded over my chest. "What's so funny?"

"You are Mummy. Will said you'd get cross if I said dat, what is poker?"

I try to glare at William, but his smile is too damn enticing and I end up smiling too. "Just because I'm smiling doesn't mean you're not in trouble. Was he okay?" I ask and look over at Ben, suddenly feeling shy and insecure around William. I can't stop the doubt from forming in my mind. What if he didn't enjoy spending time with Ben and this will be his way out.

"Nell, we had a blast. Didn't we bud? Go give your mum a hug. I think she needs it after that trick we played on her." Ben hops down and bounds towards me and I sweep him up and cuddle him. My eyes lock with William's and he mouths, "Stop worrying. We had fun," and blows me a kiss.

I smile back, all my insecurities pushed to the back of my mind, and put Ben down. "Right, mister, for being a good boy today, I thought we could go out to eat on the way home, what d'you fancy?"

Ben thinks for a minute and then says, "Pizza, Mummy. Will, can you come wiv us?"

I freeze, not knowing what to say. Dinner seems very intimate for the three of us, but I really want him to come. I want him to want to come, though. I look everywhere but at William, trying to let him make the decision for himself. He bends down and looks at Ben.

"Thank you for asking, bud. I would love to, but that's up to your mum."

Ben turns his big green eyes at me and I nod my head. "If William wants to, he's more than welcome."

I turn my attention back to William and try to fill my eyes with gratitude and rid the worry of them before I bring them to meet his. "I don't want you to feel obligated though, you've already done so much for me today."

He smiles up at me, still in the crouching position next to Ben. "Anything for you guys."

My heart skips a beat at the intensity in his gaze accompanying those four little words and the hidden meaning behind them. Held tight by his gaze, I'm swept away in those eyes of his, getting darker and darker, knowing that he's feeling the heat from our connection as well. Brought back to reality, I clear my throat and shake my head a little when Ben tugs on my hand, asking when we're going.

"Erm, do you need us to wait around for a little bit so you can get ready or..."

William shakes his head at me as he strides behind his desk, turns his computer off and grabs his laptop. "All ready," he says to us both with a smile.

Ben heads out the door first, and as I follow slightly behind I feel a feather light touch on the base of my neck that runs down my spine and stops just above my bum. I shudder at the slight touch and feel my body heat up as goosebumps erupt on my skin.

Turning my head slightly, I catch his profile looking straight ahead, seemingly unaffected, but when he looks at me I note the desire in his expressive brown eyes. I smile and lower my gaze. He may have power over my body, but I have just as much over his too, and that alone is enough to make me smile.

Dinner is going to be torture. I want him to be with us, but I'm not prepared for the onslaught of desire running through my body. My knickers are soaked before I've even left the school, and my thoughts on the whole drive over to the pizza place are consumed by him. And how that little touch made me feel so damn much.

I could easily get overwhelmed knowing he's aroused when his eyes turn almost black. That thought is nearly enough to send a zing to my core and take me half way to an orgasm. His smile, the one he gives just to me, causes goose-bumps to scatter all over my body. I long to dive into his arms and inhale his scent every time I see him. I want him to domi-nate me. I want him to control my body, to go all alpha on me and take me to the highest possible realm of pleasure, but I can't give into these thoughts because I have an almost four year old sitting in the back of my car rambling on about how cool Will is and how he's his new bestie.

I smile as I look into the rear-view mirror, watching Ben chatting away, and lift my eyes to see William's car following behind us.

"Mummy, you're not listening to me. Can I?"

I shake my head a little and focus on Ben. "Of course, baby." I don't know what I just said he could do, but I'm assuming it's something to do with ice cream or dessert. He grins at me and I return it as we turn into the parking lot.

William's car scoots into the space next to us and he frowns at me as I open my door and let myself out. Laughing, I ask, "What?" but don't stop to get an answer as I head around to get Ben.

I open his door and see he's already unstrapped himself, another thing he doesn't need me to do anymore. I'm a little shocked when Ben tuts at me and shakes his head, not too dissimilar to William.

"Why are you doing that?" I point my finger into his face and wiggle it around in front of him, but he doesn't laugh.

Instead he looks at me like he wants to tell me off. "You are 'upposed to wait for him to open da door, Mummy. It's a gentleman's way." He rolls his eyes and when I look at William in a bit of confused amusement, he's smirking behind me.

Trying to keep my laughter at bay, I ask Ben, "And who told you this? I'm perfectly capable of opening my own door, thank you very much."

Ben rolls his eyes at me again and speaks to William as if I'm the child who needs a lesson in the situation. "My grandad told me dat's what you do wiv a lady, but I fink he forgot to tell my mum."

I laugh at the same time William does and pick Ben up, a bit needy to reaffirm in my own mind that he's still my little boy, and not some sassy tweenager. "When did you get so cheeky? Is this your grandfather's influence then?" I tickle him and he throws his head back excitedly.

As I place him on his feet, I look over at William who has a strange look on his face. "You okay?" I ask him carefully, still smiling but maybe with a bit of concern in my voice. He nods at me, and as he falls in step with us, he reaches down and takes my boy's little hand as we head across the parking lot. And my heart bursts with happiness.

CHAPTER 27

Nell

"I don't know where you put all that food, Ben. You sure you haven't got a dog under the table you've been feeding it all too?"

"No, silly. Mum won't let me have a dog and Nanny says I have empty legs so da food falls into dem, I guess."

Watching William and Ben interact with each other all evening has me smiling so widely my cheeks are beginning to hurt. They have talked non-stop about everything from nursery to which superhero is the best.

I look over at William and he winks, making me blush and lower my gaze from his. When he sits forward in his chair and rests his hand on my knee, I bring my hand under the table and place it on top of his, giving a gentle squeeze, trying to tell him how happy I am and how thankful I am for him too.

"Will, can I ask you somefing?" I bring my gaze up to Ben and he looks shy suddenly.

William notices too and smiles at him encouragingly. "Yeah of course bud, anything."

"It's my birfday soon and Mum said I could have a party and invite my friends. Will you come?" Ben shyly looks down at his pile of melted ice cream, waiting for the answer he's hoping for. There's a lump in my throat that I can't swallow down, and my eyes frantically dart to William who's staring intently at me.

"If it's okay with your mum, of course I'll be there."

Tears spring to my eyes and I'm overwhelmed by my feelings for him.

He's perfect. Everything he says or does is right.

He could have just jumped in and said yeah, I'll come, or maybe, but instead he asked for permission from me without asking. It's something so silly, but he knows me and how much it means to me to have that choice. He knows I don't want to rush things, so he's patient and understanding. He knows I don't want to tell everyone yet, so he waits. But he doesn't want to disappoint my boy either, and that means everything.

I'm falling a lot faster and harder for William than I thought I would. I knew he was dangerous when he handed me that first rose and quoted Shakespeare to me. I knew he had the ability to make me feel again and, slowly but surely, he's removing every brick there is guarding my heart. I gulp a drink of water to try to sift some of the emotion that's clogging my throat.

Ben does a fist pump and tells us, "Yes! It's fine by Mum. I asked in da car and she said sure. Mum will send you an invite when she has dem printed. It's gonna be a superhero party and you'll hafta dress up." He's beaming at William who's smiling right back at him.

As the waitress brings our check, William and I reach for it at the same time and Ben tuts at me again. I huff out an exasperated sigh at the snigger coming from Mr. Shakespeare and round on my son. "Is this another piece of outdated information from your grandfather? Let me tell you now my boy, women can do whatever the hell they want. I asked William to dinner, so I will be paying for dinner. Yes, it's nice to treat people, but whether it's a man treating a woman or a woman treating a man is irrelevant. No one is obligated to do something for someone else because of their gender, understand?" I look at them both as they nod their heads and look down at the table, the same expression of remorse on both their faces.

With a smirk of my own, I gather my things and ask them, "Now, shall we go?" in my best mum/teacher voice as I saunter towards the door with a swagger in my step.

CHAPTER 28
William

"Hey man, where you been?" Marcus is on me as soon as I walk in the house, and as much as I don't want to talk, I do need some perspective.

I head towards the kitchen and sit down on one of the chairs. "Today has been interesting. I met Ben, spent the afternoon with him while Nell had a work assessment, and then had dinner with them both." I wait for a second knowing that as soon as the news sinks in his dramatic self will reply with the information and the counsel I need.

I smirk as his eyes go wide as saucers, his mouth gaping open like a fish out of water. "How...where...when? WHAT? Oh, just ducking speak, will you?" he explodes and sits next to me as I laugh and tell him the story of how my today started.

"So how did you feel when she said she'd let you watch him? You get how much of a big deal that is, right?"

I nod at him and blow out a breath before answering. "Yeah, I do. She told me no one watches him apart from her family, so I know it meant a lot today. Marcus, man, that kid is special. He's something else," I say, smiling at him. "He's so funny, and hell, he's so fucking smart. I took him to my office and was going to practise his numbers by playing cards..."

"Fun educational games," he says to me, rolling his eyes, so I give him a very ungentlemanly hand gesture.

Ignoring his laughter, I continue. "He knew his numbers, all of them. The kid isn't even four yet. He was telling me about his teacher and how he loves her, but don't tell him I told you that because I pinkie promised I wouldn't tell anyone. Shit, I broke a pinkie promise. You have to pinkie promise you won't tell anyone. I know how close you are with Emilia now." Marcus laughs at me but stops when he realises I'm deadly serious.

I hold up my hand with my pinkie extended. When I tip my chin at him to show just how serious I am, he slow blinks in bewilderment, but then links his pinkie with mine. "I promise I won't tell his secret or that you told me, okay?"

I nod, happy that he won't say anything, and he smirks at me. "I think you fell in love today. And yes, I did think the first boy you would love would be me, but it seems little Ben has gone ahead and stolen that heart of yours."

My head shoots up to look at him and I laugh. "Shit. You could be right. He's unbelievable. He asked me if I was his friend now that I was his mummy's friend, and his little face lit up when I said I was his friend regardless if I was his mummy's. He has this way of just making you feel at peace when you're around him. Fucking amazing little guy. Watching Nell with him today was..."

I stop myself as an image of her cradling and tickling him shoots through my mind, and my fear from earlier resurfaces. She's an amazing mum. Ben would be an amazing big brother, and what if I can't give them that? I'm terrified I won't be enough for them and, in time, they'll want what I can't give them. I feel like the most selfish man in the world, and I know I should let them go, but I can't.

187

I won't let go of my lady. Or of Ben either.

"What's going on? You went from happy as Larry to as sad as Susan in the blink of an eye."

I huff out a breath, run my hands over my face and groan in frustration. "I can't give her that again. Ben will be her only kid, the doctors said I wouldn't be able to..."

"Will, they said might not be able to. You've still got one good ball. Yeah, I know they said your sperm count was low, but there's still a chance." He frowns at me and slaps my arm from across the table. "Didn't she tell you before not to make her decisions for her. She might be okay with only having Ben, or she might want to adopt, who knows. Don't let a what if ruin a sure thing."

I nod my head at him and grin. "He invited me to his birthday party in a few weeks and Nell didn't say no, so maybe we're closer to telling everyone about us too."

Marcus smiles at me but the usual gleam in his eye isn't there. He takes a big breath and I wait to hear what he says next. As usual, his clarity is both comforting and contemplative.

"That's a big step. Let me ask you something, Will. Are you ready for all of this? Being a step-dad, being a part of her family, marriage and all that jazz?"

I tilt my head to the side, look at him and without hesitation say, "Hell, fucking yeah," and watch as his smile and the gleam in his eye come back.

He smacks the table with his palm and shouts, "Right ducking answer, my brother. I'd beat some sense into you if you'd said no. And then I'd have no qualms about turning you over to Emilia. You love her?"

"No, she's way too fierce for me," I deadpan, and watch as he screws his face up in confusion. "Plus, I'm kind of in love with her sister anyway."

I see the moment realisation hits, and he rolls his eyes so

far back in his head, I wonder if he can see his own brain. "Ha, ducking ha, Will. You dick. You told her how you feel yet?"

I'm still chuckling at him, so I shake my head. "No. She isn't ready to hear it yet, and I don't want her to feel rushed or pressured. I'll just show her how I feel instead."

Marcus scoots his chair closer to mine and throws his arm around my shoulder. "So, what are we getting him for his birthday? Oh, is it fancy dress?"

I laugh at him and shake my head. "Who invited you? And yes, it is. Superhero theme."

Marcus's eyes light up. "I'm so ducking excited to dress up. I'll be..."

"No one because you aren't invited."

He narrows his eyes at me, and I smirk back at him. "You're a bastard, Will. You know I love fancy dress. This isn't over!" he calls to my back as I stroll out of the kitchen and up to my room.

A few minutes later my phone buzzes in my pocket and I look down to a message from Nell.

Nell: Why are you being mean to Marcus? I just invited him to Ben's party, so stop being, and I quote, a bastard lol. Thank you for today xxx

Instead of replying, I bring her information up on the screen and hit call. She answers instantly and it makes me laugh.

"I wasn't being mean, for your information. Marcus heard fancy dress and decided to take over. You'll regret inviting him." She chuckles, and I feel my whole being calming and settling just hearing her voice.

"He said you wouldn't let him come, and he sounded very upset. Everyone thinks it's a great idea that we all dress up as well. My sisters are here, one minute." She takes a little breath and I hear footsteps and what sounds like a door closing before she says, "Thank you, William. For today and for everything. You go above and beyond for me and now for Ben too, and I appreciate you."

I'm smiling like a buffoon and I couldn't care less. She sees me. She's mine and I'm not letting her go.

"That's what you do for the people you care about, Nell, and I do. I care about both of you so much. I know I only met Ben today, but I can already see just how amazing he is."

I take a breath, ready to tell her that I am so in love with her and Ben, completely forgetting what I said to Marcus a little while ago. The door opens on the other end of the line, and I can hear her sisters' muffled chattering. She huffs and mumbles about having no privacy in her own house.

"Have you discussed costume ideas with the girls? Mark my words, Marcus is downstairs right now deciding who should go as what." She laughs again, and it's music to my ears as well as my dick. I shift uncomfortably as I sit on the bed and try to relieve the hard on I'm sporting from talking to my lady.

"I haven't yet. I was in the middle of telling my sisters about today when Marcus called Emilia to complain about you. Why were you being mean, William?"

I don't even try to suppress my sigh, silently cursing Marcus and his bloody friendship with Emilia. "He's dramatic as anything, that one. I just told him he wasn't invited. Yes, I did tell him it was fancy dress just to annoy him as he does love a costume party." I chuckle and she laughs along with me.

"Hey Shakespeare. You upset my boy again and I'm coming for you. When you make him dramatic, I have to deal with him."

I can't help but laugh out loud at Emilia and tell her, "Good for you. I've been doing that all my damn life so, enjoy. He picked your costume yet?"

"He keeps telling me who he thinks I should be, but I'm ignoring him now. He'll probably start to pout at you about it, so enjoy yourself," she shoots back in the sweetest voice I've ever heard her use. It makes me laugh and shudder at the same time.

"Sorry, she snatched the phone away and I had to wrestle Cleopatra for the last cookie."

"Next time they're there, we're talking on facetime. I would've paid good money to see that. Did you win?"

"What d'you think?" she says through a mouthful of what I'm assuming is cookie, and I can hear Cleo in the background complaining about Nell cheating.

"That's my girl. Nell..."

My door is pushed open, and Marcus flounces into my room, pouting. "Emilia's ignoring me now. Why is everyone being mean to me? I'm going to make new friends and screw you all off." He plops down on my bed and I sigh into the phone.

"Tell your sister she's a wench for me, please. I have to go and show Marcus some attention before he flounces off in a meltdown. I'll call you tomorrow. I wanted to talk to you about some stuff, nothing bad. God I just realised it sounded ominous. It isn't. I promise. I just wanted to see... Nell, I'll call you tomorrow." She laughs down the phone and I put my head in my hands in frustration.

"Okay, William. Everything's okay. I'll talk to you tomorrow. Thank you again. I really enjoyed tonight. I want to do it again. I hope that helps with what you wanted to talk about, and if not, I wanted you to know. Night."

Before I can respond, she's hung up. How did she know I wanted to tell her how much fun I had tonight and how right it all felt? Is she feeling the same as me?

"Probably, Will, but she might not know it properly yet."

My head whips around to Marcus who's still laying on my bed and I realise I must have spoken out loud.

I nod and tell him, "Come on, Bro, let's go downstairs and watch a film. No costume talk though." He moans but gets up and smiles at me and I sigh and shake my head at him like I always do.

CHAPTER 29

Costumes people! Group text

Marcus: We need to discuss costumes guys. No one wants a double at the party. Tell me your ideas please so I can get my contact to order them?

Juliet: A contact? Wow! I'm impressed.

Cleo: I'm Gamora, I call it. Marcus, you better make sure NO ONE else turns up as her, that includes any of the kids too!

Marcus: I'm not in charge of the invites, you need to speak to your sister about that I'm afraid.

Cleo: You weren't in charge of costumes either, but you bossed your way into that job title so get in on the invites as well.

Emilia: It's fine, I've already sorted the invites for his friends and I accidentally forgot to mention it was fancy dress on them. I told Ben this afternoon, he's on board as now he gets to be the only kid in a costume. It is his birthday after all. I have your back, Sis, see?

Cleo: YES! I thought I was going to have to full-on fight with a four-year-old. Now I'll be the only Gamora.

Juliet: Why are you so obsessed with being her anyway?

Cleo: Oh, my sweet little Princess. Gamora is a kick arse woman who takes no shit from no one, not even her family. She's my hero.

Juliet: (woman shrugging her shoulders emoji, monkey covering its eyes emoji, witch emoji)

Cleo: (woman smacking her head emoji) Who are you going as, Princess?

Juliet: No freaking idea and stop calling me that, please.

Cleo: We've called you that near enough your whole life and now you have an issue with it? Get over it, Princess, cause I ain't stopping.

Juliet: Ain't? Really? (Eye roll emoji) I just don't think it's an accurate description and the origin of it is rude and ridiculous.

Connor: I gave you that nickname, Princess...

Juliet: Exactly, refer to the last two R words in the text above.

Connor: (Blowing a kiss emoji) you know you (purple heart emoji) me really.

Juliet: (swearing face emoji)

Emilia: Anyway, who are you going as Marcus?

Marcus: All will be revealed later but I've checked with Ben and he said it was okay. And I love a cape lol. I've got Will and Nell's costumes sorted too. So Connor, it's just you out of the men.

Connor: I don't really know a lot about superheroes. Not really into them. Who's left?

Emilia: Starlord, Drax, Bucky, Loki, Hawkeye, Hulk, War machine, Spiderman, Vision, Falcon and Thor.

Marcus: Wow, that was surprising

Juliet: A rare insight into Emilia Cooper, people. She is a nerd.

Cleo: Just why and how?

Emilia: Oh, shut up you bunch of fuckers. Ben loves

those stupid films and watches them constantly, so of course I'm going to know them all.

Connor: That was impressive. I'm going with Thor as he's the only one I know. Plus, we all know I'm the only one who can compete with Hemsworth when it comes to looks and body (winking face emoji)

Juliet: (laughing hysterically emoji)

Cleo: (laughing hysterically emoji)

Emilia: (laughing hysterically emoji)

Marcus: (laughing hysterically emoji)

Connor: Marcus, you as well?

Marcus: Sorry. You're fit as fuck, but no one compares to Hemsworth. No one!

Emilia: Enough with this nonsense. Marcus already has my costume sorted. Just Juliet to decide.

Juliet: I know who I'll be now. I won't be a double so don't worry, but I am keeping it a secret. I'll text you privately Marcus. Bye bitches xxx

Marcus: If I'm in on it I don't care lol.

Cleo: That's payback for the Princess comments. That's your fault, Connor.

Connor: Everything's always my fault. Laters

CHAPTER 30

Nell

"I promise they'll be here, Ben. The party doesn't start for another hour. Stop worrying." I don't know what my little boy is more excited about, his birthday party or spending the day with his new BFFs William and Marcus.

A couple of days after our spontaneous after-school pizza date, my sisters were over and Emilia invited Marcus. I think William's words were, "If he's invited to Ben's party because it wasn't fair, I'm invited over today because it isn't fair too. You get one of us, you get the other. We're a package deal."

I may have responded something about liking his package. And that may or may not have resulted in a smacked bum later that night when Ben went to stay at Auntie Emilia's with her and Marcus.

But, anyway, since then, Will and Marcus have become regulars over at our house on the weekends. Ben had made two new best friends that were invited to his costume party, and I had no say in it.

Not that I'd have said anything bad about it anyway. I love seeing my little boy's eyes light up when I mention either of them, and I love that he has two more people in his life who love him and want to be his friends.

Of course, having Marcus there to distract Ben when I want to sneak a kiss with William, or when he wants to talk dirty in my ear, is a nice perk.

We haven't told Ben about us yet, but I'm feeling more and more ready as the time goes on. Knowing he loves William already removes a bit of the fear surrounding his potential reaction. I'm nervous about the finality of it all though. Once Ben knows, there's no going back. I mean, I don't want to go back, but I'm scared William might once he realises exactly how much he's taken on with us, and I don't want to risk breaking my boy's heart again. I know it's stupid, but it's just been going so well, I don't want to rock the boat. I know I have to do it soon though. William deserves that. I deserve that.

Whilst we haven't told Ben, we have told our boss. The day before summer break we broached the subject with him and he was fine with it. Happy about it, even. Which has left us to enjoy our summer together with one less worry.

I've told my parents as well. Not that I needed to, as my mum already knew. Like all mums do, she could see a differ-ence in me apparently. Today will be their first time meeting him, and the thought sends a wave of nausea through me.

I grip the side of the sofa and take a deep breath. Today's already stressful enough. Mix a bunch of kids and their parents with your boyfriend meeting *your* parents for the first time and it becomes stress city.

This stupid costume isn't helping, either. Who ever thought a rubber catsuit would be a good idea when running around after a small boy's birthday party? I take another deep breath as my stomach rolls over and the doorbell rings.

Ben runs across the hallway to the door and shouts over to me. "Mummy, is dat dem?"

Laughing I walk over and tell him, "I don't know, My super power isn't seeing through doors."

He giggles at me and bounces onto his toes as I open the door. We're met by Marcus and William dressed in full on costumes, hair done the same as their alter egos, and I can't help but grin at the smile on my boy's face. "Oh my God. Oh my God! You two look sooo good. Welcome to my party." Ben sticks his hand out to them, and I watch each of them do their secret handshake.

My mum calls Ben into the kitchen and he looks at his guests then me and smiles. "I'll be back in a minute, guys. Mum, will you look after dem please?"

"Of course I will, my little superhero." I wink at him and he smiles back as he runs off calling out to his nan.

"Well, you look amazing, Marcus. Thank you for organising these costumes. I know it probably took a lot of time but I'm so grateful. He already said it was the best day ever, and that was just seeing me in this. You could've gotten a bigger size by the way. This thing is too tight."

He laughs, but before he can say anything, we hear William growl. I turn my gaze to him and catch the feral look in his eyes. This outfit seems to have awoken the beast in Mr. Shakespeare. He grabs me by the arms and walks me backwards into the front room.

"I think he likes it that tight, Nell. I'll keep Ben occupied for a bit. You're welcome, Will." Marcus laughs as he closes the front room door.

William wastes no time circling his arms around my body, his hands landing on my bum. He pulls me closer to him, our bodies pressing against each other, and I wish we were alone and could devour each other like animals. When he brings his nose to my hair and inhales my scent, I melt even further into his embrace.

His mouth finds my jawline and he nips along it, up to my ear where he whispers to me, "Nell, you look so damn sexy I want to fuck you right here, my lady. I want to bend you over that sofa and bury my dick inside your pussy. I want you screaming my name. Fuck, woman." His mouth crashes onto mine, and I groan as our tongues collide, his hungry lips taking control of mine as he lifts me up, cupping my arse, and my legs wrap around his waist.

I break away from our kiss and he growls at me again, making me giggle. "William, we have to stop. As much as I want everything you just said, my mum and dad are in the next room." I pop a quick kiss onto his lips and slide down his body, eliciting the most satisfying groan from him. "Later," I promise as I kiss his cheek.

He shifts uncomfortably and laughs at me. "At least I know why he has a fucking shield now."

Laughing, I walk over to the door just as the doorbell rings. "I've got it," I call out to my mum as I open the door to six of Ben's friends. As Ben and his guests head out to the bouncy castle in the garden, I laugh when he tells them he has loads of superheroes coming today.

CHAPTER 31

Nell

"Mum, Dad, I'd like you to meet William Blake. William, this is my mum and dad." Mum coos over him, and dad immediately launches into shop talk about teaching and Shakespeare, and my nerves fade away.

Emilia creeps up next to me. "How's it going, Sis?"

I turn to look at her and laugh. "You look amazing! Just as good as Scarlett Johansson."

She laughs and shakes her head, pointing outside to Cleo. "No, she looks amazing. She hired a makeup artist to get her to look just like her. She's so fucking extra." We laugh but stop quickly as Mum looks over at us with one eyebrow raised. I point at Emilia and she shoves me from the side.

"Behave girls. It was lovely to meet you William, but I have some party food in the oven. We'll talk again in a bit."

William smiles, and as he turns back to me my mum mouths, "I love him," and my dad gives me the thumbs up. I can't hold back my laughter when William tells me he saw them in the window reflection.

We head back into the living room and I let my eyes roam over him in his costume. It looks like it's been sprayed onto his sculpted body, the carved-out ridges of the plastic abs a poor substitution for the real deal. His body is outstanding and I can't wait to run my tongue all over it later on.

The front door opening and closing interrupts my lust filled mind, and when I meet William's gaze his black eyes tell me that, somehow, he knew what I was thinking. I bite my lip and the look he gives me makes me whimper. He smirks, knowing exactly what he's doing to me.

My attention is snatched away from him as Connor walks in dressed as Thor, cape and hammer included but not much else. "Wow, not bad. No Hemsworth, but not bad." William laughs, but Connor just gives me a dirty look.

Marcus comes in and does a double take as he looks at Connor. "Well God damn you are fine as duck, Mr. Shay. I need a minute," he quips, as he fans his face dramatically.

I burst out laughing as Marcus reaches out to stroke Connor's abs but is thwarted when William grabs his wrist. "Marcus, we've spoken about this before. You can't touch men without permission."

Marcus pouts and tells him, "But they're so pretty." Connor chuckles, Will laughs in exasperation and I can't breathe through my own laughter.

"You can touch them if you want, I don't mind," Connor says and Marcus's eyes light up like he's the birthday boy.

He reaches out and strokes Connor's abs, wiping imaginary drool from his chin before grinning at all of us and clapping his hands together. "Right, we need Juliet now. I want a picture of all of us before we get ruined. Where is she?"

"I'm here." We all turn in unison to see Juliet standing in the doorway. She's dressed in a tight black leather catsuit, a black cape billowing behind her. Her face is as white as a ghost with black eyeliner around her gorgeous green eyes. Topped off by a black wig with these crazy horns coming out of her head, she looks absolutely terrifying. I stand in front of her gobsmacked.

Emilia breaks the awkward silence first. "Juliet, wow. I thought Cleo took the best costume award, but you have spanked her. What made you pick Thor's sister?" I turn my stunned look on Emilia, who sighs and shrugs as she challenges us, "Yeah, yeah, yeah. I'm a nerd, so what."

Everyone laughs as Marcus calls Cleo in and asks our dad to snap a picture. My mum watches the kids as we all huddle together. William stands in the middle next to me, Juliet on my other side.

We get one picture in just as Ben comes in and shouts at Juliet, "No, I don't like dat. I don't like you like dat, Auntie Princess."

He closes his eyes, his face contorting in fear and Juliet springs into action. "Baby, look, it's just me. Look Ben." She's snatched the wig and horns off and her blonde hair tumbles out.

He looks at her and relief washes over his face. "Dat's better, I don't like you wiv black hair and horns."

He runs back outside, and Juliet turns to face us, devastation written all over her face. "I'm sorry. I didn't think he'd be scared."

I instinctively wrap her in a comforting hug. Before I can blink, our sisters are there, all of us surrounding her, letting her know we're all here. "It's okay, he's fine. Come on, let's get you a drink." She sniffs and follows us into the kitchen. I give William a look to say I'm sorry and he blows me a kiss. Sisters before misters, always.

CHAPTER 32

William

"Why the fuck would she dress like that? It's a kids' party for fucks sake." Connor brings the water to his lips and takes a swig. I'm still standing with Marcus and Connor in front of the fireplace where we just had our picture taken.

Marcus laughs and puts his arm around Connor's shoulders. "You don't know who she is?" He asks with a smirk on his lips.

"No, should I?" Connor shrugs his shoulders and I chuckle because the man is clueless.

"She's Hela." Marcus says, like that explains everything.

His grin gets even wider when Connor looks blankly at him and asks, "Who the hell is Hela?"

I choke back the sip of water in my mouth, coughing and splutter-laughing at him.

Marcus rolls his eyes in frustration and shakes his head. "She's Thor's sister. She hates him and tries to kill him. How do you not know this? Did you not learn about mythology when you were younger?" Marcus retorts incredulously.

"Nope, but it figures." He swigs his water again and his shoulders sink, defeat clearly written on his face, and I can't help but feel sorry for him.

"What's going on with you two, man? Marcus here is pinning you as the next greatest love story, but I'm not so sure." I focus my gaze on his eyes and see a plethora of emotions shine in them. Shit, Marcus might be right. The pain and despair that just flew across his face could only be caused by the woman you love.

"Maybe in another life we would have been, but I don't think so. Not anymore. Sorry, Marcus." He gives that sad look again and I don't know why, but I'm compelled to say something.

"Don't give up. If you want her, Connor, don't give up. That's all I'm saying." He nods his head at me and sighs. I think he's about to give up more about their relationship, but Ben comes flying into the room, effectively shutting down our conversation.

"Hey bud, you having a good time?" I grin down at my new best friend.

"Yeah, it's da best party ever. Did I upset Auntie Princess?" He asks, biting his bottom lip.

I bend down as Connor ruffles his hair. "Nah, she's fine." I don't want him to be sad on his birthday, and I know Juliet wouldn't either, so I flash him a reassuring smile before telling him, "She said the wig was itching her head anyway."

"Good because she looks soo much better wiv her blonde hair."

"That she does little man, she looks damn near perfect," Connor says whilst smiling down at Ben.

"Uncle Connor, we aren't 'upposed to say da D word." This boy just knows how to make everyone feel better without even trying.

Connor scoops him up in his very Thor-like arms and Ben squeals in delight. "When did you get so big, huh? I remember carrying you around in one hand dude, now you're a giant." Ben laughs as Connor puts him down, his mood instantly lifted by this amazing little human. As little green eyes look up at all three of us, Ben beams in happiness.

Connor nudges him with his hip. "Did you invite your girlfriend, Ben?"

He screws his little face up and shakes his head. "No, girls are yucky, apart from my mum and Miss Ali and my aunties." We nod at him as Marcus mutters, "amen little brother," whilst taking a swig of his beer.

Connor agrees with Ben and Marcus which causes a snort to erupt out of Ben's little nose. "You don't fink girls are yucky, you love my Auntie Princess. And you," he points at Marcus, "love my Auntie Emilia."

I smirk at Connor's blush and Marcus's splutter. "Ben, you are so right about those two." Marcus's eyes narrow at me and Connor mouths *dick* over Ben's head.

But the smirk falls quickly from my face when Ben points a finger at me and narrows his eyes. "And you Will, you love my mum, but dey aren't yucky girls so it's okay." The seriousness in his little voice belies his youth, and I'm once again taken aback by how much he's affected me in such a short time. Standing with my mouth wide open I watch as he turns from us and goes to run back outside, but freezes by the door.

"MUM, MUM!!!"

The terror in his little voice is apparent and I'm over to him in a flash. "What's up bud, what's the matter?" He points to the floor where there's a big spider. He jumps back as it starts to move, and I follow him to make sure he's okay.

Nell gets to the doorway, takes one look at Ben and asks, "Where is it?" Shocked that she knows exactly what the problem is, I point to the floor and she stifles a sigh and quite possibly a giggle as well. "I'll get the jar and paper Ben, hold on okay." Her gentle tone tells me they've been here before.

Marcus points at the offending eight legged arachnid and asks, "Do you want me to kill it, Ben?"

"NO! Don't do dat. It might have a wife and a baby, and I don't want dem to miss deir daddy like I do."

And right there, my heart breaks at the sadness and compassion on this little boy's face. I can't take my eyes away from him, but I don't need to see their faces to know every adult in this room just felt the floor give out beneath them at his pain and empathy.

"We won't kill it, I promise," I tell him as his head dips down, avoiding my gaze, but not before I see the worry in his eyes.

"I'm not a baby," he murmurs, although I'm not sure if he's justifying his reaction to us or himself.

I place my hand under his chin and bring his head up to look at me. "Hey, can I tell you a secret?" He doesn't look at my eyes, his gaze hovering around my shoulder, but he nods his head. "I'm scared of spiders too. They freak me out. When we're at home, I make Marcus get them out of the house for me."

I give Marcus a wide-eyed look to get him to play along, and he laughs as he tells Ben, "Once there was one in the bathroom on the actual toilet and Will peed himself because he was so scared to go in there." I give him a dirty look and he smirks at me. Well played, but he'll pay for that later.

Ben's head comes up and he looks at me with narrowed eyes. "Really? You're scared too?" I nod at him. "And you really peed ya pants?" I aim another dirty look at Marcus, who's giggling like a schoolkid next to a smirking Connor—both out of Ben's eyesight—and sigh.

"Yes, I did, Ben," I say through gritted teeth. He giggles and I continue, "The thing is bud, I don't want anyone to know I'm scared. Especially the girls. They'll tease me, so do you think we can pretend to be brave together?" He thinks about it for a second, then nods up at me just as Nell comes in with a big jar and a piece of paper.

She bends down and expertly catches the offending arachnid in the jar, but just as she's about to leave, I ask her to wait. I pick Ben up and whisper to him, "So, will you help me, Ben. Will you hold on to me whilst I try to be brave? We need to get a bit closer to it so I can try to stop being so scared. We are superheroes after all. We aren't supposed to fear little spiders, are we?"

He shakes his head at me and frowns in concentration. "No, we aren't 'upposed to." He leans his head in closer to me and whispers, "I don't like its legs when dey move. Dey scare me."

I tilt my head back to his and whisper, "Me too. Why do they have to have so many of them?" I give a little shudder for effect, and he laughs back.

"You really are scared, aren't ya, Will?" I know I shouldn't lie to him but a little subterfuge won't hurt, especially if it helps him get over his fear.

I nod at him and make myself look scared. "Terrified bud. Will you help me? If we go closer, you hold me tight and see if you can stop me from being scared." He nods at me and I look over to Nell who has a very concerned look on her face. I wink to let her know it'll be okay, and she holds the jar up near our faces.

Ben recoils, but I tighten my hold and whisper, "Squeeze me please, Ben. I'm scared." Instantly his grip tightens but it's one of support rather than fear.

He pats my shoulder and says, "I've got ya, Will." Distracted by comforting me, I inch us closer until we're standing right next to the jar. The spider moves and Ben flinches, but brings his face a fraction closer.

"Will, are you looking? It's not dat scary. Look." I've got

my eyes closed to make him feel braver than me, but I open them a little and see that he's smiling.

"You're right bud, it isn't that bad."

"Are you still scared, Will? 'cause if you are, I'll stay, but I really wanna go outside and bounce."

I chuckle and place him on the floor. "Nah, I think you cured me, bud." He high fives me, says 'bye' to the spider, and runs out of the room.

When I turn to face Nell, who looks sexy as hell in that costume, my laughter dies and my triumphant smile is replaced with concern. She looks as if she's about to cry.

"Nell, baby, are you ok?" She shakes her head a little, as if to clear her thoughts, takes a couple of steps towards me and kisses me hard on the lips. The spider is still in the jar between us so I can't get as close to her as I want. I faintly hear whooping and cheering from Marcus and Connor, but everything else fades away. It's just me, her, a likely pissed-off spider in a jar, and our kiss.

She finally pulls away, our breaths coming out fast and our chests rising and falling in sync, looks into my eyes and tells me, "I fucking love you, William." My jaw drops open as I watch her turn on her heel and walk out of the front room, a little extra swish in her hips as she goes.

I'm frozen to the spot, highly aware that we're at a party with her parents a few feet away from me, and her son who doesn't know we're in a relationship yet. Torn between going after her and fucking her right here and now, and waiting until later to tell her and show her how I feel, I spin around, confusion etched on my face, and see Connor and Marcus grinning back at me. I raise my arms as if to say, "what do I do?' And drop my head down as I walk towards them.

Connor stops me with a pat on my shoulder. "I'd leave her for a while. It's her son's birthday and everyone's here. Talk to her later, Bro."

Marcus nods his head in agreement. "I agree with not quite Hemsworth over there. Be happy though. She loves you, man, and she said it first."

I smile at him and nod my head as Connor nudges Marcus with his shoulder, nearly sending him to the ground. I shake my head as they start play fighting, and catch sight of Steve's picture on the mantle. I smile my thanks to him and let my thoughts go wild. I can't believe she said it first. I wanted to tell her the other night, but I didn't think she was ready. I should've. Shit, I should've told her I loved her back. I just stood there, like a fish out of water. What if she thinks I don't feel the same way? Fuck. As soon as I get a second alone with her I'm going to tell her. I just hope I haven't lost my chance.

CHAPTER 33
William

Nell's been huddled in the kitchen with either her sisters or one of her parents all afternoon, and between playing with Ben and his friends, and her family getting in my way, I haven't had a chance to tell her I love her back.

I'm sure she knows though. I mean I've shown her how I feel when I kiss her, or hold her close, even the way I am with Ben. She must know how much I love them both. I've been outside with the kids playing superheroes for the past forty-five minutes and Emilia just informed us they're getting ready to do candles and cut the cake. She stands next to me and tells me, "Nell's alone in the kitchen. You have five minutes. Get in there and put her out of her misery." I turn and look at her, confusion etched on my face. "She doesn't know, Will. Everyone else here does, but she needs to hear it. Go!" I squeeze her shoulder and rush inside the kitchen, for once thankful for the way this family intrudes on every aspect of our relationship.

I freeze in the doorway at the sight before me. Nell is standing with her back to me, her hands on the counter and her head down in defeat. Her shoulders sag and she breathes deeply. As quietly as I can, I walk up behind her.

I get close to her ear and whisper, "'My bounty is as boundless as the sea, my love as deep; the more I give to thee, the more I have, for both are infinite.' I've loved you from the moment I saw you, Nell. I'm sorry, I should've made sure you knew that, my lady."

Her head snaps up and she turns to look at me, eyes shining with unshed tears. "Really? All that time?"

I nod and push a piece of hair off her face and tuck it behind her ear. "All that time. And I always will. It's infinite, Nell."

She stares up at me, smiling, and as I bend down to kiss her, Emilia pokes her head through the garden doors. "I said five minutes, Will. Hurry the fuck up. The kids are going to stage a coup any minute and I will not be taken down by four-year-olds."

I rest my forehead on Nell's as she giggles at her sister, then kiss her nose and whisper, "Later," as I go back outside, leaving Emilia to help with cake duties.

A few minutes later she brings out Ben's amazing super-heroes cake with four candles on it and I watch as he snuggles into Juliet's arms. As we sing happy birthday to him, I'm overwhelmed with happiness. This is everything I want. Kids' birthday parties, sneaking hugs and kisses with Nell and being surrounded by family. Maybe next year my mum and Frank will be here too.

I smile thinking about it all, but a chill swoops down my back and causes me to shudder just as Ben blows out his candles. Everyone cheers and I smile, but an unknown feeling of unease has taken root in my stomach and I don't know why.

CHAPTER 34

Nell

He loves me.

My jaw aches from smiling so much, and I swear my feet are floating on cloud nine rather than treading on something as mundane as the kitchen floor.

Once the candles were blown out, wishes made and cake devoured, my mum and dad told us they were taking Ben home with them so we could tackle the mess of the house. My sisters, William, Marcus and Connor decided to throw a cleaning party with William driving Connor and Cleo to get alcohol supplies for everyone.

I can see in William's eyes that all he wants is for everyone to leave so we can be on our own, and I do too, but these guys are my family. They've just spent the day celebrating my boy and I'm not going to kick them out, especially when they're offering to help set the house to rights after the chaos of the day's revelry.

Standing at the kitchen sink, washing up some of the dishes, a wave of nausea hits me again. It's so strong, I find myself holding onto the side of the sink and breathing my way through it. A conversation I had with one of the other parents about a stomach bug doing the rounds at Ben's nursery floats into my mind, and I send a silent prayer that it isn't that. Last year we caught something similar, and it wiped the whole family out with it. Cleo and Emilia had to take time off work, and Ben was so ill he had to be taken to the hospital and given fluids. The only upside was I lost half a stone in weight from not being able to eat for days.

The wave leaves as quickly as it came, and I stand up straight, blowing out a relieved breath. I won't be drinking anything tonight. I don't want to be throwing up drunk and with a stomach bug.

I finish the dishes and head into the front room to see what Emilia, Juliet and Marcus are doing and am pleasantly shocked by how clean it is already. "Wow, you guys really do have superpowers," I laugh.

Emilia and Juliet are throwing paper cups into a black bin liner like they're trying out for a basketball team. Marcus, whilst keeping score, smiles over at me and says, "If you make it fun, you can get it done in half the time."

Juliet puts her hands on her hips and pouts at him. "Who died and made him Hairy Poppins?"

We all burst out laughing, and Emilia puts her arm around Juliet's shoulder, telling her, "I love you baby sis. You should hang out with us more often."

Juliet looks at me with a smile I haven't seen on her face in a long time, and I wink at her. I know she's always felt Emilia avoided her, or didn't really like her, and although I can see where she's coming from, it's not from a place of spite on Emilia's side. It's simply because they haven't spent any time together. Growing up, Juliet was always with Cleo and Emilia was with me, our ages made it easier that way. My heart's happy looking at them both, and I'm so thankful that Juliet came home when she did.

I head back into the kitchen and manage to get most of the mess into black bin liners before the front door opens and

Cleo announces, "We got some really dodgy looks and I got ID'd to buy alcohol, today is a good day. Put some music on, Sis, we are here to paaaarrrrrttttttaaaayyyyy!"

I laugh as she swings her hips around to imaginary music until Juliet's playlist begins blaring from our home's speaker system and she joins Cleo in dancing around the sofa. Emilia and Marcus take the alcohol into the kitchen and grab the left-over superhero paper cups from the table.

I start to follow them back in there, but slow down when I sense William close behind me. An excited shiver races through me when I feel his finger trace a line from the back of my neck all the way down my spine. Suddenly, he grips me around the waist and spins me so I'm facing him, his arms locking me in place as they wrap around me.

"Hi," I smile up at him and pull my bottom lip between my teeth, knowing exactly how it affects him. His eyes are almost black. He growls at me and clashes his mouth with mine. It's a kiss filled with passion and desire and I feel my body heat up from my toes all the way to my head. My pussy is throbbing with need and my breasts are aching to be touched, licked, sucked.

"Knock it off or I'll douse you in cold water." We snap back to reality when we hear Emilia shouting at us. "Jeez, us singletons do not want to see that. Especially when it's your sister, dude."

I smile up at William and he groans out a frustrated sigh, but grins at the same time. His eyes are fixed on me, his arms locked around my waist so I can't move too far away from his body even if I wanted to. Which I don't.

He calls over to the girls, "Is someone jealous? You need to go and find yourself a man, Emilia." Marcus snorts, and when Emilia kicks him, he squeals in pain.

I turn my attention and narrow my eyes at her. "Emilia?"

She shakes her head, grabs a drink and heads straight past me into the front room and starts to dance with our sisters.

William and I turn back to Marcus who's smirking and rubbing his shin. "Oh no, don't you look at me. I'm saying nothing. I've already got a bruise coming here." He does a shot, offers one to me and William, and when we refuse, he heads into the front room with the tequila bottle and shots loaded onto a tray.

Once we're alone, William looks back at me and smiles. "Now, where were we?"

He lowers his head to kiss my neck and I giggle. "William, we have to slow down. I'm not going to have sex with you whilst my sisters, Connor and Marcus are in the next room. Anyway, I think we need to talk, don't you?"

He sighs and rests his head against my forehead. "Not fair, Nell. I've waited all day to strip you out of that suit, but you're right, we do need to talk. Want a cup of tea?"

I squeal in delight and laugh. "That sounds perfect. You're not going to have second thoughts about being stuck with an old fuddy duddy who prefers tea to tequila, are you?"

I'm joking, but there's a little truth in it, and relief washes over me when he smiles and tells me, "Nell, if you're an old fuddy duddy for wanting tea over tequila, then sign me up as one too. I love you."

I rest my head on his chest and sigh, "I love you too, fuddy duddy."

∾

"We're heading up to bed guys, we'll see you in the morning. I've left water and painkillers on the counter for you all. Drink the water before you go to sleep, please." I point my finger at all of them and fix them with my best mum stare.

When William and I turn to head towards the stairs, Juliet

plays Ginuwine's "Pony" on the speakers and they catcall and whoop at us like a bunch of children. I turn my head and narrow my eyes at them as they all gyrate their hips like they're working in a strip club. There's no way to keep a straight face at their antics.

I start laughing even harder when I see Connor stalk towards Juliet. Her face turns bright red as he starts to push himself up on to her. Take that little sister, payback is a bitch. I can't hold my cackle back as she sends me a dirty look, but I manage to catch the little smile that plays at the corners of her lips. She doesn't want to like him, but she definitely does. I hope they sort their shit out.

As we get to the top of the stairs, Emilia calls up, "We'll keep the music up for you guys. How many songs do you need, Will? I'm guessing two will do."

Laughing, William shouts back over to her, "It's longer than you'll be getting tonight, Sis."

I smack William's arm but hear Emilia laugh. "Mother-fucker's right, too. Go enjoy. And for the love of God, be fucking quiet. I'm talking to you, Nell."

We walk into my room and William sits on the bed. As I watch him, an overwhelming sense of calm and love rushes over me. This is right. He is right.

Earlier downstairs, we discussed telling Ben about us tomorrow. I'll talk to him alone and then call William over so that we can be together with him. I smile at the thought, knowing that Ben will be over the moon, especially after hearing what he told William earlier about him loving me. My boy is too clever.

I smile at William and walk the last few steps to join him at the foot of the bed. "Everything will be perfect tomorrow, William. You're still sure you want this? A ready-made family? You can still run if you want to."

I laugh as he grabs me around my waist and lifts me onto

his lap, my legs straddling his. He looks straight into my eyes as he tells me, "Nell, I want you and Ben. I want us to be a family, our little circle. The three of us forever, it's perfect. He may not be mine by blood, but I love him, just like I love you. I can't wait to spend the rest of our time together, just us three."

We smile at each other and I shift a bit on his lap trying to get comfortable. "My lady, if you keep doing that the talking will have to wait. You're making things very hard for me right now."

I smirk at him and wiggle some more. "Well, maybe I'm ready for my mouth to be occupied by more than words, William. Kiss me." With no hesitation his lips are on mine and his hands are reaching the zipper on the back of my costume. He lowers it and kisses my neck as his hands slide down my body.

I sigh as he peels the costume off me and captures my lips again, laying me on the bed. "Are you going to make love to me, William?"

He grins down at me. "My lady, I've always made love to you. Even when I was fucking you like crazy, I was still making love to you. Now how do you want it, Nell? Hard and fast or slow and deep? Either way I'm going to be buried inside this pussy, so you choose."

Panting from his words alone, I bite my lip and groan as he sucks on my nipple and circles his finger around my clit. "William. Hard and fast. Fuck me hard and fast. Please."

He chuckles as he thrusts into me, and I cry out in pleasure. "What my lady wants, my lady gets. I love you."

CHAPTER 35

Nell

The sun shines into the bedroom, and as I stretch my body out I feel deliciously sore in all the right places. I look over to the other side of the bed and smile at William laying there watching me.

"I love waking up next to you, my lady. Good morning." He leans over me and gives me a gentle kiss, but I feel my tummy start to turn.

Jumping off the bed, I throw on my robe and dash out to the bathroom, making it to the toilet just in time to empty the contents of my stomach from last night. I hear the door open and turn my head to find William standing there.

He takes in the scene in front of him and jumps into action, kneeling beside me in seconds, rubbing my back, soothing me until the retches subside. He stands up and grabs a washcloth, soaks it in cold water and places it on the back of my neck.

"Thank you, William. I'm so sorry. I think I've caught that stomach flu going around Ben's nursery. Maybe you shouldn't be near me in case you get it too."

He chuckles and wipes the hair from my sweaty forehead. "My lady, I haven't caught a bug in years, I'm virtually indestructible. Are you feeling better now?" I nod at him and smile, the heaving having subsided and the sweats from being sick have finally gone too.

"Yeah, I'm hoping it was a one off. I'm going to brush my teeth and get ready for today. Once I'm done, I'll head downstairs to sort breakfast out for everyone."

He frowns at me and crosses his arms over his chest. "They can cook for themselves, Nell. You need to rest. You've just been throwing up, woman."

I laugh at his serious stance and secretly adore the protectiveness he feels over me, but this is who I am. I'm the big sister, the caregiver, and that won't stop anytime soon.

"William. I'm fine, honestly. It's just a little bug. I always cook breakfast for them when they have hangovers, and that isn't changing." I get up off the floor and stand opposite him, running my hands over his still folded arms. I watch as his face softens with my touch.

"They're my family, William. I'll never stop looking after them. I want to kiss you right now, but you know, vomit breath and all." I turn to face the sink and take a step towards it, only to find my wrist being pulled back and I'm spun around, William's lips landing on my forehead. I sigh in contentment and pull away from him as he attempts to kiss my mouth.

He grins at me and rolls his eyes as I slap my hand over my lips. "A bit of vomit isn't going to stop me from kissing you, Nell. Let me."

I shake my head at him and say through my hand, "That's grossly romantic, William. But still not happening." I turn back to the sink, earning a smack on the bum, and laugh as I clench my legs together to stop my arousal from coating my thighs.

～

I'm dancing about the kitchen, making sure that all the fried food I have on the go is cooking to perfection, when I hear footsteps pad into the room.

Without turning around, I sing, "Morning Emilia, coffee and painkillers by any chance?" She groans back at me.

I spin around chuckling, placing the tablets and cup on the table in front of her. "You are definitely my favourite sister. Thank you." I smile at her and wink at William as I turn back to my cooking.

A few minutes later I can hear muffled voices from the hallway and I'm not at all shocked to see Connor and Juliet come into the kitchen at the same time, both with frowns on their faces and looking thoroughly pissed off. I tilt my head at Juliet, and she shakes her head slightly.

"Coffee and painkillers, Connor? Tea for you, Princess?" They both nod at me. I see the grin on Connor's face, and the frown deepen on Juliet's for calling her Princess. I snicker at them—they have to get their shit together sooner rather than later—as I hand over their cups and pills.

"The food will be ready in a bit, guys. William, will you go and wake Marcus up in the front room and see if he wants anything please?"

"If he does, he can get it himself. He's a big grown boy, he can look after himself, Nell, now sit down."

I huff out a sigh before turning my back to him and Emilia laughs. "You may as well give it up, Shakespeare. Nell's a caregiver, always has been, always will be. If you're in her house, she's feeding you, looking after you and basically treating you like royalty. It's who she is."

"Their mum is the same. I'm a qualified caterer, years at culinary school, and *if* I'm allowed to cook it's with them hovering over me. It's in her blood, Bro." I smirk as Connor confirms what Emilia and I have said to William.

I raise my eyebrows at him and with a sigh and a shake of his head he relents.

Cleo comes in as William's heading out and I have her coffee and tablets on the table before I even speak to her. Out of all of us she's the worst in the mornings. I giggle at the sight of her, hair a mess, eyes barely open and her face still bright green from last night's costume.

I turn back to the stove and another bout of nausea whacks me from out of nowhere. The dizziness that accompanies it makes me stumble and reach out to steady myself on the counter. William, who's just walked back in, is by my side in a second, asking me if I'm ok, but I can't answer as I run to the bathroom again.

Once the heaving stops, I stand up and look at myself in the mirror. I shake my head and rinse my mouth with mouthwash before heading back out to the kitchen, praying someone has been watching the food I was cooking.

As I turn into the kitchen all conversation stops and everyone's eyes are on me. William is the first over to me, gently leading me to a seat away from the food. "Nell, sit down. Do you want some water?" I nod my head, keeping my gaze on the tabletop, and even though I don't see who puts the glass down in front of me, I still mumble a thank you into the air.

I can feel all of their eyes on me. "Guys, I'm fine. There was a bug at Ben's nursery, remember. I've just caught it. That's all. Stop worrying please."

Connor, who has thankfully taken over the cooking, gives me a worried look. He hands everyone their plate of food and gives me mine. "If you don't feel up to it, I can make you some dry toast to settle your stomach."

I laugh and shake my head at him. "Are you mad? I've got nothing in my stomach now, I'm starving. I'm sure that was the last time anyway." I can feel everyone's worry on top of me and I lower my head and start to eat, hoping they'll follow suit.

William stands behind me, his hand on my shoulder, drinking a coffee. I turn my head to look at him as I ask, "You're not eating?"

He shakes his head and smiles at me. "I'm not hungry, my lady."

Frowning, I turn back to my food and eat like I haven't had a meal in months. By the time I look up, everyone is watching me. I throw my cutlery onto my plate and shout at them, "What now!"

Their eyes are now avoiding mine as Juliet quietly asks me, "Nell, are you sure it's just a tummy bug?" I look at her confused and then at William and the realisation dawns on me, they think I'm pregnant. I roll my eyes and William nods at me, letting me know I can tell them.

"I'm not pregnant, guys. William can't have kids. He had testicular cancer a few years ago and they told him he couldn't have children, so I'm not pregnant, Princess." I grip the hand he's resting on my shoulder as my sisters start to say how sorry they are, but Marcus cuts them off.

"Will, they said, might not be able to." My head shoots over to Marcus so quickly I think I give myself whiplash.

"What?"

I hear William sigh behind me, and Connor gets up, motioning for William to take his chair so he can sit and talk to me.

"The doctors told me there was only a twenty percent chance I'd be able to conceive naturally after they removed my testicle." I catch Connor wince out of the corner of my eye, but I ignore it.

"You told me you couldn't."

He takes my hand and looks me in the eyes. "That was before they tested my sperm count, Nell. After they removed it, they tested my sperm count in the one I had left, and they said it was low. It decreased my chances to less than ten percent, and that was with help. The doctors basically told me it wasn't possible."

I remove my hand from his and place it in my lap. I look at my table as I try to digest this little nugget of information and realise, I'm fucking angry. He lied to me. He told me he couldn't, not that there was only a slight chance that he could.

I look up at him and he must sense the anger radiating off me. He starts to speak but I cut him off, "No, William. You told me you couldn't. You lied to me." He shakes his head and tries to grab my hand back, but I move it away again.

"No, Nell, I never lied. The doctors told me I can't. Besides you're on the pill so there's no way you're pregnant now. I didn't lie, they said I wouldn't be able to."

Marcus clears his throat and my attention falls on him. "Nell, I don't want to get involved but why would I change a habit of a lifetime where you two are concerned, eh?" He's trying for humour, but I just stare at him as he continues. "Will believes he can't. I don't think you can count that as lying. From the minute he was told 'less than a ten percent chance with help' he's heard in his head 'can't have and won't be able too.' It's not his fault. He didn't lie to you."

I ignore Marcus and turn back to William. "I've missed some of my pills. I didn't think it was that big of a deal as I thought you couldn't..." My head starts to spin as the words fall from my mouth. "Shit, William. I could be pregnant."

I watch as his eyes light up and his mouth starts to turn up at the corners. He looks so happy and I'm in a state of shock. Numbness overtakes me. I don't know what my face is doing. I vaguely hear Juliet say she'll go pick a test up, Connor offers to drive her and then I hear footsteps, but I'm trapped in my own world. I could be pregnant.

The last time I *was* pregnant was so different. Steve and I were different. We were established, happy, in love and had been together for so long. The baby was planned and wanted.

Yes, I love William and I'm happy with him, but I never planned this, I never even thought about having someone else's child because I never had to. I thought William couldn't.

I don't know how to feel. Do I want another baby? I always did, but that was when Steve was here. How would he react to this?

He wouldn't. Because the reality is, if he were here to react, William wouldn't be. This would be Steve's baby and Ben's full sibling.

Shit, Ben. I haven't even told him I have a boyfriend let alone springing on him a new sibling as well.

My head is spinning again. I can't get enough air into my body quickly enough. The room starts to whirl around me and my stomach rolls again. I jump up and run to the bathroom, bringing up the contents of my stomach yet again. But this time it isn't possible morning sickness or a bug that made it happen. It's fear. I'm terrified. This wasn't in my plan. Plans work. They keep things structured. Shit!

CHAPTER 36

Nell

We're back around the kitchen table, seven pairs of eyes staring at the little stick that's been placed in the middle of it. The little egg timer flashes on the screen of the digital test, reminding us that in a short time we'll have our answer. I don't need to see it on the screen though. I know. I know that there's a baby inside of me. William's baby. I just don't know how that makes me feel.

I know I'm scared. We haven't been together that long, and everything has gone at warped speed between us. We don't live together, we aren't married, I don't even know if I want to be married again.

Does William want to get married? He thought he couldn't have children. I know he wants this baby and me more than anything, but that's now. Our relationship is still new. He hasn't had a chance to even experience the boring and mundane ways of my everyday life. He's only been around Ben for the fun times, coming over on weekends, going out for dinner, birthday parties, none of the normal tasks that I have to do daily with him.

What if he gets bored? When I'm huge and swollen with this new baby and Ben's acting up, will it all be too much for him? Will he leave me? Will I be alone again, raising a baby on my own? Again. Left unprepared and unready. Again. Will I be abandoned? Again.

I put my head in my hands and let my fingers sink into my scalp. I hear a gasp and shouts of congratulations as William's arms wrap around me. I hug him back, not wanting to take anything away from him at this moment. Remembering how special it was for Steve and I when we found out we were having Ben. I paste a smile on my face and excuse myself to go upstairs, feigning feeling dizzy again.

"I'll come with you, Nell." William steps beside me and I nod my head at him, knowing I won't be able to get him to stay downstairs.

Silence envelops us as we walk up the stairs to my bedroom. We enter the room and I know this isn't going to go the way I need it to go. I don't want to hurt him, but I'm terrified, and I need to figure out what I'm meant to do right now. I sit on the edge of my bed and again put my head into my hands. William sits next to me and places a hand on my back between my shoulder blades.

"Nell?" Almost whispering, I hear him try to engage with me.

"I'm still mad at you, William." I can't look at him. I don't want to see the excitement on his face or the twinkle in his eyes about our baby because I know my eyes are blank.

"Nell, I honestly believed I couldn't. The doctors told me that the less than ten percent chance was with their help, so naturally it was even less. This is a miracle, Nell. One that I don't regret. Do you?"

I sigh and stand up. I start to pace around the room, needing distance between us to think and speak without hurting him. "William, I'm so confused right now, I don't know what I'm thinking. Everything is muddled up in my head. If this happened to us, William, how do you know it hasn't happened before? You could have children out in the world you don't even know about."

He starts to laugh gently and my eyes zero in on him. Nothing about this is funny, why is he laughing? "Nell, is that what you're worried about? I've never not used a condom with anyone but you. You're the only one, my lady."

I stalk over to the chair in the corner of my room and sit down. I exhale a deep breath and try to get some words out of my head. "William, I don't want to take anything away from you right now. Finding out you're going to be a parent for the first time is an amazing feeling. One that you should cherish. But I'm struggling here. Everything has gone so fast with you and, whilst I've enjoyed the ride, I feel a bit motion sick right now. There are so many things worrying me."

He stands up and towers over me. "Like what, Nell? Talk to me." He crouches down and takes my hand in his. I let him for a minute and then take it back.

I start pacing again. I see his head and shoulders sag, but I can't focus on that. I need to get my head together. I'm now a pregnant mother of two. I need to be in mum mode again. I need to focus. I need to prepare. I need control back.

"William, we have to be practical here. We haven't been together that long. We don't live together. We barely know each other, and we're having a baby together. We need a plan for when things go wrong. Something that's set in stone for both of us so it doesn't take us by surprise." I look at him for the first time and all I can see is anger and hurt in his face.

"For *when* things go wrong, Nell? I see where your thoughts are. I know you pretty well, Nell, and you know me too. Even if you want to pretend like you don't. Let me ask you though, did you have a plan like that when you and Steve found out about Ben?"

I know where he's going with this and instead of taking a breath and regaining composure and not letting this escalate now, I let my frustrations and anger out on him. I have to. I need the control back so I can focus and look after Ben and this new baby too. I have to make him walk away from me. It's the only way. I can't stay with him and have him leave me later, my heart won't survive that again. I need to be able to control my situation and make him leave now so I can prepare myself for the heartbreak. I can't be blindsided again.

"Don't be ridiculous, William. Steve and I were married. We'd been together for years and we were actively trying to conceive. Ben wasn't a product of miscommunication."

He snorts his disgust at me as his face twists in contempt. "Nell, let's just be honest here. The problem isn't that we haven't been together that long. Or how well we know each other, is it? The problem is the baby's mine and not Steve's. That I'm here and he isn't." He folds his arms over his chest.

I stand facing him, rage flashing through my eyes, but also guilt because I know what he's saying is partly true. "How dare you. I've never hidden the fact that I love Steve and that if he hadn't been killed, I'd still be with him. Yes, I thought when I had another baby it would be Steve's, so yeah this is hard for me because it's another reminder that you aren't him." I clap my hand over my mouth once I realise what I've just said.

"William, I didn't mean..."

He cuts me off with a wave of his hand. "No, it's okay, Nell. I've always known he's your number one, I just hoped I could've been up there with him. I told you I'd share you. I was prepared to be second best for you, but I won't stand here and have you tell me that our innocent little baby is an afterthought—sorry, a product of miscommunication, that's what you said wasn't it?—and not a product of the love that we shared. You can't deny that you love me, Nell. I know you do. You're just too scared to do anything about it."

I want to scream at him, of course I love him, but I stay

silent. I need him to walk away from me now and not later on. I get to choose this time.

"I have stood back and watched you love another man, even though it kills me, because I never wanted to take that away from you. I thought you had enough room to love me too. Are you telling me I was wrong? Was I just a filler for your time, someone to help you get back to the old Nell again?"

I can't speak. If I open my mouth to answer him, I'll beg him to forget everything that's just happened and forgive me. To stay with me. But that leaves me open to heartbreak, and I can't do that again. I can't lose another man that I love. So I stay silent and let him continue.

"I was in this for life, Nell, but you know that. I didn't leave you, HE left you, not me. I want to stay, but I'm not wanted enough."

He walks towards the door as tears are streaming down my face and I try to call out to him, but my voice is lost. I'm watching him walk away. No, I'm pushing him away. He's right about that, but he isn't right about me not wanting him. I want him so much that I'm breaking my own heart. Because it's better to lose him now, when I can control the situation. If he were to be taken from me later, when I'm content and happy and unaware, with no hope or control and two kids this time, I wouldn't survive. I can't do that again.

He stops at the door, his hand on the handle and his back to me, and quietly begs, "Please let me be there for that baby, Nell. Please don't shut me out of their life too. I love them more than you'll ever know."

My face is drenched in tears as he storms out of my room. I sink to the floor as my silent sobs wrack my body and the front door slams closed. I curl into the foetal position, ironic I know, and sob.

Within seconds my sisters are here. Emilia spoons me

from behind. Juliet gently lifts my head, places it on her lap and strokes my hair, whilst Cleo lays next to me, face to face and holds my hands. The Cooper circle of comfort.

I cry for what feels like hours. I cry for everything. I let out the tears I've held inside for Steve and what we could have had. The tears for Ben and the loss of his dad. For William. My sweet, loving, caring William, who doesn't deserve any of this. I cry for our baby. For what I've done to it already. For pushing its daddy away so that I could control a situation because I won't be able to live through another heartbreak where I'm left alone without being prepared.

I can't do it again. I have to be strong. I can't afford to break. I must protect myself and my heart in order to be the mum that I need to be to my children. In order to survive. William will never understand that. I'll forever be sorry to him, but it has to be this way. It has to.

CHAPTER 37
William

"Will. Will! William, get the fuck up." I can hear someone calling my name in the distance, but my eyes are too heavy to open. The bottle of whiskey I consumed last night might be the contributing factor for that. I roll onto my side, intent on shutting out the noise, but the voice just gets louder and clearer. "Will, if you don't get the fuck up, I'm going to do something you'll regret later on."

I groan at Marcus to leave me the fuck alone, but he starts shaking me instead. I try to lift my arm to swat him away, but I don't realise how close to the edge of the bed I am and end up tipping onto the floor. Marcus's laugh is now ringing through my ears, making my head pound so loudly I'm sure he can hear it.

The room is spinning, and I feel like I'm going to throw up, but then I'm being hauled up and back onto the bed, sitting this time. Marcus hands me a massive glass of water. Thankful for it, I chug it down in one go and hand him the glass back. He exchanges it for another glass—this one's full of green shit that looks like chewed up grass from a cow—and tells me to drink it all in one go.

I know what it is, and it's not a good sign. It's his secret hangover cure that he only breaks out in dire emergencies. Grimacing in pain and disgust, I take the glass and bring it to my lips. I hesitate and look up at him, pleading to not have to drink this concoction, but he folds his arms across his chest and tells me to drink as he stares me down like the petulant child I know I'm behaving like. I do as I'm told and chug it. It's vile, and makes my stomach want to expel it immediately, but I force it to stay down, knowing it'll help me feel somewhat human again soon.

"Thanks, Bro, I needed that."

He nods his head at me and gives me an awkward smile. "Don't thank me too soon. Emilia's on her way to see you."

I groan at him and drag my hands through my hair. "I don't want to fucking see her. Tell her I'm not in."

He laughs and shakes his head. "Will, come on. We both know that girl is like a shark and can sniff out her prey from a mile away. Besides, she might help."

It's my turn to laugh, except mine is derisively at him. "Help? Why would she help me? Her and her sisters are thicker than thieves. She's probably here to rip into me for leaving Nell. It'll be all my fault, the arsehole who leaves his pregnant girlfriend for no reason. I don't want to argue with her."

He places his hand on my shoulder and gently tells me, "She isn't as bad as you think. She won't be here to argue either. It's been four days, Will, and all you've done is lay in bed drinking yourself into a state. It's not healthy, Bro. You, more than anyone, need to stay healthy."

I look up into my friend's eyes and can tell he's worried sick. Guilt washes over me and I lower my head down in shame. "I'm sorry Marcus. I just needed to escape for a bit. I had everything I've ever wanted for a second and then it all went to shit. I'll go and freshen up before Emilia gets here.

Hopefully, she won't rip into me too badly." He throws a sad smile at me as I get up and head into the bathroom.

Leaning my hands on the counter to hold myself up, I stare into the mirror and recoil at my reflection. I barely recognise the man looking back at me. My eyes are shadowed with dark circles, I have at least five days' worth of growth on my beard and my complexion is pallid and grey. It's reminiscent of my cancer days, before the treatment started, and I hate that haunted look in my eyes.

This stops now.

I grab my razor and get to work at hacking off this beard as the shower heats up. If nothing else, Emilia can go home and tell Nell that I look somewhat normal.

CHAPTER 38

William

I've been sitting on my bed for the last five minutes trying to get the nerve to go downstairs and face Emilia.

Marcus let me know she was here, but I told him I was just finishing up. It bought me a little time, but I know that I have to go down and face the music now, before she storms up here to find me. I'd rather have this conversation in neutral territory, not my bedroom.

I breathe out a resigned sigh and force myself to stand up and go into the hallway. Taking slow, deep breaths as I walk down the stairs, trying to calm my racing heart, I head into the kitchen.

"Hey." I offer them both, and Emilia greets me with a smile that unexpectedly puts me at ease.

Marcus flips the switch on the kettle. "Emilia, do you want another? Will, I'm assuming you want a strong, black coffee." He gives me a knowing look and sheepishly I nod at him, as does Emilia.

"Will, how are you?" she asks me. Her voice is kind, almost gentle, and I motion for us to sit at the table.

"I'm okay." I pause and blow out a breath. "No. You

know what? I'm lying, I'm fucked. I had everything I'd ever wanted and then it was gone. How's my lady?"

Emilia gives me a small smile. I can see the worry and concern in her face and I feel bad for her. "It's nice to hear you call her that, Shakespeare."

I shrug at her as Marcus places my coffee in front of me and sits in the chair next to Emilia. "I still want her to be mine, Emilia. Nothing's changed there. She just never really was, was she? She's always belonged to someone else."

Emilia frowns at me and I brace myself for her onslaught, the protection of her sister being the only thing that she cares about. "She stopped belonging to him when he left her, William. She just needs to realise it." My head whips up to look at her, and when my mouth drops open in surprise, she grins at me. "Didn't expect that, did you?"

Confusion sweeps over me and Marcus chuckles at my expression. "Definitely didn't expect that. He thought you were here to rip into him."

She feigns a shocked look on her face and puts on her sweetest voice. "Why would you ever expect that from little old me?"

Marcus chuckles and Emilia giggles, totally unaffected by my disbelief. "Oh, I don't know, probably because when we first met you threatened to cut my balls off and wear them as earrings. Joke's on you anyway. I only have one so you'd have been lopsided."

She smirks at me and raises her eyebrow. "That promise still stands, Shakespeare." I throw my hands up in exasperation, but she just laughs back at me.

"God, you're dramatic aren't you. It still stands because you didn't hurt her. She hurt herself." I sit back in my chair and motion with my hand for her to continue. "She told us what happened, what she said to you about Steve and the baby. That's not Nell, Will. This isn't her. She's scared and she's trying desperately to regain some form of control. She did similar things after Steve died."

I fold my arms over my chest. I've seen this side of Nell all along. The need to control elements of her life. Struggling to let people in because it's easier if she does it on her own, her way. It's why I gave her time, space, so that she could get used to me being there.

I want Emilia to tell me why she believes Nell is doing this, though, so I wait. We aren't going to get anywhere with me speaking.

"Did she talk to you about Steve?"

I nod at her. "Yeah, we spoke about him a little."

She lowers her eyes, clearly struggling with being here, likely feeling she's betraying her sister's trust. "Did she talk to you about after Steve died? In depth, not the 'I just got on with it' crap she spins to everyone?" I shake my head at her, and she sighs. "I'm going to tell you some things that might help you understand Nell. I shouldn't be here really, but I figure we've gotten involved in every other aspect of your relationship, so why stop now."

Marcus nods his head and then stands up. "I think this should be a private conversation between you two. Call me if you need me. I'll be in the front room." Emilia smiles at him and he grabs my shoulder as he leaves. I'm so fucking thankful to have him in my life. He may be dramatic and needy, but he's my best friend and will always have my back.

Emilia clears her throat and continues, "You know Nell and Steve got together when they were ridiculously young, right? They were perfect for each other, they lived for each other. They decided on universities around their relationship, they did everything together. They were never apart. Nell went from living at home, to living in dorms with Steve, to living in their house together." I knew this, but I nod at her to continue, still unsure what all of this is meant to explain.

"She'd never been alone in her whole life. Not until the night she was told he was gone. She went from being part of a team to being alone in the blink of an eye. She was lost. She lost herself when Steve died."

She shuffles on her chair, uncomfortable at the emotions that she's evoking in herself in front of me. I reach out and take her hand, squeeze it gently, and let go again. She smiles her appreciation and continues.

"Did you know that she only cried a little when she found out? She was sobbing these gut wrenching, body wracking cries when we got to her, and then stopped as soon as Ben was placed in her arms. She later told me she was distraught that he'd seen her break down.

"I tried to reason with her, reassured her that he wouldn't remember and she was allowed to grieve, but she wouldn't have any of it. She didn't cry again. Not one tear. Until after he was buried.

"All day at his funeral she was composed and collected, then when we got home, she went upstairs and shed a few tears, but only a few." A bitter smile graces her face as she remembers her sister's pain, and my heart breaks for her and all of them. Still, I say nothing, needing Emilia to carry on.

"She vowed to remain strong for Ben, and she has. Too strong. She hasn't allowed herself to grieve for Steve, for the loss, for the betrayal. He let her down. He left her. Broke his promise of forever to her, and she's terrified of history repeating itself. She doesn't want to be caught unawares again. Does this make sense so far?"

I lean forward and consider what she's told me. "She didn't grieve properly, that's what you're saying? I get that, I really do, and I'm so sorry for everything she lost, but it still boils down to the fact that she doesn't want me, Emilia. She wants Steve. She wants her marriage to him, this baby to be his. She doesn't love me, Emilia. Nothing's changed since I left the other day."

She shakes her head at me, annoyance radiating off her. "I knew I should've let Juliet come, she's better with these feelings and crap."

She rolls her eyes and takes a deep breath. "Shakespeare, you're right, she hasn't grieved properly for him. Or at all, really. Part of grieving is being able to let someone go. To be able to say goodbye to them. Nell hasn't, and for some reason still isn't able to do that yet. You're wrong about her not wanting or loving you, though."

I scoff at her, lean back in my chair and rake my hands through my hair. "Yeah, because when you're happy and in love and find out you're pregnant, you always push the other parent away. And tell them you're upset because they aren't your dead husband. I wish you'd have told me this before. I'm so fucking stupid," I deadpan at her, and her scowl actually makes me recoil a bit in my seat.

"Funny, Mr. Sarcastic. If you let me finish, I'll explain why you're wrong and be happy to rub your face in that fact." She pauses to see if I have anything else to say and I dip my head for her to continue.

"She pushed you away *because* she loves you and wants you so fucking badly. She knows if anything were to happen to you or your relationship she wouldn't be able to come back from it. She'd end up that sad, desperate, lost woman again.

"She had to rebuild her whole life once, she doesn't think she can do it again. She only had Ben the last time, but now she's about to be a mum to two babies. If it was hard before, imagine how much harder it would be now.

"She's basically so fucking terrified *because* of how much she feels for you. She loves you, William. She wouldn't have done this if she didn't." She looks me straight in the eye and continues whilst hope flickers in my soul. "She pushed you away now to stop herself being blindsided in the future. Even though she's that sad, lost, and desperate woman again now anyway. She just needs help to see it.

"Now, see how wrong you were."

She smirks at me and I roll my eyes at her. "Emilia, that's stupid. I wouldn't leave her. I love her more than anything."

She looks up at me, a grim expression on her face. "So did Steve."

Her words hit me harder than any physical punch ever could. I blow out a breath of air and sit back in my chair again, the impact still sitting on my chest.

"No one can promise the future though, Emilia. I don't know how long I'm going to live for. Who ever does? This was one of my reasons for backing away at the beginning, you know?"

She shakes her head at me, confusion marring her face. "What do you mean?"

I pause before I tell her. My mouth is as dry as the desert, thank you lingering hangover. I stand and grab a cold drink from the fridge, needing both a second to gather my thoughts and relief from the sudden cotton mouth. I offer her one, but she declines, so rather than head back to my chair, I lean up against the counter. A little distance may make this easier for me.

After I've downed nearly a whole bottle of water, I continue. "Do you remember when I became distant with her, before you guys set us up at that meal?" She nods at me, so I carry on. "One of my reasons for doing so was because I'd been ill before and I was worried about putting her through that again. I didn't want her to have to deal with another partner dying."

Her eyes grow wide, and she shifts in her chair. "But

239

you're okay now. Nell said you were alright. Why would you push her away because of that?"

I shake my head and smile at her worry for me. "Four years cancer free. It's always in the back of my mind though. It could come back. I was scared to put her through that. She brushed it off and told me if that happened, we'd deal with it together."

She thinks for a second and replies back, "It would still be different from losing Steve, though. She would have some warning. She could take control of the situation. I think what's playing with her mind is the not knowing. Not being able to see when tragedy is going to strike. She wasn't prepared for it with him. She's worried it'll be an out of the blue moment again.

"But that's what love and a relationship is. You put your trust into someone, hope for the best and enjoy the good times, so when the bad times come you have those memories to see you through."

I sit back down opposite her, nodding my head. "So where does that leave me? A part time dad who's in love with the woman having his baby, but can't do anything about it because she's too scared to trust me and enjoy the good times."

She slow blinks at me and bites her lip, evoking memories of Nell doing the same and making my dick remember all of the fun times we had with her. "Emilia stop looking at me like that, you're reminding me of Nell." I shudder, a look of horror on my face, and she instantly drops her lip and kicks me under the table.

"Fucking gross, Shakespeare." I rub my shin and laugh.

She frowns at me, smirks and then drops her eyes to the table. "Please don't give up on her. Give her some time. I just wanted you to know that the woman that said those horrible things to you and pushed you away isn't the same Nell that you love, but we'll get her back." She reaches over this time and takes my hand. "I promise I will do my best for you, Shakespeare. For both of you." She squeezes my fingers and smiles at me.

"Thanks. I'm not sure it's going to be a happily ever after situation for us, Emilia. Like I said earlier, I can't switch my feelings off. I can't stop loving her. So, I have no choice but to wait. Especially as she's carrying my baby." I can't help the smile that creeps onto my face when I think about that, and she smiles back at me.

"No matter what happens between you and Nell, you'll always be that baby's daddy. That alone means you are a part of this family, Will. Whether you or Nell like it or not, you're a part of us now and nothing will stop that. Us Coopers may take the piss out of each other, but we look out for our family. That includes Connor, Marcus and now you.

"You have my number and everyone else's too. Text us, call us whenever you want to. I'll keep you updated on things as well. We will bring her back, and then it's up to you to decide if you want her or not."

I nod at her and smile as she stands up and heads out. When I hear her say bye to Marcus, I know it'll be seconds until he's in here with me.

As if on cue, he appears in the doorway, a huge grins on his smug face. "I told you she wasn't that bad."

I laugh at him and rub my shin under the table. "Yeah, tell that to my shin. She kicked me."

He laughs back at me and pulls a tracksuit leg up to show a big blue and green bruise on his shin. "Yeah, that's one of her favourites. You know what I did but what did you do?"

I shake my head, grinning at him. "Let's just say she looks more like Nell than she likes."

He starts to laugh, and I join in with him. These past few days have felt like an emotional roller-coaster. On the one hand, I have something I never thought I'd be able to have—a baby of my own. On the other hand, I've lost the only woman I've ever loved. Whether I'll be able to have them both at the same time is unknown to me yet, but I really fucking hope I can.

CHAPTER 39

Nell

Super-mum to the rescue. If all else fails, rely on the fact that you have to plough on and do what's needed for the sake of your child.

Ben has no idea what's going on with me, and I have no intentions of telling him either. It's been just over a week since his party, and he's asked on several occasions where his new best friends are and if they can come and see him. Thankfully, I've managed to convince him they're both very busy. He isn't happy about it, but it's tough. I can't exactly phone William up and ask him to come and spend some time with my son after what I did to him.

I close my eyes and try to force the image of him out of my mind. The one where the pain is etched on his face and the hurt from my words is flashing through his eyes. I did that to him. I made him hurt to save myself from pain in the future. I'm a selfish bitch, but I had to. Self-preservation and all that. I shake my head and mentally reprimand myself for letting those thoughts in again.

"Mum, are we going to Nanny's now?" I look down at Ben, standing in his doorway with his little overnight bag on his shoulder, smiling away at me. Normally his smile makes me sad and reminisce about Steve, but that's another thought I'm forcing out of my mind.

I'm struggling with my memories of him. Everything I remember is now tinged with anger at his abandonment. It's ridiculous to feel this angry with him this many years on, but I can't help it. I hate that he isn't here. I hate that *because* he isn't here, I'm having to do what I'm doing to William.

And I hate that I'm alone again. I also hate that I hate being alone as well. That's a lot of hate running through me. The resentment I feel towards him is unhealthy, I know, but it's there in my head and I have to force myself to push the bitterness out of my mind and focus on Ben.

"Yeah, baby, we are. I'm going to pick Auntie Princess up from there as she was helping Nanny with something, and you'll stay there tonight if that's okay?" He nods at me and heads downstairs as I follow him.

A wave of nausea makes me stop at the bottom step but I'm able to breathe through it. I've been having sickness every morning, but the nausea lasts all day. I was the same way with Ben. The little comparison makes me smile, but then I remember William and my smile fades away again.

He should be fussing around me and making sure I'm okay, like I know he would be if he was here; but he isn't. He needs to keep a distance now, one I can control, to protect us all.

Today the sickness seems a bit worse, but I think that's down to guilt. I have my first scan and I haven't told William. In my defence, I never intended on keeping him from any of the scans or anything to do with the baby, but I didn't expect to get a scan so quickly.

I thought I'd have more time to get used to the empty feeling in my chest without him before I had to see him again, but the midwife explained they needed to do a 'dating' scan as soon as possible. I know it's not right and he should be there, but I can't face him yet, and the guilt is eating away at me. I know I'm being unbelievably selfish, but I have to be to protect my heart.

I tried to explain that to Emilia when she ripped into me and told me just how selfish she thought I was, but she wouldn't listen. She made me promise her that I'll let him know about the 12-week scan. She also informed me that no matter what, he would be at that one. I know she's right and I'm wrong, but I can't deal with my feelings for him as well as everything else.

I need to pack him into a box in my brain labelled *William* and leave him next to the one that says *Steve*. It's the only way I can cope.

I manage to get Ben into the car and to my mum's house in record time and without feeling too sick. I rush him inside, tell my parents that I'm late, and grab Juliet as quickly as I can. I need to avoid an inquisition from my mum and any kind of eye contact from my dad as he'll know there's something wrong straight away. It's where Emilia gets her senses from.

"Jeez woman, you nearly pulled my arm out of its socket dragging me out so bloody quickly. What gives? We aren't late, we have plenty of time." Juliet rubs her shoulder gingerly.

I wince and apologise to her. "Sorry. I didn't want to have to deal with Mum or Dad. I haven't told them anything yet." She nods at me and looks out the window.

I know my sisters don't agree with what I'm doing, but it's not their choice to make. I've never fallen out with any of them before, especially not Emilia.

As soon as William left that day, and I'd picked myself up off the floor and was able to tell her what had happened, she told me off big time. Then she walked out and has only spoken to me on our group chats or via group video calls, never one to one. It's killing me, but it's another thing I have to let roll off my back.

I can't sit around and wait for something to happen to William like I did with Steve. Something that leaves me alone and lost again. Not with two children to look after. I barely survived when I had one, and I was younger and my heart was stronger then.

This way is better for everyone, they just need to trust me. Emilia will realise it soon enough. I'm trying to be strong, but it's hard. My sisters are the people I rely on for everything, and to know they're unhappy with me hurts.

I clear my throat and Juliet looks over at me. "Are Emilia and Cleo meeting us there?" I ask tentatively.

She gives me a small smile and nods her head. "Cleo's already there waiting for us, but Emilia said she wasn't sure if she could make it. She has a client meeting or something." Juliet looks down at her lap and fiddles with her hair. I know she's trying to cover for her.

I smile and nod my head but can't find the words to say anything, so we continue in silence.

∼

"Well, that's gross." Cleo looks down disgustedly at the sample of urine I'm holding.

I smirk at her. "Part of the job, I'm afraid," I tell her as I sit back down next to her.

It's 10:40, my appointment is at 10:45, and there's still no sign of Emilia. She's always been my shadow, my rock, and to not have her here now is crushing me. I know she's angry with me, but a small part of me hoped she'd put it aside for today.

"Nell Vickers?" I look up and see a young woman holding a clipboard standing in front of me. I smile, stand up and head towards her, both of my sisters following closely behind.

We enter the little room and the familiarity of it all smacks me in the face. I take a step back, recoiling from the memories of being here with Steve and the happiness I felt compared to now. Being here without William leaves a desolate feeling swarming inside me.

Cleo grabs my arm and Juliet's arm goes around my waist as I put my head on her shoulder and listen as she tells me to breathe. I follow her instructions and hear Cleo tell the sonographer I was having an anxiety attack.

I want to scream at them, "No I'm fucking not. My heart is broken because the man I love isn't here with me." But I can't, because it's my fault he isn't here. I stopped him from being here.

I try to focus on Juliet's voice, the one telling me to breathe in for four seconds and out for four seconds, and follow her instructions. After a while, the darkness starts to subside, my breathing regulates, and the dizziness stops. I smile at the sonographer, embarrassment written all over my face, and apologise to her.

She isn't fazed by any of it and gets to work, having me lie down and lift my top up. I stare at Juliet as the jelly is placed on my tummy and the scan starts. Juliet's eyes cling to mine and I swallow, trying to clear the fear and emotion clogging my throat.

The sonographer turns the screen to us and smiles. "Everything looks good. I'd estimate that you're about 6 weeks along. Does that sound about right?"

I nod at her, tears spilling down my cheeks. I look at Juliet, my voice barely a whisper, "It must have been one of the first times we..."

She smiles down at me and whispers back, "Meant to be, Nell."

I close my eyes tightly, swallow my doubt away and turn my head back to the screen.

"If you look here, you can see the little blinking part? That's your baby's heartbeat. It's nice and strong. Just what we like to see." I cry harder and whisper my thanks to her.

I go through the formalities in a zombie-like state, unaware that I'm doing them, but somehow they get done. It's only when we get outside, and I have to pay attention to the midwife giving me my next scan date in six weeks' time, that I fully grasp that I just saw mine and William's little baby in there. My hand shoots to my belly and rubs it gently as I whisper, "I'm so sorry."

CHAPTER 40

Nell

After a silent drive back from the hospital I open my front door and I'm shocked by what greets me. Emilia is sitting on my sofa, drinking a cup of tea, reading one of my Shakespeare books. And something inside of me flips. A red rage descends on me and I fly into the front room.

"How fucking dare you. You can't show up to the hospital, but you think you can waltz into my home and act like you've done nothing wrong?"

She places the book on the table and slowly takes a sip of her tea before slowly placing her mug back on the table. Each movement is intended to anger me more, and it's working.

I growl at her and she smirks at me before calmly replying, "I didn't do anything wrong, Nell. I had a meeting. I couldn't make it. And if I'm honest, I still don't think it's right having us all there when William doesn't even know you went today. I came here to see how it went. I never expected so much hostility, but it's okay. You and I both know who it's really meant for. You're just too much of a coward to say it out loud."

Rage is seeping out of my pores, my breathing is laboured and if I were a cartoon character, steam would be screaming from my ears right now. "What the fuck are you talking about?" I spit out at her as she smirks at me again. "Stop fucking smirking at me, Emilia. I punched you in the face enough times when we were younger, I'll fucking do it again now."

I hear Juliet gasp from the doorway and Cleo tell her to shush, but my head is focused on Emilia and what she said a minute ago.

She stands to face me, eye to eye, and I can see her working hard to remain calm when she shakes her head and tells me, "I'm not who you're angry at, Nell. There are two people that you're raging at and I'm not one of them. So why don't you save your 'she hulk' impression for when you figure that out."

"Stop talking in riddles and just fucking spit it out. You're a joke, do you know that? Standing there judging me when you've never had a real fucking relationship in your life." I hear Cleo shout my name, but Emilia and I ignore her, eyes focussed on each other.

She smiles at me. "Do you know what, Nell, you're right. I haven't. I haven't found anyone that was worthy of spending my time on, let alone giving my heart to. But you, you found someone who's perfect for you. You're having a baby with him for Christ's sake. But instead of enjoying that, you push him away. You get angry at him, when, in reality, the people you're most angry with are yourself and Steve. So out of both of us, who's really the joke here, Sis?"

I start to maniacally laugh and scream at her, "Definitely you. I'm not a fucking joke, Emilia. You're deluded, you know that right? Steve's dead, why would I be angry at him?"

My head is screaming she's right. I'm so fucking angry with him for everything, but I don't want to tell her. It would be too much like admitting how true it is. And then I'd have to face the reality of how angry I am with myself, as well.

She spins on her heel, grabs the picture of him off the mantel and shoves it in my face. "Tell him how you feel, Nell. How you really feel. Do you want me to start you off?" I ignore her and refuse to look at the picture. "Steve you're a fucking, stupid man. The one bloody night you decide to go out and you don't come back. You should have come back, Steve." She thrusts the picture into me again, "You go."

I look at it, trying to block out the screaming in my head but it takes over my every thought. '*Why did you listen to me? Why didn't you stay in the pub for a bit longer or leave earlier? Why did you get yourself involved? I don't care if you were helping someone else, what about me? What about Ben? You left us. You promised you'd never leave us. We're all alone because of you and your fucking hero complex. Why couldn't you have just walked home? You were needed here. I needed you more than that woman. I didn't know how much to pay on the gas or the electric, Steve. I didn't know how to fix the boiler when it started playing up. I didn't know how to snuggle Ben in the special way that he liked you to. They were your jobs, Steve. I needed you. We needed you. You lied to me. You promised me forever. You said we'd grow old together. You promised me more. I want my life back. I want me back. You broke me. You left me a shell of a woman and you shattered my heart.*'

Suddenly I'm on the floor with all three of my sisters wrapped around me and I don't know what happened. Emilia is stroking my hair and kissing the top of my head. Juliet is by my feet, rubbing my legs and Cleo is holding onto my hand for dear life, all of them touching me, comforting me.

Emilia shushes my sobs. "Nell, you're allowed to be angry with him. You're allowed to hate him, as well as love him, but you're not allowed to hold onto him anymore. He's gone. You need to let him go. Properly let him go.

"William loves you and you love him and that's allowed too. Steve would want that. William isn't going anywhere, and even if he does, you will be okay. You have all of us and you'll never be alone. You know everything now. The boiler, the gas, the electric. You won't be blindsided again."

I blink up at her and realise I must have said everything out loud. The words in my head must have spilled out without me even being aware of them. The tears fall down my cheeks and I look around my front room, the one still decorated the same as it was when Steve was alive.

It's been trashed.

Steve's picture is smashed against the mantel, pieces of glass scattered everywhere. The coffee table has been flipped, New Jersey Housewives' style, and all the contents are all over the floor. Emilia's tea is splashed all over my cream rug, which would normally make me wince but not right now. I try to speak but no words come out.

Cleo looks at me kindly. "You're allowed to be angry at yourself too. Be mad that you told Steve to go out that night. Be mad at yourself that you fell in love with Will. Be mad that you fell pregnant. And especially be mad that you pushed Will away.

"But don't be that idiot that stays mad and doesn't learn from it, Nell. Accept it all and move on from it and be happy. You and Will, you have a chance of being so happy with Ben and this little baby. Let yourself be happy, Nell. Show the rest of us how to do it."

Again, I try to speak and can't. My ability to form coherent sentences is lost and I'm just a crying puddle on the floor. After a few moments, I manage to get myself together. I wipe my nose and eyes on my sleeve, run my hands through my hair, and take in a deep, shuddering breath.

Looking over at the picture and then to Emilia, I whisper with as much strength as I can muster, "Please clean that up whilst I make tea, but I don't want it back up there. I'll put it in Ben's room once I've replaced the frame." She nods at me and I walk into the kitchen alone.

My head feels like it's going to explode. The adrenaline that was coursing through my veins is causing a major crash now and all I want to do is sleep. I sit down whilst the kettle is boiling and close my eyes for just a second.

I wake up to find my sisters sitting around my table in the kitchen, drinking tea and coffee and smiling at me.

"Hi," I sheepishly say to them.

"Oh, is Luce Banner back in the room? The She-hulk has gone, has she?" Emilia jokes and we all giggle. My sisters and I have always had the ability to move on from things, no grudges held. I especially love this about us today.

"Emilia, I-I'm so sorry. The things I said to you..."

She waves her hand in front of my face and grabs my hand, her beautiful green eyes sparkling up at me. "Don't, Sis. I know that wasn't you. It was grief and fear. They've gone now?"

I smile weakly at her, still feeling awful for being so wretched to her, and nod. "Yeah, I think so. For years I've felt so bad for even contemplating those feelings towards Steve, but yeah, I'm angry with him. It feels like he chose to help that person over me and Ben, and he left me alone, with our baby. I had no knowledge of how to run the house or..." I stop and take a deep breath. "I-I guess I buried it all so deeply that it stopped me from healing and being able to move on. God, I've kept this place in the exact same way. A shrine to our time together. I want to redecorate. Or sell it all."

253

I put my head in my hands and feel comfort when Cleo starts to rub my arm. "You don't have to eradicate Steve from your life, Nell."

Emilia smirks as Juliet says, "Eradicate. Dad would be impressed with that one, Cleopatra."

Cleo looks over at Juliet, sticks her tongue out and rolls her eyes at our baby sister. "Whatever, Princess." Ignoring the narrow-eyed, dirty look Juliet throws at her, she continues talking to me. "By all means redecorate, but selling this place is a bit drastic. It's a beautiful house, Ben's only home. It's around the corner from your job and Mum and Dad and soon you'll need their help again. Plus, Ben's going to have a lot of change to deal with. Let him stay in his home."

I take a deep breath and gaze around my kitchen. I've always loved it here. I can picture Steve standing at the stove, cooking us pancakes. No shirt on, wearing dark denim jeans and barefoot. I can see myself with Ben as a newborn, him in one arm whilst I'm warming his bottle up and trying to stop his crying by pacing around the table.

I also see William, standing behind me and telling me he loves me for the first time. It feels like such a long time ago. My heart aches for him. I want his arms around me. I want to hear his voice calling me his lady. I need his kisses and his touch like I need to breathe, but I pushed him away. He won't be back in this kitchen, playing happy family with Ben and I. He won't be here at night when I'm making our new baby its bottles.

I made him leave. Worst of all I told him it was because he wasn't Steve when I don't even want Steve anymore. I love him, I always will, but I love William more. A realisation I held back for fear of disrespecting what Steve and I had.

Tears spill from my eyes again and Emilia grabs my hand,

Cleo, the other and Juliet stands behind me, her hand on my shoulder, all of them touching me again.

"William." I manage to croak out, as more tears come and the sobs that wrack my body leave me breathless.

Emilia shushes me again. "William will be there when you're ready to talk, trust me, Nell. You have to focus on you for a bit. You need to see a grief therapist. I have an appointment on hold for you when you're ready. It's with the one I saw after Steve died."

My head shoots up to look at her. "What? You saw a therapist? When? Why didn't you tell me?" Shock radiates through me and I cling to her hand.

She smiles a sad smile at me and tilts her head to the side making her long, blonde hair fall over one of her shoulders. "After Steve died, I struggled a bit with my emotions. I knew him for a long time, Nell. I stalked you two for most of my life. I felt like I'd lost my big brother...and my big sister too."

She whispers the last bit and I grab her hand tighter and cling to her. "I'm so sorry I wasn't able to be there for you, Emilia."

She laughs and I look back at my other two sisters, startled, and see they're both smirking as well. "Nell, you shouldn't have been there for anyone except you and Ben. You needed us more than we needed you. I wasn't clouded by grief and depression and pure pig headedness like you were, and I went and sought out help. It was Mum's suggestion. She said she tried to tell you to go but you put a stop to it rather quickly and dismissed her idea."

I look down at the table remembering that conversation I'd had with Mum. A month after Steve's funeral she came to the house, cleaned and cooked for us, and told me about a great therapist her friend had started seeing, suggesting I visit them too. I scoffed at her and told her I didn't need anyone, that I had my family and Ben and that was all I would ever need. She tried to push me, but I stood up and told her Ben was tired and that I had to put him to sleep. An hour later I came downstairs, and she'd gone. It was never mentioned again.

"She told me it was a friend of hers that was going, not you." I told Emilia. She smiles and rolls her eyes at me and I can't stop the laugh that comes out of me thinking it must be a Cooper family trait, seeing as we all do it, quite a lot as well.

"If she'd told you, Nell, you would've gone into protective big sister mode and pushed your thoughts and feelings even further down. I told her not to. Begged her actually." She grimaces at the memory and we all laugh, knowing it must've been torture for our super strong sister to beg anyone for anything.

I sit up straighter in my chair, square my shoulders, and let the tears flow. I've spent too long holding them in. "I'll go. Book the appointment for me, tell me when and I'll be there." Emilia nods at me and Juliet and Cleo both smile, relief flooding their faces.

"If I'm staying here, I need it to be redecorated. As cheaply as possible, but I need it to look different everywhere. I need it to be for me this time, not an 'us'."

They all nod their heads and Cleo grabs her phone. "A friend of mine owns an interior design company, she'll do mates rates and get it sorted in a few weeks." I nod and tell her to find out a price for me, anxious of the cost as I don't have much left in my savings account, but Emilia cuts me off.

"I'll pay for it. I have the money, it's my gift. I don't want arguments, Nell. I want to do this for you, Ben and my new niece or nephew. It better be a niece this time." She gives me a steely look and I know there's no way I'll be able to change her mind, so I lower my head and thank her.

Within a few hours, my new life is set into motion. I have an appointment to see a therapist starting on Monday. I'm moving in with Mum and Dad for three weeks whilst the house gets redecorated, and I have my appointment for my twelve week scan in six weeks' time. By then, I have to decide what to do about William. I know I want him back, but I don't know if he'll want me anymore. Only time will tell I suppose.

CHAPTER 41

Cooper Clan check in. Group text

Marcus: I just wanted to touch base and do my weekly check on best friends' baby mumma and the Cooper clan. I miss you guys.

Emilia: Awwwwwwww

Cleo: (Red heart emoji)

Juliet: I actually miss you too.

Emilia: How's Shakespeare doing?

Marcus: He's okay, been at the gym a lot.

Connor: He's a beast in the gym at the minute. Working off his heartbreak. He seems very calm about it all though.

Juliet: You go to the gym with Will? How did that happen?

Connor: I reached out to him after the shit hit the fan. Wanted him to feel like he was still a part of all of us. I know what it feels like to be taken into the Cooper clan and treated as one of them, you never want to lose that feeling.

Emilia: You'll never lose us. You're stuck with us now for life.

Cleo: Fo' Life, homie.

Juliet: What they said...

Connor: (Purple heart emoji)

Marcus: Well shit, I'm tearing up over here. Distraction time... is Nell really doing okay?

Juliet: She's hating living with Mum and Dad again and can't wait to move back home this week. She isn't Moody Margaret like the last time. She's more Sad Susan. She misses Will.

Emilia: She tells me about her therapy sessions. Her therapist sounds amazing. She's in a good place.

Cleo: Her morning sickness has subsided as well.

Juliet: Is Will open to talking with her? We don't want to broach the subject with her if he isn't ready.

Marcus: Oh Princess, that man is so in love with her he would do about anything to talk to her, but he doesn't want to push her into anything. That's why he hasn't contacted her.

Cleo: He's doing the right thing. Her therapy sessions and giving the house a remodel will help her move on, but she needs to figure everything out herself. Tell him to hang in there.

Emilia: We're all on the same page. They will be together before my niece gets here.

Connor: Nephew. We need to tip the favours to the boys in this wacky family.

Cleo: Dream on, she's having a girl.

Emilia: Cleo, what time will the house be ready for us to go over there?

Cleo: They'll be finished tonight so anytime in the morning. Shall we say 11am? Juliet can get Nell there. Connor, you coming?

Connor: I'll be there at 11.

Marcus: Take lots of pictures for me. I hate that we won't be there (crying face emoji)

Emilia: We'll all be together there soon enough. I'm heading back to the office. Speak to you later.

Marcus: Bye Coopers...

Cleo: I'm out too, love you all.

Connor: I love you all too. ALL of you (purple heart emoji)

Juliet: (Purple heart emoji)

CHAPTER 42

Nell

"And how did that make you feel?" Dr. Montgomery is asking her favourite question again. I have to fight myself to stop my eyes from rolling. It's my ninth session with her and as much as I think she's helping me through my issues, she's also a pain in my arse. She wants to know how I feel over everything. I know that's the point of therapy, to delve into your emotions and discover why you feel them so you can start to move on from them, but that question is beginning to get on my last nerve.

I sit straighter in my chair, tuck my hair behind my ears and clear my throat. "Out of control." I hope that answer will satisfy her, but I see her smirk and my inner eyeballs roll at her. I take a breath and sigh. "Fine, when I found out I was pregnant again, I was scared."

"Scared of what, Nell?" She leans forward as she asks that question and on instinct I slink down in my chair.

"Scared of history repeating itself. Something happening to William. Him leaving me and having to go back to the person I was after Steve died." I look down at my shoes, trying to avoid her face. This shit is hard for me to admit.

Somehow avoiding eye contact makes it easier. I'm not sure if I'm worried about seeing pity or judgement in her expression, but it all hurts.

"So, you were scared that you were going to feel out of control, out of your depth? Why would you feel like that again, Nell?"

I sigh and look over her shoulder at the framed diploma on her wall, my default item to stare at to stop tears from escaping my eyes.

"Because I'd be alone again." I cross my legs and shift on my seat. She sits back and writes something in her notebook, and I swallow my insecurities at what she's writing.

"Nell, you understand that when Steve died you felt overwhelmed by everyday life tasks, like..." she flips through her notebook and quotes me, "'paying the electric and gas bills, putting Ben to sleep in a certain way, fixing the heating' and other things. You felt like that because you allowed Steve to take the lead in your relationship and do things without your knowledge. Mundane tasks that you felt you didn't need to know because Steve had it handled.

"Then when he died you were forced to learn about all those tasks. You had to learn how to cope on your own and raise a baby that way too, which was never in your plans."

I take a deep breath and furrow my brow. I did let Steve deal with everything. He never controlled me in the sense that I wasn't 'allowed' to do what I wanted, but he did take care of a lot of the everyday things. Things that, after he died, made me feel incompetent.

I keep silent and let the doctor continue as she sits back in her chair and speaks with confidence and poise. "If you and William were to start a romantic relationship and anything DID happen to him, or said relationship was to break apart, you wouldn't go back to the person you were after Steve died because you've learnt how to be independent.

"Most people learn this after they leave home, Nell. To stand on their own two feet. But you went straight into a relationship with Steve and were happy to let him guide you. Unfortunately, you had to learn to navigate your way through grief, motherhood and independence all at the same time." I nod my head at her, everything making perfect sense.

"Being independent doesn't mean that you can never be dependent on another person again. It just means that you *can* do everything alone, but you choose whether you want to or not. You can accept help; share the load, so to speak. You can be independent and maintain your abilities to run a house, parent, be a strong woman *and* be in a relationship with someone as well. It's all about balance, Nell. It's not one or the other."

I look over to the diploma again but this time a tear escapes and runs down my cheek. Dr. Montgomery gives me a gentle smile and pushes the box of tissues on her table closer to me before she continues.

"You spent a long time being part of a couple, time that you would normally have spent learning how to be alone and independent. You went through the motions of moving from your parents to University and your own home, but you were with Steve then.

"When you were finally forced to learn how to be on your own, it wasn't through choice. So it's understandable that you want to control elements of your life, that you feel nervous about being with someone again. You have a choice as to where you take your life from this point forward." She looks me right in the eyes, which are now leaking more of those tears that were trying to escape earlier, and smiles at me.

I lean forward to grab some tissues and ask her, "Do you think I made the wrong decision about William?"

She gives me a subtle smile, pushing her dark rimmed glasses to the top of her head before she speaks. "Nell, officially, as we have a minute or two left, I think you did what you felt you had to do to survive. I also think seeking help to deal with the abandonment issues Steve's death caused was an incredibly brave and smart decision in moving forward with your life."

She looks at her watch and her smile gets bigger. "Off the cards, as our session has officially ended, I think you need to give you and William a go. You love him and he loves you, and that's hard to find. Believe me. Don't be afraid. You have a wonderful family to support you no matter what. And now a wonderful therapist too."

I reach over to her and grab her hand smiling. "A wonderful therapist and friend as well."

She squeezes my hand and pops her glasses back down onto her nose, signalling for me to get the hell out of her office.

"Princess, I'm nervous to see my house. What if I hate everything after all the money Emilia has spent?" I groan to Juliet who's sitting next to me in the passenger seat of my car, Ben strapped safely in his seat behind us.

"Nell, don't be silly. Cleo's friend is one of the best in the business, they wouldn't have done anything that you won't like. Just relax and make sure your blood pressure stays low for my little..." I shoot her a look and if I could shoot daggers through the air at her, I would. Luckily, she stops before she mentions her niece or nephew in front of Ben. When she rubs my arm and whispers *sorry*, I shake my head to tell her it's fine.

"Mummy, will my room be da same?" A worried little voice comes from behind me. I catch his eyes in the rear-view mirror and send a reassuring smile his way.

"It will be even better than before. You're getting a new bed, a big boy one. Your toys will all be the same though, so don't worry."

He smiles back at me, the worry disappearing from his eyes as Juliet picks up the conversation. "Seriously dude, your room is the best one in the house. I might move in there with you. Nell, do you think Ben's new bed will fit me in it as well as him?"

He giggles in the back, replying for me, "No Auntie Princess." I snort with laughter as she frowns at me furiously. My boy has picked up on the family nickname for his auntie and she certainly isn't impressed.

"You won't fit. I don't need to sleep wiv you, I'mma big boy. D'you still need to sleep wiv someone, Auntie Princess?"

I laugh uproariously as Juliet splutters through laughter. When I catch Ben's innocent frown in the mirror, I try to bring myself together. "Auntie Princess might need to sleep with someone still, but it won't be you Ben, so don't worry," I tell my boy as Juliet frowns at me furiously.

"She can ask Uncle Connor. Dey can get married and live happily ever after and she won't hafta sleep on her own. I bet Uncle Connor'd sleep wiv you, Auntie Princess."

I can't help the smirk on my face as she knocks her forehead on the window when I tell Ben, "I bet he would too. Maybe we should ask him today."

He nods his head and then catches my eye again. "Mummy, I bet Will would sleep in your bed. You know, because I'm too big to sleep in dere now. Can I show him my room today?"

The smile that was lingering on my face at Juliet's discomfort slides off at Ben's words. I'd give anything to have William sleep in my bed again.

I clear my throat before I try to answer Ben. "Erm, no, not

today baby. Will is working." He must be able to sense my tone as he doesn't press it any further, but Juliet reaches over and grabs my hand that's resting on the gear stick and squeezes it. I give her a quick look, a sad smile, and squeeze back as we turn onto my driveway.

CHAPTER 43

Nell

"It's amazing. Cleo, Emilia, thank you so much. I can't believe this is my home."

I look around the house that I've lived in for years and I'm shocked at the transformation. Gone are the boring white walls and dark grey accessories, and in their place is white panelling on the lower half of the hallway with a light silver damask wallpaper at the top. It looks spacious, warm and homey.

I walk into my front room, the room that used to be my favourite, and gasp. It's stunning. The bottom half of the walls are papered in a light gold colour with flecks of glitter all over that, when the light hits right, twinkles. The top half is a brilliant white. I feel like I've walked into a show home. The fireplace is still there, but on top are two candlesticks and three pictures. The first photo that catches my attention is of me and Ben, and happy memories swim in my head as I remember our trip to the farm. We were laughing because I'd stepped in a massive patch of cow poop and Ben thought it was hilarious. My parents are smiling at me from within another frame, a memory from one of their many cruises. The third is a recent photo of me and my sisters with Connor. Two people are missing from those pictures, and the thought makes me incredibly sad.

Emilia walks over and reassures me, "You can change them when you want too. We wanted you to have your family up there when you came home. I know we'll need to add to them soon, hopefully with more than one person though."

She motions to my belly and squeezes me tightly as Cleo comes stomping into the front room. "I'm such an idiot. Nell, I forgot to stock your fridge. There's no milk, bread, nothing. I can't drive over to the shops either as I've had two glasses of champagne now."

I shake my head and laugh at her. "Don't worry, Sis, I'll take Ben and pop over there now to grab a few bits. I'm sure he'll want to pick some snacks as well. I'm not cooking though, so order pizza for everyone. And I'm buying."

I call up to Ben to come down and from the corner of my eye I see Connor heading Juliet's way. She must see it too as she quickly says, "I'll grab him, Nell. I'll come with you guys. I want some chocolate anyway." I smirk, knowing she's just trying to get away from Connor as she runs full pelt up the stairs to drag Ben away from his new superhero room.

"Ben, you can grab a couple of sweets but none of the chewy ones that get stuck in your teeth. I hate those sweets." I tap my foot and send my best teacher look at Juliet and my son, both of them standing at the side of my car pulling faces at me. They look at each other, then turn their conspiratorial grins on me. I do my best to hide my smile as I turn my back to them and head towards the small supermarket.

"Ben, Ben stop." Juliet is shouting behind me and before I have the chance to look back and see what's going on, a Ben-like blur darts past me.

Panic rises in my throat. "Ben. Stop now!" I shout at him, terrified that he'll be hit by a car. But all the panic subsides when I see a familiar figure stooping down and scooping him into his arms for a hug.

I stand rooted to the spot as beautiful brown eyes look over Ben's head and lock with mine. My heart beats rapidly, my mouth goes dry and a lump the size of my fist lodges in the back of my throat. I take him in whilst he stands, takes Ben's hand, and walks towards me. His hair is longer. His eyes are still as beautiful, but they carry a sadness that cuts me deep to my soul.

I caused that.

My gaze scans down his body, and I feel heat surge through me at the sight of his firm, athletic build covered in a simple white t-shirt. His hard, muscular legs are encased in dark blue denim that sculpt him perfectly. I know what that body feels like on top of me, surrounding me and inside of me. I shift on the spot and hope to God he doesn't notice.

I'm trying to decipher the grin on his mouth as he approaches, when I feel a slight pain in my lip and quickly release it from between my teeth. I don't want him to think that all I wanted him for was sex. Or to be a 'filler' as he suggested that night. I desperately want him to tell me he still wants me, still needs me, the same way I crave him. Even though I know I don't deserve it after the way I treated him.

When he stops in front of me, I give him a sheepish look and apologise to him before turning my concern and fear on my son. "Ben, don't ever run off when we're in a car park again. A car could've run you over. You're in big trouble mister."

Ben looks down at the ground and mumbles to me. "I just wanted to see my friend."

Guilt washes over me and tears prick my eyes. I bend down and reach out to him but he sidesteps me and goes to

Juliet, who's standing behind us. She motions that they're heading into the shop and I take a deep breath before I stand and face William.

When he looks me straight in the eyes and smiles, my insides turn to mush. "Don't be too hard on him. I had eyes on him as soon as he started running, he was safe." I nod at him and go to bite my lip again, consciously stopping myself this time, but the amusement that flashes through William's face tells me he caught it.

"How are you?" I ask him tentatively, and he gives me a sad smile.

"I've been better." He looks away and I want to slap myself silly for hurting this man. "How's the baby? How are you feeling? Do you need anything?"

"Nothing yet. The morning sickness has subsided a bit now, which is good." He nods at me, and I try to ignore the guilt that hits me when I realise he should've been there, would have been there, with me to help me through the sickness. I don't deserve him.

He runs his hands through his hair and blows out a breath. "I better go. Phone me...," a flicker of hope surges through me and I'm just about to open my mouth and ask if we can talk about us when he says, "You know, if you need anything for the baby or any appointments come through. I'd like to be there for everything."

I force a smile onto my face and nod at him. And then I watch him leave again. My head is spinning. He doesn't want me anymore. He only wants to be there for the baby, not me. I can't blame him. But I can blame myself. He's walking away. Protecting himself from me. He'll have a new woman to quote Shakespeare to and kiss, fuck and love. I'll be alone with my children again. And this time I have no-one to blame but myself.

CHAPTER 44
Nell

"Auntie Emilia. I saw Will. I told him about my room."

Emilia's eyes dart from me to Ben and finally to Juliet. Panic flashes through them as she takes a breath and leans down to speak to Ben. "Really? That's amazing. I bet he was so happy to see you. Do you want to go outside and see the new swing set we've set up for you?"

When he squeals in delight and flies out the back door like a cheetah, Emilia spins around to me. "What the fuck happened?"

Cleo walks back into the kitchen from outside, eyes wide open. "Ben said you guys saw Will. What happened?"

Emilia rolls her eyes and grits her teeth as she says, "She was just going to tell us when you interrupted."

Cleo pulls a face at her and sticks her tongue out before turning to me. "Well, don't just stand there, tell us. Connor will be able to keep Ben entertained outside for a while. Spill, Sis."

I take a deep breath and shrug. "He isn't interested in me anymore. He didn't ask how I was or even mention anything about us. I thought he was going to, when he said to call him, but he just wanted to know about the baby. I've lost him."

I look at my sisters, expecting some sort of support from them, but they just look at me, Emilia by the oven, Juliet sitting at the table and Cleo perched on my new marble counters, frowns on their beautiful faces. I throw my arms up in the air and shout "What?" at them. Emilia turns her back to me and Juliet shakes her head. Cleo clears her throat, but says nothing.

Finally, when I'm just about ready to storm out of the room and take refuge, alone, in my bedroom, Emilia pipes up, still with her back to me. "Maybe you should give Dr. Montgomery a call. Talk it through with her. Anything we say to you now will go in one ear and out the other. She can make you see sense." With that she walks over to the back door and motions to the other two to follow her. And they do.

I'm completely flabbergasted at them but before I can start to get angry, I reach for my phone and dial Dr. Montgomery's number. She answers after the third ring.

"Hello, Nell, are you okay?"

I take a deep breath before I speak. "Yeah, I'm fine. Well, I'm not really. I just had a run in with William and Emilia suggested I call you to go through it." I frown at my words as I still don't understand why she wouldn't talk to me about it. I mean, I know they've all become friends with each other, but sisters before misters and all that jazz. Right?

My thoughts are interrupted by Dr. Montgomery's slight chuckle and then her apologies. "I'm sorry, Nell, it's just that if Emilia suggested you call me it's because she knows you wouldn't listen to her about it. I'm flattered that she thinks highly enough of me to think I can talk sense into you. Tell me what happened."

I explain everything to her, trying not to leave out any details. I want to be able to gloat at Emilia when she confirms what I know. That he's moved on.

She pauses for a brief moment and then asks me,

"Throughout your relationship with William, what have you always asked from him, Nell?" The question throws me off kilter and I search my mind for an answer. Before I can think of one, she answers for me. "Sorry, Nell, my next client is going to be here very soon so I have to be quick. You always asked him to give you time and you'd let him know when you're ready. He gave you time with your relationship becoming physical, remember? And you went to him when you were ready to be intimate. What makes you think this is different?"

I slump down in my chair and sigh out a breath I wasn't aware I was holding in. "I hurt him. I could see the pain in his eyes."

"What was one of the last things he said to you, Nell? In your room, the day of your argument, do you remember?" I nod my head, tears streaming down my face, but I know she can't see me.

My lack of answer forces her to answer herself. "He told you he was in it for life. That he wouldn't leave and he wanted to be there, but he wasn't wanted enough. Maybe, Nell, you need to tell him he is wanted before he can come back."

The air leaves my lungs in a whoosh and I sob into the phone unable to speak. The back door opens, and my sisters come running over to me. Emilia takes the phone and puts her hand on my shoulder, Cleo is in the chair next to me holding my hand and Juliet is mirroring her on the other side. Emilia places the phone on the table on speaker and tells the doctor they're there.

"Nell, tears are good. Let them out. You're supported as always. Your relationship with William was based on him chasing and then waiting for you to be ready. He's still waiting. Are you ready?"

I try to get words out of my mouth, but none will come

and instead I drop my head, so my chin is resting on my chest. Am I ready? Do I want William in my life, with me, not just as a co-parent? Do I want his arms around me? Do I want to wake up to him every morning and go to bed with him every night? Do I want to be a family with him, me, Ben and the baby?

Realisation swallows me and I cry out, "Oh my God." Through my sobs, I manage to splutter, "Yes. I am. I'm ready. I'm so fucking ready."

There's a collective sigh of relief from my sisters and Dr. Montgomery. "About fucking time, Sis." Emilia says from behind me and kisses the top of my head as Dr. Montgomery says goodbye.

Mopping up the tears on my face with the tissues that Emilia passes to me, I shake my head at them. "What if he's over the wait?" But they just stare back at me. Again.

The tension is broken when Connor walks in with Ben who runs straight upstairs grabbing his crotch area and shouting, "I need a wee wee." Cleo snort laughs and Juliet rolls her eyes.

"He isn't. Over the wait by the way." Connor says as he walks over to the fridge and grabs a bottle of water from it.

"They're not going to be cold, I just put them in there. And how would you know?" I ask him, confusion written all over my face.

He shrugs nonchalantly and takes a big gulp of water before telling me, "I've been training with him. He isn't over the wait. The ball's in your court, Sis."

When the doorbell chimes, Connor's eyes skim over all of us and he sighs when none of us move to open the door. "I'll go, shall I? You just want me to pay for the fucking pizza."

He stalks out of the kitchen as I turn around to my sisters. "Did you guys know they were spending time together?" They all nod.

Emilia bites her lip and then looks annoyed at herself and shivers. Weird. "Yes, we did, Nell. We've all been in contact with Will too, just an FYI. Marcus has been checking in with us and asking how you are, as well as Shakespeare. They both care about you. William loves you. He gave me that plant over there for the 'new' house."

I look to where she's pointing and see a small white rose plant. I put my head down and mumble *shit*.

Juliet giggles and claps her hands. "It's time for a plan, Nell. What are you going to do to win back your man?"

I bring my head up, square my shoulders and show her my most determined face, hopefully making her think I have a plan. But they know me too well, and when all I get is silence and side-eye, I admit, "I don't know. But you're all going to help me figure it out. Emilia, get Marcus, we need his help too. I have to convince William I want him and I'm sorry. I don't want to lose him again."

"Don't you worry, Sis. We'll devise a plan that will knock him on his arse. Cooper Clan, assemble."

Juliet and Cleo laugh, whilst shouting, "You're such a nerd, Emilia."

And for the first time in a long time, I have hope that everything will be okay.

CHAPTER 45

Cooper Clan to the rescue!
Group text

Emilia: Marcus, you there boo?

Juliet: Are you doing this to annoy me?

Cleo: She calls him that all the time when they're out, so I don't think so.

Juliet: It's just so unlike her. She's normally so prim and proper and boss-like.

Emilia: You two little brats realise I can read everything you put, don't you? (Woman smacking her forehead emoji)

Nell: Oh Emilia, emojis? Really?

Juliet: NO NELL! You will not take away my right to free emoji speech in this group. You already have the sister group. I will not give up my right to speak emoji.

Nell: Jeez Sis, dramatic much...

Cleo: I'm with Princess. #freeemojispeech #mylifemychoicetoemoji #nellisanemojifascist

Marcus: What a fabulous day to be alive. We have a very dramatic debate going on about the freedom of emoticon (the correct terminology for speaking emoji), the sun is shining and Nell has finally (girl, you took your damn time!) come to her senses regarding my boy Will. Princess, emoticon all you want (Princess emoji, blowing kiss emoji)

Juliet: I will be seeing you very soon, Marcus, and I will remember all of these Princess references. And you will be punished.

Connor: Erm what did I stumble onto here? (Embarrassed face emoji)

Juliet: (Eye roll emoji, woman smacking forehead emoji)

Nell: I fucking hate emojis.

Emilia: (Laughing hysterically emoji) Is everyone set with the plan? We all know our roles?

Connor: Yep...

Juliet: (Thumbs up emoji)

Cleo: (Thumbs up emoji)

Marcus: (Boy and girl kissing emoji)

Nell: (Eye roll emoji)

Juliet: Have we converted you? YAY!

Nell: No, I just needed to roll my eyes before I exploded. You're all bonkers, but I love you all so much. See you tomorrow. Good luck Cooper clan.

CHAPTER 46
William

I'm not in the mood to go out on a session. I want to wallow in my room and hate the world in peace, but Marcus and Connor have other ideas.

Ever since I saw Nell the other day, they've been on my arse about going out this weekend. Probably because seeing her completely threw me for a loop. As soon as I spotted her, I wanted to wrap my arms around her. I wanted my lips on hers, to taste her and hear her moan.

Instead, I asked some generic 'how's the baby' question and felt sick to my stomach when she told me about her morning sickness easing off. I should've been there to go through that with her. I did tell her to call me, but quickly added if she needed to for the baby when I saw the panic and fear cross her face.

She either isn't ready to get back together and still needs time, like Emilia suggested, or she doesn't want me because I'm not Steve. I think option two is the more likely reason. And that is what's making me absolutely miserable. I've been slumped about the house since then, only leaving when Connor made me go to the gym with him.

Now, against my will and better judgement, I'm getting

dressed up and preparing for a night of drunken antics from the guys. They'll have fun, and I'll be the designated sad sack sitting in the corner trying to smile, when really, I just want to wallow in my bed again with a bottle of whiskey.

"You ready yet, Bro?" Marcus is calling up from the downstairs hallway and I sigh as I take one last look in the mirror. The gym sessions have been a good thing. Besides being a good outlet for my anger and frustration, I'm looking more shredded than ever before. The tight white shirt I have on, sleeves rolled up to my elbows, shows my biceps off nicely and my jeans are a bit tighter around my thighs too, so that's a plus.

When I head downstairs and see Connor and Marcus looking up at me like proud parents watching their child about to head off to prom, I give them a confused look. "What's wrong with you two?" They both look away, like they've been caught doing something they shouldn't be, and I shake my head at their strange behaviour. "Right boys, are we ready?"

I grab my keys off the table next to the street door, turning back to them, arms opened wide, and they both grin as Marcus nods.

"Oh yeah, we are definitely ready, Bro."

As the doors open to our local pub, I feel a sense of calm I haven't felt in a long time. I want to analyse what this means, but decide to just roll with it and let myself try to enjoy the night.

Marcus heads straight to the bar and Connor ushers me towards the seating area in the far right corner. The corner that Nell and her sisters sat in all those months ago. God, it feels like a lifetime ago now, not a few months.

As we sit, Connor slaps me on the back in that manly way us men do, because emotions are for sissies and all. "You okay? You've been quieter since you had your run in with Nell."

I nod my head at him but feel my shoulders slump when he mentions her name. "Yeah, I'm fine. I miss her. I love her. I want to be with her, Ben and our baby. But I can't make her feel the same way."

I look down at the bottle of beer Marcus places in front of me and pick it up to take a swig just as Connor tells me, "You never know, she might finally come to her senses. Don't give up." I stare at him, he knows I've heard it all before, but he just smirks back at me.

The door opens and I hear the Cooper sisters enter the bar in all their typical boisterous noise. Their voices are a welcome intrusion and miserable reminder, all at the same time. My head whips around, my eyes instantly seeking Nell, but to my relief and disappointment, she isn't here.

Cleo, Emilia and Juliet strut over to the bar, seemingly unaware that we're here, so Marcus heads over to them. I look at Connor, the love emanating from him as his eyes land on Juliet. I tip my head over towards her and ask, "Connor, what's stopping you two?"

He drops his eyes and smiles the saddest smile I've ever seen on his face. "It's complicated. Let's just say, I fucked up but for the right reasons, and she doesn't agree."

Marcus and the girls join our little party, and I watch Juliet closely as she looks at Connor. I can't hold back my own smirk when I see the pink tint hit her cheeks.

I lean into Connor's space, so only he can hear me, and whisper, "You never know, she might finally come to her senses. Don't give up." I chuckle as I use his own words as encouragement to him. He whispers, "fucker" back at me, but his happy smile is firmly back on his face as he stands to cuddle each of the girls, deliberately leaving Juliet for last.

Emilia sits next to me and slaps my thigh. "How you been, Shakespeare?" She asks me, with a happiness in her voice that's off putting. Emilia as a bad arse, I'm used to. Emilia all happy and smiley, I am not.

"Meh," I shrug my shoulders at her, and she laughs. I shoot her a 'what the fuck' look but she just grins at me.

"And you're the one that's supposed to be good with words. The children of our future are doomed with the likes of you teaching them."

I laugh at her quick wit, and try to very casually find out where Nell is and how she's doing, but Emilia sees right through me.

"Oh, Shakespeare," she starts whilst holding in her laughter, "she's doing better. She's still going to therapy and has had some really good sessions. She's good, and that's all I'm saying about her tonight. We're here to have a good time and celebrate you becoming a daddy."

The smile on my face is one of pure elation until Cleo pipes up, "Oh, Emilia's getting all kinky with Will. Is he your daddy, Emilia?" She has this sultry voice on and is biting her lip trying to look sexy. Both Emilia and I heave at the same time.

"Cleo, you're a fucking sicko," Emilia manages to get out without puking whilst I sit looking dejected.

I manage to look at Cleo, who's grinning like a Cheshire cat, and tell her, "I think you've just ruined the word daddy for me, Cleopatra." She frowns at the use of her full name but her smug smile returns quickly as my joke hits her.

Laughter comes from all sides of me, and I bask in the knowledge that even though Nell and I are, well fuck knows what we are, this family is still treating me like I'm one of theirs.

A drink is placed in front of me, and I look up to see the barman with a tray full of drinks, shots and a white rose. I'm just about to tell him that we didn't order these, when he catches my eye and grins.

"This is for you. But I'm under strict orders to tell you that you can't turn around until you've read it all." He places a letter and the white rose in my hand then turns and leaves.

Everyone else fades into the background and I'm too preoccupied with my racing heartbeat and erratic breathing to care. I turn the paper over, finding a quote with the same elaborate mistake I once made, '*there was a star danced, and under that was you born.*'

Several things become clear simultaneously: this has been an elaborate ploy to get me to come here, this note is from her, and she's here somewhere.

What's not clear is what it means.

Is she wanting to start again, to see where we can go? Or is she trying to let me down gently so we'll be amicable for the baby's sake?

I want to open it, but at the same time, I don't want to. I look up and see ten expectant eyes studying me, and then looking away sheepishly when they realise they've been caught.

Marcus clears his throat and Emilia shouts at me, "Don't just sit there staring at us. You'll never know unless you open it, Shakespeare." I shake my head at the lack of privacy they give me and open the note.

Mr. Shakespeare, William,

I'm sorry. I never intended to cause you pain, but I did, and by doing that I've inevitably caused myself a world of it as well. I'm sorry I ruined a moment that should have been one of the happiest of your life, and I'll feel guilty about that forever. I spoilt a moment you truly believed you'd never experience, and I should never have done that to you. You didn't deserve that. I know you didn't lie to me about not being able to have children. It was just easier to be angry with you over something and push you away than to try and understand my need for doing so. I think you probably have a fair idea as to why I did it anyway.

*I'm sorry for telling you that I didn't want you because you weren't Steve. That couldn't have been further from the truth. Therapy has helped me understand that too. I loved Steve. I really did. But not as much as I **love** you. I don't expect you to believe me, I've given you no reason to trust me, but I will no longer deny myself, or you, the truth.*

The feelings I have for you are more intense, more passionate and more fierce than what I experienced with Steve. We got together so young that I think puppy love developed into a contented love, and I was happy and comfortable with that. When I started to realise my feelings for you, I got scared, but I managed to push through the fear because I was so immensely happy.

Finding out about the baby tipped me over the edge of happiness into panic. I've told you about Steve dying and how I felt at the time, but I didn't tell you the full extent. I know Emilia has filled in some gaps for you, and I'm grateful that she did, but I'd like the chance to explain everything to you as well. I won't write it all down, as you'll be here reading forever, but I need you to understand something I've just recently accepted.

For most of my life, I was that thirteen-year-old girl who started dating Steve. I never lived on my own, and sort of traded being looked after financially and emotionally by my mum and dad to Steve. When he died, I was alone in the world with a baby, a tiny life completely dependent on me, and I was completely clueless. It terrified me and, as I picked up the pieces, I vowed never to go back there again.

I was scared that because my feelings were so much more

intense for you, that it would be a million times harder to fight back if anything were to happen to you. Or us. Plus, I'd have two children to care for this time. I thought it was easier to push you away now, so I wouldn't be blindsided when the inevitable happened. My therapist thinks I have a slight control issue. I'm not even arguing about how true that is. I hope that makes sense.

I want you to know I've come to realise I never dealt with Steve's death properly. Hiding from grief doesn't make it go away. Who would've thought that, eh? It festered until I built this image of him and us through rose coloured glasses. We weren't perfect, and he wasn't perfect either, but fear and loss painted him that way in my memory. My anger at him finally surfaced when I blamed him for losing you. And that aware-ness and release forced me to deal with these issues.

I even redecorated my house. It's been done for me, the way I wanted it - that control thing reared its head again but this time it was good. Or so my therapist says.

William, I'm so sorry. I love you. More than you'll ever understand.

Now you know my heart as well as my mind, and if you can see any chance in us being that family you spoke of, I'm here for that journey. You need only turn around.

If not, I fully understand. Just know I will never not love you.

"One half of me is yours, the other half yours,
Mine own, I would say; but if mine, then yours,
And so all yours."
Forever yours,
Nell xxxx

I can't look up from the paper straight away knowing they're all watching me, waiting for a reaction. I'm too conflicted to face anyone just yet. My heart wants to jump up, run over to the bar and find her and never let her go. But my head reminds me we've been here before. Does she really means it this time or not? I don't think I can take another blow to my heart. I know I'm running out of time to pretend I'm still reading the letter, and that I need to decide what to do, but I'm still so unsure.

"We know you've finished the letter, Bro, stop faking it. You read fucking Shakespeare's thee, thou, thoust, crap for fun. You ate Nell's words up about a minute ago. Talk to us." Marcus's smart arse voice invades my head and I instinctively look up at him, seeking the comfort he's offered since I met him.

Except, it's not just him this time. It's the whole Cooper clan, minus the one I truly need. If I go by her letter, she's waiting for me at the bar. I know she is even without checking. I can feel her eyes on the back of my neck. Can feel her very presence in my wounded soul.

I take a deep breath and relay my fears to my new family, who just happen to be Nell's too. "What if she changes her mind? I can't take it again. I won't do that to Ben and the baby. I want a life with her. An always, not just a now." I look into each of their eyes and see the same thing: respect, love, and hope.

Juliet steps forward. "Will, you need to tell her that, not us."

Connor steps behind her to speak to me. "Sometimes it takes losing the person you love more than anything to make you realise what you had. If you don't take this chance, you'll spend every day for the rest of your life living with the knowledge that you turned away the best thing that ever happened to you. Even if you believe you had valid reasons for doing it. Trust me, you don't want to live with that regret. I know."

His eyes dart to Juliet and when she lowers her head I swear a tear slides down her cheek. Before I can be sure,

Connor continues, "It looks like she came to her senses man, now it's time for you to come to yours." When he smiles at me and nods his head, I stand up and hug him before turning to face my fears and my future.

~

She's there, staring down at her drink, and my heart urges me to head to her, to my home, my family. My feet move swiftly through the small crowd, everything but her fading into the background. When I place my hand on her lower back, the breath catches in my throat as I inhale her scent.

She turns on her stool and looks up into my eyes, hers glistening with unshed tears. I smile at her and when I gently stroke her cheek, she nuzzles into my hand. I key in on the music in the background as the song changes, and chuckle.

My whisper in her ear causes her whole body to shiver. "This song was playing as you walked towards me on your birthday. After you read my note..." I pause for a second trying to get my timing perfect. "I'm thinking now what I thought back then..." I pause again so she can hear the chorus of "Marry You" by Bruno Mars.

She gasps and throws her arms around my neck as the realisation sinks in.

I laugh as I wrap my arms tightly around her. "We still need to talk, Nell, but I want it all. You, me, Ben and the baby. Together forever. Is that what you want?" I lean back to look into her cat-like eyes and take in her beautiful smiling face.

"Yes, William. A thousand times yes."

I pick her up off the stool and swing her around before crashing my lips to hers in a fierce, passionate kiss. With my lips still on hers, I whisper, "No more running."

She breaks away and kisses me all over my face, whispering back, "No more running. I'm all yours, William. Forever. I love you. I'm so sorry." She apologises over and over again, until I take her lips in another blistering kiss and silence her.

Our moment of reunion bliss is interrupted by some serious heckling and cat calling from the Cooper clan, and we finally break apart, laughing at them. As we head back over towards them, I stop mid-stride and turn to her.

"This is it now, Nell. Me and you?"

She smiles up at me and tells me, as much with her words as with the love in her eyes, "Me and you. Mr. and Mrs. Shakespeare." Then she tiptoes up to kiss me briefly on the lips before taking my hand as we walk over to our family.

Epilogue

Nell

"Are you ready?" I look up to William and smile. He's nervous. I can see it in his eyes. I squeeze his hand and give him another reassuring smile. I place my other hand on his chest, over his racing heart, and feel him relax under my touch. He blows out a shaky breath and we walk towards the darkened room.

The sonographer looks over her notes and I take my position on the bed, already rolling my top up as I know the procedure. William hovers near me, raking his hands over his face and the sonographer laughs, "First baby?"

I giggle back. "For him, yes. I have a son from a previous relationship." She gives me a smile, free of judgement, and explains what she's about to do as I peek at William.

He's listening intently, like he might be quizzed later, and I grin at how cute he looks. Minutes later, a black and white image appears on the screen. William's grip on my hand tightens as tears pool in his eyes and fall down his cheeks.

Happy tears, if the smile on his face is anything to go by. "Nell, it's our baby. I-I-I can't believe it. Thank you, thank

288

you." He bends his head down to kiss me, and as our lips meet, I feel an exhilarating jolt of electricity zing through my body and take up residence in my core. He moves back a fraction and rests his forehead on mine, telling me, "I love you Nell. And when we get home, I'm going to show you just how much." He kisses the tip of my nose and I giggle like a schoolgirl and blush furiously.

This man of mine gives me all the feels.

"Ben, come in here for a minute please." I walk into my front room and sit on the sofa, staring at the little image of our baby on the scan picture that we got today. I'm about to tell my beautiful boy that he's going to be a big brother. The excitement's bubbling inside of me. I know Ben will be over the moon with the news, just like he was two weeks ago, when I told him that William and I were in love and he'd be moving in with us.

His first question had been, "Can Will stay in my bedroom when he lives here?" There was no awkwardness or worry about losing time with his mum, just pure excitement about the prospect of having his new best friend around more.

"Hi, Mummy." Ben walks into the room with a smile on his face and a spring in his step, followed shortly by William.

"Did you guys have fun on the swings?" Ben nods his head frantically as William takes the seat next to me on the sofa but leaves enough room for Ben to sit in between us. As he wiggles in what has become his spot, I hold onto William's hand behind Ben's back.

"Yeah. Will pushes way higher dan you do. He's gonna be my new pusher. Did I say it right, Will?"

William chuckles next to me and I can feel the vibrations

through our clasped hands. "Yeah, bud you did. Pusher not pusherer. Perfect Ben." I laugh at their little conversation, imagining Ben saying it wrong and William correcting him. God, I love them both so much.

"So, Ben, we have something to talk to you about. You know how you, me and William are going to be living together soon?" He nods his head enthusiastically at me so I carry on. "Well, how would you feel if someone else came to live here too? Maybe a little baby that you could be a big brother too? Would you be okay with that?"

I bite down on my lip, a rush of nerves hitting me when Ben's face changes from contemplation to pure happiness. "Am I gonna be a big brover? Am I gonna have a baby to play wiv, Mummy?" I smile down at him and nod. His face stills for a second as he asks, "I don't want da baby to be sad dough, Mummy, when it starts to miss Daddy. Like I do."

A small frown is on his face and tears well in my eyes, but before I can regain my composure to reply to him, William is already speaking. "Bud, I'm going to be the baby's dad, so they won't be sad. I'd like to be yours too, if that's what you'd want."

I glance at Ben, who's got his inquisitive face on and then steal a glance at William, who looks sick with nerves.

"So, I'd have two daddies? One here and one in heaven?"

I nod at Ben. "If that's what you'd like. Or you can have William as your best friend instead. It's up to you. But whatever you decide for you, William would still be the baby's dad."

Ben looks worriedly at Will. "If I pick you as my dad will you stop being my best friend?"

William and I both start laughing as he answers. "No bud, you'll always be my best friend. Just don't tell Marcus. I can be both Dad and your best friend."

Ben gets up and launches himself at both of us, tears

falling from all three of us. "I've never had a real-life daddy before."

Too choked up to speak, I leave it to William and wait for his reply. "Well, I've never had a real-life son before. We can learn as we go, together. Yeah?" Ben looks up at him and nods and gives him the biggest bear hug I've ever seen.

He turns to me, sitting in William's lap and clasping him around the neck, and asks, "Is it a girl baby or a boy baby?"

And my heart melts.

"We aren't sure yet. We might be able to find out a bit later on, or we might have to wait until the baby is here before we know, but we can have guesses."

He thinks for a second and then tells us, "It's gonna be a girl. I'll hava sister, I bet ya." Confident in his declaration, he gets up and bounces out of the room and upstairs to his bedroom.

William captures me in his arms, and I snuggle back into him. "I think that went well. What do you think we have?" I ask him.

He squeezes me tightly, kisses the top of my head and smiles down at me. "I think we have the most amazing little boy upstairs, and whether we have another boy or a little girl in there doesn't matter to me. Either way, I'm more blessed than I ever thought possible. You've given me everything, Nell. You've given me your heart, your trust, your love. You've let me become a dad to Ben and the baby, and I'll forever be in your debt."

I reach up and kiss him, slow and with love flowing from my lips to his. I want him to feel how much I love him. I break away a tiny bit but leave my face next to his.

"William, you've given me so much more. You've given me myself back, and for that I will be forever grateful. Thank you for never giving up on me. For taking the chance on a single mum with issues. Thank you for your patience too. I love you so much. You've given me and Ben a family. Mr. Shakespeare, I would not wish for any companion but you. I'm so sorry it took me so long to get here."

I frown as a grin spreads across his face, unknowing what I said that was so funny. "Nell, we did what we had to do to get here, and as the big man himself said, *'The course of true love never did run smooth.'* We have true love, baby."

His grin gets bigger, and he picks me up so I'm straddling him. Instantly, my core starts to throb and heat pulses through my body, pebbling my nipples against my top. William's eyes zero in on them. He licks his lips and his smile conveys all the dirty things he wants to do to me. Before I can even blink, his lips are on mine.

And before we can take it any further, Ben calls down for William.

He groans and puts his head in the crook of my neck, and this time it's me grinning and giggling. "Welcome to parenthood, Daddy."

He shudders. "No, Nell. Don't call me Daddy. Cleopatra ruined that for me."

He grimaces and I laugh again as Ben shouts down, frustrated at being ignored. William settles me back on the couch and I watch as he jumps up and runs up the stairs to spend time with his son.

I can't believe how lucky I am that I finally found the courage to say those three little words to him *'I'm all yours'*.

THE END

Acknowledgments

Where do I begin? Jeez, this writing lark is easier when it's about fictional characters.

I need to thank you, the readers, because without you, I and so many other authors, wouldn't be able to make our dreams come true. I love that so many of you took the chance and read Mine, always, (if you didn't, go do it now - ha, sorry my bossiness came out. I mean if you want to go read it, you can, I guess lol). The support and feedback is appreciated so much. I've read all your reviews and I'm beyond grateful. Thank you!

To my sister, who read the very first draft of I'm all yours and after four chapters told me to take it away and redo the whole thing, thank you! At the time I wanted to unalive you but I'm so grateful that you called me out and told me I can do better. With your support and encouragement (more like cracking the proverbial whip at me but hey-ho) it helped shape this book into what it is today.

To my arc readers for always telling me the truth, for being amazing at recommending me and my books to others and for being the best people ever, thank you.

Valerie, no words are needed, but I'll use a few anyway. You're my strength, my rock, my voice of reason and I love you. Thank you!

To my editor (I love calling you that) we are soaring together, onwards and upwards! - Sorry if the commas aren't in the right place (monkey covering mouth emoji).

To my family, my girls and my hubby, I love you all more than words can say.

And to everyone else in Romancelandia, I adore you all. You are the best people and I love each and every one of you!

About the Author

Koko Heart is a romance writer who lives in London, United Kingdom with her husband and their four daughters. She writes from her heart and has always been fascinated with happily ever afters. She still believes in fairytales but likes them a little bit dirtier now.

Also by Koko Heart

Mine, always - https://books2read.com/minealways Amazon and KU

Mine, finally - https://dl.bookfunnel.com/4um95dy6pa A book funnel freebie

Printed in Great Britain
by Amazon

87697419R00172